The Melancholy Virgin

Also by Annabel Laine

THE RELUCTANT HEIRESS

ANNABEL LAINE

The Melancholy Virgin

ST. MARTIN'S PRESS
NEW YORK

M/

For my aunt
Jenny C. Wylie
who would, I hope, have
enjoyed it.

Library of Congress Cataloging in Publication Data

Laine, Annabel.
    The melancholy virgin.

    I. Title.
PR6062.A359M4   1982   823'.914   81-16730
ISBN 0-321-52865-5   AACR2

Historical note

Although all the major characters in the plot of *The Melancholy Virgin* are fictional, many of the minor ones were real – not only Mrs Siddons and Edmund Kean, but Robert Elliston, John Townsend, and a whole range of others, from the great Catalani, by way of the regrettable Mrs Porter, down to the Twamleys, the Toozes, and the Horribows. All of them behave in the book as they did in life. Or as their critics said they did.

Chapter 1

Prefacing his words with a discreet cough, Brandon addressed himself to the unyielding air above his master's head.

'Begging your lordship's pardon,' he began.

His lordship, frowning over a long, closely-written document in his hand, paid no attention.

Brandon waited.

'Yes?' said his lordship at length.

'There is a Person who wishes to see you, my lord.' The capital letter was perfectly audible.

'And?'

'And he refuses to go away, my lord.'

The earl laid the paper down on his desk and surveyed his butler in mild reproof. 'Brandon,' he said. 'When I told you I did not wish to be disturbed, that was precisely what I meant. But since I know you are eminently capable of fending off a mere Person, however obstinate, without reference to me,' his dark brows rose enquiringly, 'you had better tell me the rest.'

'Yes, my lord. It is a person from the Bow Street police office.'

The earl regarded him thoughtfully.

'One of the Runners, my lord.'

The earl's expression could not have been said to change, but the faintest gleam of something that might have been amusement crept into his cool blue gaze.

'A Mr Townsend, I believe,' said Brandon, conceding defeat. This was by no means the first time he had admitted Townsend to the house in St James's Square, but it gave him obscure satisfaction to act as if each occasion was not only the first but destined to be the last. Bow Street Runners, no doubt, had their place in the order of things, but that place was not, he held, within the portals of a gentleman's residence. The fact that Townsend was allowed to run tame at Windsor Castle, Carlton House, and Brighton Pavilion, where he fulfilled the occasional role of royal bodyguard, did not moderate Brandon's view in the least. Rather the opposite.

The earl thanked him politely. 'You may show him in, in about five minutes. And Brandon,' he added, surrendering to his baser instincts, 'bring in the refreshment tray, if you please. With the Mountain Malaga, I think, as well as the sherry and port.' As he began to clear his desk, he grinned to himself. One of these days he was going to try Brandon's patience too far.

Brooding invisibly over his lordship's iniquities, Brandon paced majestically back towards the main hall, his basset-hound features inscrutable. To be serving refreshment to a Bow Street Runner! It was all of a piece. And the tale was bound to leak out – it always did – so that he would be duty bound to administer a severe setdown to a number of his acquaintances among the upper servants of the *ton*. Not that he didn't enjoy it. Lord Alvanley's steward would comment, in his niminy-piminy way, on Mr Brandon's positively saintly forbearance in putting up with it, and wonder how in the world he could contrive to maintain his marvellous – quite, quite marvellous! – standards in such an unconventional household. And Viscount Detherage's valet would say, in a shocked undertone, that the earl wasn't a *radical*, was he? No doubt it came from his being a diplomat, and having to associate with all those revolutionary Americans and Frenchies. But he wouldn't, personally, care to be in service with such a gentleman. Oh, dear me, no!

To all such provocation Brandon was accustomed to reply, in his loftiest tones, that much could be forgiven one who had A Brain, which was more than could be said of *some* people whom Brandon could, but in deference to present company would not, name. In fact, wild horses would not have dragged from him the fundamental reason for his devotion to the earl. It was not just that he was, in general, an unusually considerate employer. Rather more important was the fact that, for Brandon, service within the orbit of Charles Edward Graham Dornay, fifth Earl of Moriston – aristocrat, diplomat, and occasional detective – was as good as a play and very much better than some he had paid good money to see at the Surrey Theatre or the Olympic. The unique privilege – nay, the truly sybaritic pleasure – of being allotted a walk-on part in a production of such unfailing interest was more than enough to compensate Brandon for the occasional affront to his professional susceptibilities.

Even if sometimes it was a close-run thing, he thought, as, after lurking for the requisite five minutes under the staircase, he emerged into the front hall again to confront the colourful figure of John Townsend, pillar of Bow Street since he was a lad in 1781, and now in his middle fifties the most experienced and successful thieftaker of them all.

Townsend was clad in knee breeches, gaiters, and a coat of voluminous cut in a blinding shade of blue. In one hand he carried a knobbly cane, which he refused to relinquish, and his wide-brimmed hat was still on his head, partially hiding hair that was curled under after the fashion of a medieval pageboy, and was mud-brown at the back and incongruously flaxen in front. He grinned at Brandon without rancour. 'Well, cully? Right, was I? Happy to see me, and bring in the booze tray?'

With quelling hauteur, which did not quell the Runner in the slightest, Brandon invited him to step this way, and in frigid silence and at a funereal pace the two men progressed back through the staircase hall and the long, sunlit dining room to the great double doors of the library.

The earl was waiting. 'How are you, Townsend? What can I do for you?'

The Runner, small, portly, sharp as a fistful of razors, looked up at him and remarked, 'Now, that's one of the things I like about your lordship. Not, "What do you want?" but "What can I do for you?" I wish more people would take your tone. It 'ud make my job a lot easier.'

'But dull, Townsend. Dull!'

'I grant you that.' He sighed gustily. 'Ay, the day this country has a properly organized, properly manned police force, with the authority to insist on cooperation from the public, will be the day I elect to retire, no doubt. But it isn't likely to come yet awhile. In the meantime, I'm kept pretty well as busy as a tick in a sheep shed.'

9

The earl waved him to a chair as Brandon reappeared with the tray.

'I thought there was some talk of increasing the Runners' numbers?'

'Ay, there was. The port'll do me nicely, thank you. But when it came to the bit, what with having to stump up for the magistrates, and the clerks, and the caretaker, and the messenger, and the assistant gaoler, and the foot-patrol men, and the horse-patrol men, the Treasury just couldn't find the extra guinea a week to pay another man. And supply your own clothes,' he added moodily. 'So, six Bow Street Runners there are, and six there will remain.'

The earl surveyed the Runner's eye-catching attire in sympathetic silence. But when Brandon had withdrawn, he remarked, 'I think you might risk putting your hat on the floor, you know. It must weigh heavy with all that lead in the brim.'

The Runner smiled a trifle guiltily and did as he was bid. 'I'd forgotten you knew about that, your lordship.'

'And I know what an effective weapon it is. A running man at twenty paces, if I remember?'

Townsend smiled again, absently. A faint summer breeze, soft and sweet-smelling, stirred the curtains at the windows overlooking the garden. He sniffed appreciatively. 'Stables must be to leeward today,' he observed. 'Queer to be in the heart of London and not smell horses. In fact,' he took a genteel sip of port, 'I was surprised to find your lordship in town at this time of year.'

Coming from one of the best-informed men in London, this had an implausible ring, but the earl took it without a blink. 'I have been in France for the past few weeks. The Duke's victory at Waterloo raised more diplomatic problems than you might easily imagine, and I found myself chained to the conference table for longer than I expected. I returned to town only yesterday.' His chin resting lightly on his steepled forefingers, he watched the little Runner quizzically. 'I have a good deal to catch up with before I will be able to leave for the country.'

Townsend shifted slightly in his chair and bobbed his head towards the neat piles of papers on his lordship's desk. 'I should have thought that efficient secretary of yours – what's his name? Mervyn? – would have taken care of all that for you.'

'He is on holiday.'

'Gone to the seaside, has he?'

The earl looked at him. 'My secretary is on holiday. My estate manager is at Atherton, which, as I am sure you know, is my home in Wiltshire. My sister, Lady Susan Gregory, is in excellent health, thank you, and so is my brother John. And so am I.' He paused, considering. 'The weather in Wiltshire has been fine this year, and the harvest prospects look good. The factor on my Scottish estates tells me it has been raining there. As usual. But the sheep seem to enjoy it.' He paused again. 'Yes, I think that covers it. Cut line, Townsend! There is really no need for all these polite preliminaries. What's afoot?'

A muscle twitched at the corner of the Runner's mouth. 'Yes. Well,' he began. 'The thing is, my lord, that I am engaged on a case at the moment ... '

'Yes?'

'And I'd be obliged for your help.'

'Yes?'

'Trouble is,' he went on, delicately scratching one eyebrow with a blunt forefinger, 'I don't rightly know where to start.'

'At the beginning?' suggested his lordship drily.

'Ay, but it's not so simple. In fact, it was really your secretary, not you, I wanted to talk to. But he seems to have vanished.'

'Hardly that,' said his lordship. 'I imagine he has gone to visit his family at Worthing.'

The Runner shook his head, and the flaxen fringe bounced distractingly. 'Not there, my lord. Not at his father's Rectory, and not expected.'

'You mean you've sent to find out?'

'As soon as I discovered he wasn't here.'

'Not today, in other words.'

'Two days back.'

The earl shrugged. 'There are any number of places he could be, and any number of reasons for going somewhere other than Worthing. Can't your problem wait till he comes back?'

Townsend shook his head again, positively. 'Afraid not, my lord.' There was a silence. 'You wouldn't,' he enquired

11

tentatively, 'like to tell me something about Mr Mervyn's background?'

'No, I would not,' snapped the earl, exasperated, and then laughed as the Runner opened his mouth to protest. Throwing up his hand in a gesture of conciliation, he said, '*Pax!* I know – what has happened to my famous cooperation with Bow Street? Very well, then. Francis Mervyn is twenty-seven years of age, the son of a parson, and has been my secretary since he came down from Oxford six years ago. His manners and morals are unimpeachable, his judgement excellent, and his only fault – if it *is* a fault – is that he is laconic to a degree. I both like and respect him, and frankly I should be lost without him.'

He came to a decided halt, and the Runner, half under his breath, said, 'I was afraid of that.' But his boot-button eyes met the earl's unwinkingly as he added, 'That wasn't quite the kind of information I had in mind, my lord. I'd like to hear something of his private life.'

'Well, you won't hear it from me,' said his lordship roundly. 'What the devil *is* all this? Why are you so interested in Francis Mervyn?'

Townsend chose his words carefully. 'With anyone else, I'd keep my tongue between my teeth, and that's the truth. But because it's you ... And I'll be bound you'd find out anyway, so there's not much point in holding back. But you're not going to be best pleased. It's a case of murder.'

He waited, but the earl was unhelpfully silent.

'Yes. Well,' said the Runner. 'A young woman, aged twenty-one, with an apartment in Mecklenburgh Square. One of the new terraces. You know it?' The earl nodded. 'She was in the theatre for a while, in the chorus at the English Opera – nice enough voice, it seems – but about two years ago she found a protector who set her up in style. Nothing flash, just quiet and tasteful. Then at the beginning of this year she seems to have met your Mr Mervyn and fallen for him, good and proper. We found her diary. Seems she was desperate to marry him, but he wasn't interested; had a more respectable young lady in his eye. Anyway, the long and the short of it is that, last Friday afternoon, her sister went to visit her and found her dead. Hit over the head with a bronze candlestand, the heavy kind. One blow would probably have been enough, but

12

whoever killed her didn't stop at one. She seems to have died late on Thursday or early Friday.' He paused. 'Friday was the day your Mr Mervyn left town. You can understand why I'd like to talk to him.'

A few moments passed. Then, 'Yes,' said his lordship, idly revolving his glass between long fingers. His blue eyes were abstracted, his face and voice completely devoid of expression. 'Did no one hear any screams?'

'No.'

'Or see anything suspicious?'

'No.' The Runner waited.

'The diary. I take it that it wasn't just an appointments book, but the kind that people write up at the end of the day?'

'Ay.'

'And what did it say for Thursday?'

'Nothing. But she didn't fill it in every day, and some days there was nothing in it at all.'

'Mmmm,' said his lordship. 'In any case, it would hardly have been likely to end with the remark that "Francis Mervyn is reaching for the candlestand and is going to hit me with it".'

The Runner smiled perfunctorily. There was another silence.

His gaze unfocussed, his voice soft and reflective, the earl said, 'What was she wearing?'

'One of those *peignoir* things, all muslin and lace.'

'And her hair?'

'Hair?' the Runner repeated, momentarily perplexed. 'Oh, I see what you're getting at. Neat. Ringlets at the sides and a braid at the back.'

'So she was either preparing to go to bed, or preparing to dress. Which doesn't do anything to pinpoint the time. Any possibility that the motive was robbery?'

'Nothing was missing, as far as we know. And there were no signs of the apartment being broken into.'

'Mmmm,' said his lordship again.

Townsend waited.

'Where were the servants?'

'They have the day off on Friday. Leave before dinner on

13

Thursday evening and are – were – expected back in time to prepare and serve it on Friday.'

The earl's brows rose slightly. 'Did they have any other time off?'

'Monday nights.'

'Nights?'

'They were free at eight in the evening and expected back at eight on Tuesday morning.'

His lordship relapsed into contemplation. The Runner raised his glass to his lips, watching him covertly over the rim. There was nothing to be read in the dark, strikingly handsome face, no crease in the broad brow, and no sign of tension in the firmly sculptured jaw above the impeccable cravat – tied, the Runner observed knowledgeably, in a simple Mailcoach to suit the plain but superbly tailored dark green coat the earl favoured for morning wear. Townsend was just thinking wistfully that it would be pleasant to be thirty years old again, even if he had never had a figure like his lordship's, when the earl put his glass down abruptly and raised his eyes.

'You're quite wrong, you know. Whoever killed the unfortunate girl, it was certainly not Francis Mervyn.'

'But you'd be bound to say that, wouldn't you, my lord?'

His lordship regarded the little Runner amiably. 'You do me less than justice, my friend. Unless you have omitted some significant piece of information, I can think of at least two other people with potentially far stronger motives.'

'Two?' exclaimed the Runner, startled. He himself could think of at least half a dozen, but only one of them had figured in the outline he had given the earl.

'Of course. The protector, about whom you have been so noticeably reticent, and the young lady Francis is supposed to have preferred.'

The Runner pursed his lips doubtfully. 'Granted, I've known young women clout people over the head with a blunt instrument before now. Often enough. But it's usually their menfolk they clout,' he added with a gleam of humour. 'They're more likely to take a shiv to another woman.'

'A knife, you mean? Perhaps, but respectable young ladies of the kind we are presumably talking about don't usually carry knives. You said the killer hit the girl several times when one blow would have done. Now, what that suggests to me is either vicious rage, or a kind of weak and panic-stricken determination to do the job properly.'

'There's something in that,' Townsend admitted grudgingly. 'But either state of mind could still have applied in the case of your secretary, couldn't it?'

'You might think so, but you don't know him. I do. And I'll tell you something else. The servants' calendar of time off means that your victim was either an unnaturally benevolent employer, or else wanted them out of the house at particular times. Did they ever see her protector?'

It was in the nature of a rhetorical question, but Townsend replied, 'They don't think so.'

'Don't *think* so?'

'Well,' said the Runner defensively, 'there were quite a number of people in and out of the place, and there was no way for the servants to know which of them might be paying the bills.'

'Indeed. Well, I suggest that, if you have not already done so, you enquire into the whereabouts of your young lady's protector on Monday and Thursday evenings. It seems clear to me that those were the times he visited her. Certainly, Francis Mervyn's visits to her cannot have conformed to such a regular pattern. He, as you may or may not know, has rooms in this house, and I would have been bound to notice if he had begun to absent himself so consistently.'

The Runner's small black eyes, usually so shrewd, had become slightly glassy.

'Townsend,' the earl said. 'You do *know* who her protector was?'

The Runner's elbow was on the desk, his chin propped on his thumb and his forefinger sealing his lips. He shook his head and his flaxen fringe waggled.

The earl rose to his feet and went to refill the glasses. He placed one before the temporarily oblivious Runner and then returned to his own side of the desk where, after waiting patiently for a moment or two, he drew a writing block towards him and began to make notes.

It was fully five minutes before Townsend sat back in his chair again. Noticing the glass, he picked it up, took a gulp, and

15

then set it down. 'I'll bear your view in mind, my lord. I can't say more.' On the face of it, the earl's arguments had made good sense, but Townsend thought them largely invalidated by his lordship's natural prejudice in favour of Francis Mervyn. For his part, the Runner was prejudiced against Mr Mervyn, not only because of his own reading of the situation but by the decisively stated opinion of a certain young woman whose judgement he deeply respected. Uncharacteristically, he swore under his breath. He was in for an uncomfortable few days.

The gentian blue eyes were looking at him satirically. Townsend said, 'I'll make a bargain with you, my lord. You believe Mr Mervyn is innocent, but he still looks to me like the most probable candidate for topping. Ay, you may frown, my lord, but that's what it all comes down to. However, I don't like to see justice miscarry, any more than the next man. So I'll tell you all I know about this case. I'll pursue my own line – which, I tell you frankly, means going after your secretary – but if you can prove to my satisfaction that someone else murdered Imogen Reece, I'll not take it amiss.'

'Imogen Reece!' exclaimed the earl sharply, and caught the fleeting look of expectation on Townsend's face. He shook his head reproachfully. 'Oh, Townsend! *Two* other potential murderers? A dozen, surely?'

'Not as many, and only because the poor girl was lonely and bored.'

The earl went off at a tangent. 'I am surprised that Bow Street should be taking an interest in a case like this. Some little ladybird or other must come to grief almost every day. And what's more, since a demi-rep's – er – gentlemen friends usually come from the more fashionable and influential levels of society, I would have expected your Chief Magistrate to shy off what could turn out to be a somewhat ticklish case?'

Townsend swore under his breath again. His lordship had a nasty talent for putting his finger on the tender spot. 'Yes. Well,' he said. 'Sir Nathaniel isn't too keen. I've been privately retained. And,' he took a breath, 'I've a personal interest myself.'

'Ah,' said his lordship invitingly. 'Tell me more.'

Chapter 2

Two hours later, the Lady Susan Gregory walked purposefully into her brother's library, asking as she entered, 'Who was that I passed on the way out?' Then her hazel eyes widened under the dashing O'Neil hat, with its pink silk bands and curled white plumes, and she answered herself cheerfully. '*What* a silly question! It was Townsend, surely? No one else in the world could look like that. What did he want? But never mind for the moment.' She began to strip off her gloves. 'Goodness, but it's warm! Charles, I want to talk to you.'

Her brother surveyed her grimly. 'Not half as much,' he said, 'as *I* want to talk to *you*!'

She looked at him. 'Oh, dear!' she said, and sat down with exaggerated meekness. 'What have I done?'

Having lived with her brother for several years as a very youthful widow, she had learned to ignore it when he was out of frame. But her recent remarriage – to a husband now at sea – had taught her a new sensibility. Her brother's occasional ill humour was no longer something to be shrugged off in the interests of her own comfort, but something to be concerned about for his sake. This time, she could see, he was genuinely disturbed.

'Tell me about Francis.'

'Francis?'

'You were in command while I was away. He has gone on holiday. Where?'

'Worthing, I assume.' She caught her brother's eye and hastily revised what she had said. 'I don't really know. My impression was certainly that he was going to visit his family, as usual, but I don't recall whether he said so, or not in so many words.'

'When did he leave?'

'Last Friday morning.' Painstakingly, she corrected herself again. 'At least, he said on Thursday evening that he intended to. Brandon would know.'

'And when do we expect him back?'

'The end of next week.'

'And how, pray, was I to get in touch with him if I needed him urgently?'

Lady Susan was tiring of the inquisition. 'Really, Charles!' she said. 'How often, in the six years he has been with you, have you been so inconsiderate as to summon him back from holiday?' He shrugged, and she concluded astringently, 'Never! Precisely!'

He laughed. 'You're right, of course, But there's no need to sound so governessy about it. Now, this is important, Susan. During the last few weeks, have you noticed whether he has been going out regularly in the evenings? Every Monday and Thursday, say?'

She reflected for a moment. 'No, I don't think so.' He looked unaccountably relieved. 'I certainly saw him last Thursday evening, and I remember he dined with John and myself the Thursday before. Oh, and last Monday he had a long conference with Matthew before he went back to Athⱅrton. Matt was in town for a day or two, did you know? He wanted Francis's opinion on a new system of estate accounting he thinks would help clarify the profit-and-loss situation on the Home Farm, and possibly the tenant farms as well. Just think,' she added mischievously, 'what a lovely time you will have listening to him explain it all to you when we get back to Wiltshire. And that reminds me ... '

Her brother interrupted her ruthlessly. 'Yes, later. Now, another thing. How did he seem to you during the week or two before he left? Was he upset, or disturbed in any way?'

She looked at him solicitously. 'Dear Charles! Are you feeling quite well? You know that the world could collapse around Francis Mervyn's ears without disturbing his equanimity. No, he was his usual unexcited self. Why?'

He ignored the question. 'Have you an engagement this evening?'

18 .

'I had,' she replied with some asperity, 'but I cried off in honour of your first day home.'

'How kind!' He smiled at her limpidly. 'And John?'

'Has ridden off to Box Hill. An engagement he felt he could not break. He does not expect to be back until late.'

'In that case, we had better postpone the family conference until tomorrow ...'

'*What* family conference?'

'... at about eleven, if that's not too early for you. And this evening, instead, perhaps you would like to accompany me to the theatre?'

'Charles,' said his sister resignedly. 'This is *August*. The theatres are closed.'

'Not at all. Drury Lane, Covent Garden, and the Opera may be closed. But *we* are going to the Olympic.' He picked up a creased and faintly grubby playbill from his desk and handed it to her. 'And now, if you will forgive me, I have something to attend to.'

'But Charles!' she exclaimed as he made for the door leading to the back of the house and thence to the stables. 'I wanted ...' The door closed behind him. '... to talk to you,' she concluded pensively to the empty air. But her voice lacked conviction. Although she was perfectly sure that her brother's heart had emerged undamaged from his entanglement, a few months before, with Miss Caroline Malcolm, she was still reluctant to tell him what she had just heard about that changeable young lady.

With a sigh, Lady Susan dropped her eyes to the playbill in her hand.

It appeared that she was being taken to see *A Grand and Terrific Caledonian Drama, founded on Shakespeare's sublime Tragedy of Macbeth, interspersed with Characteristic National Marches, Choruses, Combats, and Processions, entitled The Fatal Prophecy, or The Scottish Regicide.* The part of Macbeth would be taken by Mr Elliston, and that of Banquo by Mr Megget, while the character of Scotland's great tragic heroine, Lady Macbeth, was to be played – Lady Susan blinked – by that magnificent, dazzling, superlative new star of the operatic firmament, Signora Katarina.

In the event, Lady Susan was to find it a remarkably

19

entertaining evening, although she could scarcely have foreseen that her brother would fall completely, irrevocably, and permanently in love with Lady Macbeth.

He succeeded in hiding it. But only because, at first, his sister was too entranced by what was going on on the stage to have eyes for anything else. By the time she turned to him, in a ripple of amusement over the liberties that had been taken with the Bard, his heartbeat had begun to steady again, and the breath that had drained out of him in a single rush had returned to his lungs. His nerve ends still quivering, his eyes shaded by their lids, he made some smiling response that seemed to satisfy her. He had no idea what he said, then, or later in the evening, no awareness of anything that happened in the theatre or on the stage. His attention was concentrated on one slender figure as intensely as the sun through a burning glass. He saw only great dark eyes and honey-coloured hair, heard only a voice that could charm the birds from the trees. Nothing else came within his consciousness.

He did not remember the curtain coming down, or the journey back to St James's Square, or how he contrived to talk to his sister with apparent normality. He did not remember retiring to his bedchamber, or dismissing his valet for the night. Not until dawn crept in to lighten the sky, so that the world began to take on outline and then definition, did he come slowly to himself again and realize that he must have been standing by his window, still fully dressed, for several hours. He crossed to his bed and lay down on the coverlet, hoping that sleep might overtake him. Instead, his mind began to function again, one thought chasing another round and round in his brain until he leapt to his feet and began pacing the floor, window to door to fireplace to window. On and on.

He had taken his sister to the theatre because he wanted to see Signora Katarina, whose real name, Townsend had said, was Miss Katharine Kenwood. She had been a friend of Imogen Reece, and was, the Runner said, a young woman of character who had always been convinced that Imogen's passion for Francis Mervyn would end in disaster. Who was so sure that Francis had killed her that she was actually paying Townsend to trace him and arrest him. Who was one of the few

20

people whose judgement Townsend respected. And with whom he, Charles Edward Graham Dornay, fifth Earl of Moriston, had quite blindingly fallen in love.

It was nonsensical, of course. He had seen her for an hour or two on the stage of a vulgar, noisy theatre. Had admired her face, her voice, her figure. Been intrigued by the style and gallantry she displayed as the whole ridiculous fiasco of *The Scottish Regicide* staggered on to its uproarious conclusion. Been interested by subtle evidences of taste and breeding that were uncommon among theatrical performers.

But none of this meant anything at all. And none of it explained his absolute and unalterable conviction that, at last, he had found the one woman with whom he wished to spend the rest of his life.

He lay down on his bed again and succumbed to dreams as foolish and romantic as those of any schoolboy adrift on the innocent, idyllic sea of first love. But his mind could not rest. He was neither young nor inexperienced. He was thirty years old and far from chaste. With retrospective loathing, he reviewed the long and decorative procession of wayward and amusing ladies whose names society had, at one time or another, linked with his. And those other ladies, no less wayward, of whom society knew nothing. Would she understand – his lovely, beloved Kate? Would she recognize that his life, until now, had been only a shadow play? Suddenly, he became frightened of what the tattle-mongers would make of it – the scandalous *on-dits*, the malicious speculations – if he were to show signs of having formed a partiality for her. All those mothers of nubile daughters who had condemned him as a rake because he had ignored the fluttering eyelashes and amateur flirtatiousness of the *ingénues* who appeared with such repetition, Season after Season, on the marriage mart. Who would revel in venting their spite not on him, but on Kate – young, unmarried, an actress, and wholly vulnerable. It was society's ineradicable belief that no woman who appeared on the stage could possibly be a lady. Even, he thought with a momentary twitch of humour, when she *was* a Lady. The Misses Farren, Brunton, and Bolton had all recently married into the peerage, but it had not protected them from sly innuendoes and acid asides. How could he shield her? Until he was assured that she would marry him, he could not afford to show even a flicker of his feeling for her.

Hours, days, weeks later, there was a deprecating tap on the door and Sanderson entered. With a single glance, he took in the fully clothed form of his master, the disarrayed coverlet, the open curtains, and parted his lips to speak. But something in the earl's face caused him to change his mind. Silently, he brought hot water, silently laid out fresh clothes, and silently helped his master to dress.

'Dash it!' said the Honourable John Dornay to Lady Susan some little time after. 'You might have left a message. It was only just after nine when I got in last night and I could have joined you. I always seem to miss the fun!'

She chuckled. 'You certainly did on this occasion. I don't remember when I was so diverted.'

'Mind you,' he continued disapprovingly through a mouthful of cold roast sirloin, 'I don't know what Charles was thinking of, taking you to a place like that. Not the thing at all!'

She regarded him with barely repressed amusement. At twenty-two, he was the youngest of her six brothers and sisters, and the one who most strongly resembled the earl. But although he had the same dark, aquiline good looks, and might even, she thought, develop the same supple strength when he outgrew his present undeniable weediness, he had none of his brother's polish or, as her ladyship – seven years his senior – never wearied of pointing out, his faultless grooming. This morning, as usual, he looked as if he had dressed all by guess, but she was too amused by his stuffy view of the previous evening's escapade to take him to task for it.

Instead, with a nice blend of dismay and defiance, she exclaimed, 'Oh, dear! Do you think not? Even though I wore my domino and mask?'

He looked at her suspiciously. 'That's not the point. The audiences at the decent theatres are bad enough, shouting and heckling and throwing things. And think of the lobby at Drury Lane, full of prost ... I mean whor ... drat it! I mean *females*, reeling up and down drunk, most of them! However, I suppose you wouldn't know about that. But the Olympic's far worse.

I just hope you didn't understand what they were shouting from the gallery, that's all!'

She gave way to a peal of laughter. 'Not the words, I will admit. But the sense was unmistakable. The pit wasn't too polite, either, especially when someone threw open a door and let in a gust of air that rocked the chandeliers and poured hot wax down everyone's neck!'

'Oh, that's always happening,' John said dismissively. 'Though I thought Elliston was supposed to be installing gas lighting? The first theatre in London to have it, and all that. He's always puffing off about how wonderful he is.'

'Of course, yes. I'd forgotten he was the manager as well as the leading actor. Charles says the piping is there, but the system isn't properly functioning yet. I suppose,' she went on reflectively, 'that the smell of gas won't be worse than the smell of people and oranges. I nearly choked last night when they doused the candles for the blasted heath and cavern scenes. The fumes from the wicks were quite suffocating. So was the dust.' She giggled. 'The Three Murderers stirred up so much of it that Banquo's corpse sat up and sneezed violently four times, and then lay down again!'

'Did he? How splendid!' John pushed his plate aside. 'But what was it like apart from that?'

Lady Susan cocked her head judiciously. 'I found it extraordinarily interesting. I've always known – in theory, I mean – that with only Drury Lane and Covent Garden permitted to put on legitimate drama, the other theatres have had serious problems. Like having to change the words, and add music, and grand spectacles, and so on. But I had never quite realized how much ingenuity they could bring to bear. Until last night.'

Her brother grinned. 'For example?'

'For example, having Lady Macbeth sing all her speeches. It was a pity that Macbeth himself merely *spoke* his, for it made the dialogues between them a little difficult to follow. But there is no doubt that Mozart does wonders for what I have always considered one of Shakespeare's more depressing pieces.'

'Mozart? But surely ... I didn't know Mozart had done a score for *Macbeth*?'

'Oh, not specifically,' agreed his sister affably. 'But *Figaro* is very adaptable, you know. It's just a matter of changing the tempo and intensifying the delivery a little.' She corrected herself. 'A lot.'

John groaned quietly.

'They used the Cherubino love song from Act Two – you know, the *"Voi che sapete"* – for the sleepwalking scene.'

'Impossible!'

'Nothing of the sort,' replied his sister, affronted. 'Just a moment . . . Yes. Give me a note.'

'Do, re, mi, fa, so, la, ti, do,' he warbled obligingly.

'That's a scale.' She tried it. 'So, so-do . . . '

'A bit high for you?'

'Don't interrupt. So, so-do-ti-so-fa, mi, do-fa-mi, re. The words had to be altered to fit, of course, so that it came out something like, "Out, dam-ned-spot-I-say, Out, out-I say-ay".'

'You don't mean Signora Katarina was singing *English*?' exclaimed John, disgusted. 'Not "out-a, out-a, damn' spot-a"? Not "all-a ze pairfumes of Arabia weel-a not sweeten zees leetle 'and"?'

'Certainly not. I shouldn't think Signora Katarina is any more Italian than I am. Her voice is superb and her diction perfect. Unfortunately. On the whole, I would really rather not have heard some of the words. "The scent of blood still hangs, up-on my hand, Nor will it ever fade, from this my hand, No scents of Araby . . . "' She broke off. 'Frankincense and myrrh came into it somewhere, but it was that fa-fa-fa-so-fa-fa, fa-fa-fa-re bit of the music and I cannot for the life of me remember how they contrived to fit a word like frankincense into it.'

'My God,' said John, awed. 'What did Charles think of it?'

'I really don't know. He was behaving slightly peculiarly. But I suspect he was enraptured by Lady Macbeth – a very attractive girl, I may add – and rather less enraptured by the National Marches, Choruses, Combats and Processions.' She remembered something. 'And you won't believe it! But do you recollect those dreadful children Monsieur d'Egville was always introducing into the dance chorus at the Opera a few years ago – half a dozen undernourished waifs with enormous feet, who clumped around the stage in classical draperies, simpering? I've forgotten their names.'

'You don't mean ... ?' John said breathlessly. 'You *can't* mean ... ? Not the Twamleys, the Toozes, and the Horribows?'

'That's right!' she exclaimed. 'How clever of you. Well, they were in the Combats and Processions. In *tartan* ... '

The door opened on his lordship, who surveyed the two delinquents sardonically and enquired whether they proposed finishing their breakfast in the foreseeable future. 'I have been waiting,' he said, 'most of the morning for you.'

Lady Susan rose to her feet in her stateliest fashion, shook out the folds of her extremely becoming, vandyke-flounced white gown, refilled her coffee cup, and strolled with it in the direction of the library. John, tossing down his napkin, wished his brother an icy good morning, and followed her.

Chapter 3

Half an hour later, John was saying, not by any means for the first time, 'But it's nonsensical!'

'Quite!' his brother agreed pacifically. '*We* know that, but Bow Street does not. In default of firm evidence pointing to someone else, however, I am afraid that it can quite easily be made to look as if Francis has committed murder.'

'Yes. But,' John went on, 'to be accused of murder just because one visits a demi-rep! Why, that would turn half the *ton* into murder suspects!'

'So it would. *If* half London's demi-reps met an untimely end. Take a damper, John,' the earl advised kindly. 'What we are concerned with is proving that Francis did not commit this particular murder. I assume none of us thinks he did? Susan?'

Her eyes were on the delicate muslin flounce she was embroidering, white-on-white Moravian work. Embroidery, she said, helped her to concentrate. 'You want a considered answer, not just a dutiful agreement?'

'Of course.'

'Then I confess that I have no idea of whether Francis is, or is not, capable of murder. I even think he might be, if it were planned and purposeful. But he has been with us for six years, and unless he has deceived us completely, he has the most enviable self-control. I don't think that this kind of messy violence would be in his style at all.' She looked up and smiled. 'I vote not guilty.'

'Well, really!' John exploded before his brother could speak. 'I must say that's pretty cool. Why don't you just add that he probably planned the murder to *be* messy, because he knew it would throw us off his track!'

26

His sister had turned slightly pink. 'There's no need to take that tone,' she said. 'Loyalty to one's friends is very commendable, but if *that*'s the best argument we can find for thinking him innocent, then we might as well stop right now.' John was temporarily silenced. 'And in answer to your question, if Francis was actually planning a murder, he would certainly be clever enough to plan it in such a way that he himself would not appear to be involved at all.'

'Quite so,' said his lordship coolly. 'Now, having disposed of that little difficulty, all we have to do is decide how to prove him innocent. Suggestions?'

John, still slightly nettled, spoke at random. 'Prove he was somewhere else when the murder took place.'

'And how do we do that?' John's face was a blank. 'We could,' the earl went on smoothly, 'ask him where he was at the time. If we could find him. Wake up, John! Could *you* produce witnesses to swear to your whereabouts between eight on Thursday evening and midday on Friday? Every minute? No, if Francis could do that, there would be no problem. He was probably, like you, peacefully asleep in bed for most of the crucial time, which seems to have been from about two in the morning until eight, or perhaps nine.' He paused. 'I think, Susan, you might enquire discreetly from Mrs Jameson whether Francis's rooms showed any signs of untidiness or hasty packing. And, I suppose,' he added distastefully, 'whether his bed had been slept in.'

'Well, I'll be ... ' exclaimed John. 'Dash it, you're every bit as bad as Susan!'

Wearily, his brother said, 'John, your feelings do you credit, but it would be a great deal more helpful to all of us, Francis included, if you would use your head. We are agreed that Francis did not kill Imogen Reece. But it *is* possible that, when he left London, he knew she was dead. If he did not know, why has he broken the habit of years and gone somewhere other than Worthing? And if he *did* know, then why has he gone away at all? And,' he said sombrely, 'will he come back?'

'But how could he know she was dead?'

'If he was as deeply involved with her as Townsend believes, nothing is more likely than that he should have gone to say goodbye before leaving town. He may have been one of the last

27

people to see her alive – or the first person, other than her murderer, to see her dead.'

'Oh,' said John, daunted.

Lady Susan, her glossy chestnut head bent over the delicate Moravian work, wondered frowningly whether the family had perhaps been a little over careful with Francis. She had always thought him too reserved, and had once suggested to Charles that they might encourage him to be more forthcoming. But she had been told succinctly, 'Francis Mervyn is a grown man and a highly intelligent one. He can, and must, make his own decisions.' She could readily understand what it must have been like for someone of his temperament to be raised as the fifth son in a family of eighteen children – his father, as Francis himself drily put it, being a clergyman 'of moderate means and immoderate powers of genesis.' But it was one thing to respect his desire for privacy; quite another, she now thought, to have allowed him to retreat into a fortified tower and pull up the drawbridge. The present situation might never have arisen – and the problems she foresaw for the next few days most certainly would not! – if even one member of the household had known something about his private life.

'Matthew!' she said suddenly. Matthew Somerville was a distant cousin of theirs, as well as being the earl's estate manager at Atherton. Like Francis, he was more than an employee, but not in any real sense a member of the family. As a result, the two young men, very much of an age, had found themselves in a kind of wary alliance, wary because Matthew – anxious, naive, and unsure of himself – found the earl's secretary mildly intimidating, while Francis – silent and self-possessed – continued stoically to hope that Matthew would some day grow up, and especially that he would grow out of his enervating habit of starting sentences and running out of confidence before he had finished them.

Her brothers were looking at her enquiringly. 'It occurred to me that Matthew might know something,' she explained. 'You remember, Charles? I told you that Francis and he had a long conference on Monday of last week, and it seems to me that Francis might have mentioned his holiday plans. I suppose,' she added doubtfully, 'that Matthew might even know something about Imogen Reece, too?'

The earl smiled on her benignly. 'Well done. As it happens, I sent Anderson off to Wiltshire yesterday afternoon, with instructions for Matthew to get back here at the earliest possible moment. He may indeed know where Francis has gone, though I confess I should be surprised to discover that he knows anything about Imogen Reece. I hold out more hope of Francis having told him something about his "respectable young lady".'

'Why?' demanded John. 'Why should he tell him about one and not the other? There's nothing very scandalous about visiting a demi-rep!'

The earl grinned. 'I despair of you! Matthew is scarcely noted for his smooth tongue, and I, personally, would prefer not to introduce him to my prospective wife in the virtual certainty that, at some stage in the conversation, he would blurt out something about my mistress!'

Lady Susan, an expression of the most extravagant interest on her face, said, 'Is that a situation that seems likely to arise?'

The earl pointedly ignored her. 'Let's return to the issue,' he said. 'If we cannot prove that Francis was somewhere else when the murder occurred, what are the alternatives? Suggestions, anyone?'

John, who had been through this kind of catechism before, opened his mouth to reply, but his sister demurely forestalled him. 'Find out who *did* murder her.'

'Clever girl,' said his lordship.

John, who had been ready with the same answer, felt he was being discriminated against, and reacted accordingly. 'And how,' he demanded brazenly, 'do we do that? Suggestions, anyone?'

Hastily converting a laugh into a cough, Lady Susan dropped her eyes to her embroidery. If ever the day came when John stopped trying to compete with his formidable eldest brother, she would be deprived of a good deal of entertainment.

'You have some?' the earl was asking kindly.

'I might, if you would condescend to tell us a few details. We can hardly be expected to make an intelligent contribution when we only know the bare outlines!'

'You're probably right,' said his lordship, effectively taking the wind out of his brother's sails. 'Very well. I'll start ... '

'Before you do,' Lady Susan interrupted. 'I have ordered luncheon for two o'clock. Will you have it here, rather than in the dining room? It's only a galantine, some salads, and an anchovy omelette. Unless Alexandre has been attacked by inspiration,' she added cautiously.

'Here,' said his lordship.

'I'll go and arrange it. Don't start till I come back.'

The door had scarcely closed behind her when John said, 'You know, I really do not think we should be talking in this frank way in front of Susan. It's terribly improper. And what's more,' he remembered, 'I can't think what you were doing taking her to the theatre last night. And to the Olympic, too!'

His brother smiled. 'John,' he said reassuringly. 'Susan was married at nineteen, even though – yes, I know! – she was widowed within months. But the fact that she did not remarry until last year has nothing to do with the situation. I dare say you would be astonished to discover just how much society matrons know about their lords' extra-curricular activities, and how busily they gossip about them. No, Susan is unlikely to be shocked by hearing about the world of the demi-reps. Even so, if this case affected anyone but Francis, I should probably try to prevent her from becoming involved. But if you think she can be persuaded to stay out of it, you are more sanguine than I. And as far as last night's little adventure was concerned, I had what I thought was a good reason for it. I wanted her opinion of someone. Perhaps,' he went on reflectively, 'it was a mistake.' John looked at him curiously. 'But ... ' he said as the door opened again to admit his sister, ' ... we will soon find out. Tell me, Susan ... '

She seated herself gracefully in the leather-covered chair by the window.

' ... what did you think of Elliston last night?'

'Elliston?' she repeated in surprise. 'Was *he* why you took me to the theatre? But I've seen him at the Lane, often enough! Don't you remember him delivering that extraordinary "special address" Lord Byron wrote, when it opened again in 1812 after the fire? What did I think of him? Unquestionably he is a Presence, even if he overplays it. When he kneels before the curtain to apostrophize the audience, and throws out his arms in that melodramatic way of his, I half expect him to cast himself on my breast. Which I wouldn't much care for. And he seems to have too many irons in too many fires. At least, I am told that's why he is not always word-perfect. Certainly, his straight Hamlet two seasons ago did not tally with my memory of Shakespeare's. But his aplomb! For that, I have seen no one to match him.' She looked at her brother. 'Have we digressed into dramatic criticism, or do we have some special interest in him?'

'He was Imogen Reece's first protector.'

'Oh-h-h-h!' said John.

The earl settled back in his chair. 'Miss Reece, it appears, belonged to a respectable West-country family. Her father was a physician, and I believe the grandfather was an Army major-general. Her mother died when she was only a child, and she was raised by an ineffectual spinster aunt who moved in to look after Imogen and her sister Olivia, who was seven years older. Imogen, it seems, became stage-struck at an early age. Her father arranged for her to have singing lessons, in the hope that this would divert her mind, but – not, in my opinion, surprisingly – it had quite the opposite effect. Her voice was pleasant enough, and carried her successfully through a series of Ladies' Concerts in the provinces, but proved to be really too weak for the theatre. She did, however, succeed in winning an engagement in the chorus at the Opera, more on the strength of her looks than her voice. Now, although a *prima donna* can make a very substantial income – rather more, I am told, than a straight actress of similar eminence – lesser lights have to take as much work as they can find in order to make ends meet. Outside the Opera season, Imogen found minor roles in other theatres, and this was how she met Elliston. He is something of an impresario, as you know. At the end of 1812, if I remember, he was not only playing Hamlet at Drury Lane, but running the Surrey Theatre, negotiating to buy the Olympic from Astley, and managing one of the lesser theatres in Birmingham and others elsewhere.

'Too many irons in too many fires,' Lady Susan confirmed with a satisfied nod.

31

'Indeed. Now, for some reason which escapes me, audiences adore him . . . '

'He's very handsome,' her ladyship pointed out.

'And he does have panache,' said John.

'You may be right. But my Lord High Elliston overworks and underpays his players quite ruthlessly, and is a good deal less popular on the business side of the footlights. Which may explain, in part, why he responded when Imogen Reece fell head over heels in love with him. And, of course, as a man of forty, he was probably flattered at being worshipped by an extremely pretty eighteen-year-old. In any case, he set her up in rooms near Drury Lane, and for several months she was idyllically happy. His dignity, of course, would not allow him to let her go on working, which proved to be unfortunate, since he is notoriously mean and pennypinching, and Imogen soon found herself in financial trouble. Characteristically, our friend Elliston would pay the rent if he happened to have money in his pocket when he was asked for it, but not otherwise. And most bills he simply stuffed in a drawer and forgot about.

'Not surprisingly, finding herself dunned by tradesmen and having to pawn her trinkets, Imogen fell out of love almost as rapidly as she had fallen into it. She tried to find work again, but seems to have met with some resistance, especially from people who disliked Elliston and were not averse to exacerbating *her* difficulties in the hope of increasing *his*.'

'How unkind!' Lady Susan exclaimed.

'Yes. At this point, however, she had a stroke of what appeared to be remarkable good fortune. She acquired a protector who was not only rich but reliable. They reached a businesslike agreement. He took apartments for her in one of the new houses in Mecklenburgh Square, gave her a roll of bills at regular intervals for her expenses, and visited her – or so Townsend and I deduce from her domestic routine – on specific days and at specific times. On Monday and Thursday evenings, to be precise. He may have stayed overnight on these occasions; we don't know. According to what she told her friends, he was a kindly and civilized man . . . '

John said, 'I should have thought *any* man would be, compared with Elliston!'

'Possibly. In any case, she seems to have been reasonably

happy with the arrangement. The only trouble, according to Townsend, was that she became intolerably bored. Mecklenburgh Square, as you know, is rather out of the way, so she was isolated from most of her friends and acquaintances. And her protector insisted on absolute secrecy about their relationship – which meant, of course, that he could not ride with her, or walk with her, or escort her to the Opera, or squire her to parties.'

He held up his hand. '*Yes*, John! We know there is no particular stigma in being associated with a demi-rep! Just let me finish, and then we can discuss why a man might be anxious to remain anonymous in such a situation. Where was I? Yes. The result was inevitable, even though Imogen Reece does not appear to have been cut out to be a ladybird. She began to acquire casual gentlemen friends, all of them young bucks from the *ton*. It started, apparently, when she became acquainted with a rather fast young woman who lived nearby and was accustomed to give and attend parties of the more informal kind. Townsend has been unable to find out whether Imogen's protector knew about these activities, but she certainly kept them from her sister – the father died some years ago – and from the one woman friend with whom she remained in touch.

'She seems, however, to have kept the important part of her bargain with her protector. She told no one his name, and even in her diary referred to him only by his initial. "C. gave me a roll of bills today, so I shall buy that delicious satin and tulle bonnet after all." That kind of thing. And then, at the beginning of this year, she met Francis.'

'How?' said Lady Susan in tones of wonderment. 'It doesn't sound like his kind of social circle at all.'

'It doesn't, does it? I don't know how they met, but it's possible he may have heard of her from someone. I know I had, even if only at third hand.'

'And I,' said John.

'She seems to have been quite an unusual young woman, as it happens. By no means ill educated, and possessed of excellent manners, quick wits, and some degree of charm. I am also told that she was both warm and kind-hearted.'

'Ha!' John remarked cynically.

33

His brother smiled. 'In that way, too, no doubt. But I am talking about her general personality.'

Lady Susan said, 'Pretty?'

'I believe so. Silvery-fair hair, and large pansy-blue eyes. A little on the plump side.'

John said consideringly, 'I can see why Francis should have become involved, of course, but why should such a – sociable? – girl have fallen for someone so reserved? He's hardly a lady's man.'

'I don't know,' his sister objected. 'Those saturnine looks of his are very dramatic. And his silences make a very pleasant change from other people's gabble-mongering.'

Neither of her brothers rose to the bait. The earl stood up, flexing his shoulder muscles, and turned to look out of the window. The long, narrow garden was vividly lit by the early afternoon sun, so that the shade under the trees was intensely black, while the small pool, artistically banked with rocks and shrubs, had a dark oily stillness. The beautifully manicured grass looked tired, and even the roses drooped. High above the narrow green canyon the sky was a metallic blue.

His lordship sighed.

Interpreting him correctly, his sister remarked, 'That was one of the things I have been trying to say to you ever since you came home. It would be so lovely to be at Atherton. London in August is dreadful. Surely we can leave soon?'

'You may leave tomorrow if you wish,' said her brother with unwonted sharpness. 'But I must stay, if I am to help Francis. And so must John.' He gazed abstractedly at the far garden wall, clad in creeper from ground to roof line. 'Have you heard from Adam recently?'

She had spoken without thinking. A little subdued, she replied, 'I had a batch of letters last week.' As Lady Susan Channock, she had met Captain the Honourable Adam Gregory last September and married him three months later. Three months after that, Napoleon had landed in France from Elba, and Adam had been despatched hurriedly back to sea by their Lordships at the Admiralty. Since then, she had seen him only twice, once for a day, once for two. 'He has been ferrying *back* to France and Belgium all those nervous French and Belgians he ferried *out* during the crisis. One would think,' she

34

remarked, depressed, 'that they might contrive to find their own way home. However, he believes that he might – just might – be free of the whole business soon.'

Her brother, restored to humour, smiled sympathetically. 'Let us hope so. For I need him. And so, undoubtedly, do you.'

There was a tap on the door, and it opened to reveal Brandon followed by a small procession of footmen. 'The Pembroke table, my lady?' he enquired, and receiving assent proceeded to remove from it two small ornaments and the Argand oil lamp, with its cut glass reservoir and repoussé silver base, which he placed tenderly in the space reserved for it on one of the bookshelves. Raising the table flaps, he adjusted the supports and then whisked from the drawer a damask cloth of dazzling whiteness, which he proceeded to smooth lovingly over the mahogany top. Next, with an imperious hand he summoned forward the first of the footmen, who deposited his burden on the table. When three trays had been carefully bestowed and the fourth and very junior footman had carefully set down the supper canterbury with its load of plates, glasses, and silverware, in its appointed place, Brandon removed the covering cloths from the trays and surveyed them critically. Salads on one, cold meats on the second, and a variety of breads, wafers, sauces and condiments on the third. He was satisfied.

All this had been accomplished in total silence, while the master of the house surveyed the garden, his sister her embroidery, and Mr John the elegantly gilded plasterwork of the ceiling. If Brandon had not already known that something was up, he would have guessed it by now. As it was, with curiosity seething blissfully in his breast, he merely said, 'I ventured to bring up the Volnay, my lord?' The earl nodded without turning, and the first footman reappeared from the dining room bearing wine tray and glasses. Brandon surveyed his arrangements and came to the reluctant conclusion that all was well.

'We will serve ourselves, thank you,' said her ladyship. 'And I will ring when we are ready for the omelette.'

Brandon bowed and withdrew, closing the doors slowly behind him.

Lady Susan giggled. 'Poor Brandon! He must be dying of curiosity. Townsend yesterday, and a family conference today!'

'Yes,' said his lordship briefly. 'But while I have, in general, no objection to providing the servants with entertainment, I would prefer that this time, for Francis's sake, they should be kept as much in the dark as possible.'

'My God, yes,' said John, much struck. 'It would be intolerable for the poor fellow to come back and find that even the scullery maid knew all about his love life!'

'If that happened, I doubt if he would even stay,' said his lordship gloomily. 'Hell and the devil confound it! As soon as I saw Townsend's face yesterday I knew we were in for something unpleasant. Susan, would you like some of this galantine of – veal, is it?'

They ate in preoccupied silence, and by a majority vote decided against the omelette, to the mild disappointment of John, the minority, and the Gallic rage of Monsieur Alexandre in the kitchen, who had set aside six eggs newlaid that very morning and now declared them to be *pure perte*, useless for anything other than one of the housekeeper's custards. Mrs Jameson took this very badly, and the atmosphere below stairs remained decidedly cool for the rest of the day.

When the trays had been cleared away by Brandon's cohorts, John said disparagingly, 'We don't know much, do we? We don't know the protector's name. We don't know how Francis and Imogen Reece met. We don't know a thing about Francis's "respectable young lady". We don't know why the protector should have been so secretive. We don't know ... '

'Stop!' said his lordship. 'Let me tell you the rest of what we *do* know. The girl's only living family is her sister, who is married to a parson ... '

'Another one?' Susan said.

His lordship had a momentary blockage. 'Oh, Francis's father, you mean? This one doesn't have a parish, however. He acts as librarian to Lord Ballinton.'

'Good God!' John said. 'I didn't know *he* could even read!'

'You wouldn't think so from his conversation, would you? However, he did inherit a library, and he may feel that the books ought to be dusted occasionally. I assume the position is a sinecure, and probably very poorly paid. Townsend says that Mr Iredale has no other employment, although he deputises occasionally for curates who are indisposed or in need of a rest. He has a small private income.'

'Who's paying Townsend, then?' John asked. 'If Nathaniel Conant doesn't regard it as an official case for Bow Street, *some*one must be paying. And your Mr Iredale doesn't sound as if he could afford a guinea a day plus fourteen shillings in expenses.'

'Is that what it costs?' Lady Susan asked.

The earl, who had hoped that no one would raise the question of who was paying, said gratefully, 'It's the standard rate for the Bow Street officers when they're on outside duties. Their equivalents in the other metropolitan Police Offices – the ones that were set up under the 1792 Act – are always complaining that *they* don't do so well, but since it's nearly always Bow Street that people apply to for help in solving the more difficult crimes, that's perhaps only fair. The Runners are pretty astute, and the half-dozen of them available for outside duty work very hard. They could scarcely do it if they were just on a wage. Until recently, their official pay was only eleven shillings and sixpence a week. But Townsend, and one or two of the others, like Sayer and McManus, make £200 a year *and* an allowance out of their guard duties at court, as well as a guinea a day every time they do duty at the Bank of England or the Opera. Then there's their share of the £40 reward paid to those who procure the conviction of a felon, not to mention one or two other perquisites like the sale of their Tyburn tickets, which grant the possessor exemption from a number of parish duties. Those fetch about £25 in areas like Covent Garden. No, the Runners tend to regard their official wage as not much more than a retainer. It's the outside work that gives them a reasonable living.'

'But who's paying *this* time?' John persisted.

His brother said with imperceptible reluctance, 'Well, Bow Street is next door to Covent Garden, so Townsend's pretty well acquainted with theatre people. And, of course, he sometimes does special duty at the Opera, as I said. He knew Imogen Reece when she was a singer, and seems to have had a soft spot for her. Says she's just the kind of bright, lively, pretty daughter he would have liked to have. So he may not be charging expenses. But the fee has to be paid through official channels, and it's the responsibility of a Miss Katharine Kenwood. She's a friend of the family, I believe.' He took a breath. 'Townsend seems to respect her judgement, and she is convinced that Francis killed the girl.'

'Feminine instinct!' John snorted. In his experience, females who qualified as 'a friend of the family' were always of a certain type. He jumped to conclusions. 'Why do these interfering old ladies insist on poking their noses into other people's affairs!'

'Yes,' said his brother after a moment. Lady Susan looked at him sharply, but was quite unable to interpret his expression. She went back to her embroidery – and to the something that was nagging, irritatingly, at the back of her mind.

His lordship said crisply, 'And that, I think, is all. Just at the moment, I don't, on mature consideration, see that it would be purposeful to speculate on the one thing we haven't really discussed, the protector's reasons for lying low. Those are not altogether important right now, and I am sure,' his smile was expansive, 'that you both have quite enough to think about for the time being. Until Matthew arrives, we may as well forget about the "respectable young lady". So the most urgent things to do are to find Francis, and to talk to some of the people we know are involved. In other words, the sister – Olivia Iredale – and the lady who's paying the bills, Miss Kenwood.'

John wrinkled his nose. He had a feeling he knew what was coming. And it did.

'John. If you could arrange to set out in an hour or so, you might almost reach Worthing tonight. What Francis's parents would probably not reveal to Bow Street, they will to you. Even if they know nothing about their son's private life, they must have some idea of where he has gone.'

John sighed. 'If I take the curricle, I suppose I might even manage to get there and back by late tomorrow. Oh, well ...'

'And Susan can produce one of her elegant sketches of Francis.'

Arrested, Lady Susan looked up. 'But Charles, you know I'm not very good at portraits. Landscapes are more my style.'

'Nonsense,' he replied bracingly. 'Remember how useful your copy of Mrs Malcolm's portrait proved to be last year, when we were trying to trace her movements? And this time we will need to know who entered or left the house in Mecklenburgh Square for several days before the murder.'

She took a very deep breath. 'Yes. And that reminds me...'

'So while you are both engaged on these useful endeavours, I will go and see Mrs Iredale and Miss Kenwood. Or vice versa. I find it difficult to believe that *neither* of them knows anything useful about Imogen's protector.'

'Charles,' said his sister forbiddingly. 'I am trying to say something!' He raised an eyebrow at her. 'I met Richard Malcolm yesterday, quite by chance, and asked after Caroline. He said she was to be married soon. To young Inverwick.'

'Really?' said his lordship, mildly interested. 'How splendid. They will suit very well. We must send them something nice.' He rose to his feet. 'I think we have finished for the moment, so if you will forgive me, I have things to attend to.'

Simmering, his sister watched him vanish through the door. She turned to John. 'It really is the outside of enough!' she said feelingly. 'Here have I been summoning up courage for the last twenty-four hours to break it to him that that little minx is to be married, and what does he say? "We must send them something nice". Men!'

John grinned. 'They really wouldn't have suited, you know.'

'Of course I know! And nothing could have been more fortunate than the fact that Caroline recognized it, too. He frightened her right from the start, of course, but I thought she had managed to overcome that.'

'If you want my opinion,' said her brother unkindly, 'when she got over being frightened of Charles, she started being frightened of you!'

His sister's mouth opened.

'Well, you must be quite intimidating to a conventionally-reared girl.' Relenting, he added, 'Besides, Charles didn't really care for her. It was just a new experience for him – the damsel in distress, and all that. And such a pretty damsel! But I'm damned sure that, as soon as he discovered she had no

39

sense of humour, he began wondering how to get out of the entanglement, and was much obliged to her for freeing him from it!'

Lady Susan sighed. 'Oh, well. Water under the bridge, I suppose.' But she did wish Adam would come home.

Chapter 4

Miss Katharine Kenwood's image stared solemnly back at her, a pale and cloudy oval accented only by her enormous dark eyes and the vast Elizabethan ruff that framed her face. 'Oh, well,' she said disconsolately. 'I suppose I must make the best of it.'

'You look very nice, miss,' volunteered Betsy, her maid. 'Truly. It's quite becoming, that – er – frilly thing round your neck.'

'Don't humour me, Betsy. To have to receive the man at all is bad enough.' She peered again at her reflection. 'But to have to receive him looking like a mutton cutlet is beyond bearing.'

Four years in the theatre had taught Miss Kenwood something that had never been apparent to her in the nineteen sheltered years preceding them – that the great majority of people were accustomed to judge by appearances, and that the starchier members of society, even those prepared to invite a Mrs Siddons or a Mr Kean into their homes (though they seldom invited Mr Kean twice), were only too swiftly reminded by the smells, sounds and sights of the theatre itself that actors and actresses were, after all, very inferior beings with none of the instincts of fastidiousness that were an essential part of true gentility.

There was no reason for Miss Kenwood to assume that the Earl of Moriston was going to prove any exception to the rule. Townsend had said that he was a great landowner, and that his name was a distinguished one in diplomatic circles. He differed from most of his peers in possessing a sense of social responsibility, which led him to give such assistance as he could to Bow Street, and in this particular case he had a personal interest since it was his private secretary who was involved. Miss Kenwood anticipated a somewhat pompous gentleman of advanced years, who would try to browbeat her in an odiously polite and diplomatic way. His purpose, obviously, was to induce her to call off the hunt. It was an encounter she could have looked forward to, without pleasure but with relative equanimity, in her elegant and civilized drawing room at home, surrounded by furniture, books, and ornaments that bore mute witness to the fact that her taste, education, and upbringing were very little inferior to his. She could, she thought regretfully, have worn the new *gros de Naples* dress, whose unusual buttermilk colour so effectively set off the pale highlights in her heavy honey-gold hair, while its fashionable tunic line not only suited her figure to admiration but combined style and severity in the precise proportions the occasion seemed to demand.

But the whole affair had been taken out of her hands. The matter was urgent, according to his lordship, and he proposed coming to the theatre between five and six – unless, his note had added with cursory politeness, it would discommode her – so that they might talk before the curtain went up. She could hardly reply that it *would* discommode her to receive him in the disreputable green room, whose slatternly splendours made such a perfect backcloth for the costume she wore, an antiquated confection of painted satin and imitation gems whose stage experience was far longer than her own. It did not trouble her that a whole generation of Virgin Queens had trodden the boards in it before her. What *did* trouble her was that despite Betsy's labours it was still a rather poor fit. She tugged impatiently at the stomacher, and the stitching came apart.

Betsy, clucking reproachfully, produced needle and thread. While she worked, her mistress stood dutifully still, surveying herself in the glass. Some day soon, she thought, someone was going to do something about introducing historical accuracy into stage costume. And not before time. She had seen enough Elizabethan portraits to know that, despite the ruff and stomacher, Good Queen Bess had never looked like this! And this dreadful glass did not help, either!

She moved abruptly. 'Have you done?'

42

Betsy, for whom the question had come a moment too soon, sucked the bead of blood welling from her finger, and nodded. If only her adored Miss Kate were as placid as her great dark eyes seemed to imply.

'Good! Then please go and fetch Elliston.'

Betsy gulped. No one 'fetched' Mr Elliston!

But to her infinite relief, there was at that moment a tap on the dressing-room door and Mr Elliston himself wafted into sight.

'Violin obbligato,' he murmured.

Kate looked at him. 'Certainly not,' she said. 'Violins, maybe. But with madrigals in the Elizabethan idiom, nothing is obbligato except the voices. Tell me,' she went on, and her voice was a purr. 'Whom have you found to take the other parts?'

'Others?' he inquired grandly. 'You need *others*?'

'Yes,' she said.

'There is a man called de Giovanni,' he conceded.

'I know him. He sings in a whisper just loud enough to show that he is out of tune.'

'And one named Fischer.'

'Who does, I admit, *breathe* in tune. Heavily.'

'And, if I recall, a Signor Rovedino.'

'Better,' she nodded approvingly. 'At least the audience can always tell when he is singing by the fact that he opens and closes his mouth.'

Elliston regarded her closely. 'My dear Katharine,' he said. 'Can it be that you are out of temper?'

The limpid eyes opened wide. 'My dear Robert!' she said. 'How could you tell?'

He smiled modestly.

'Look in my dressing glass,' she said.

He surveyed its foggy depths consideringly. 'You would like a new one?' he guessed.

'Oh, Lord High Elliston! Great actor! Great manager! Great man! Yes.'

'And larger?' he suggested munificently. 'So that you may study that slender, graceful figure *toute entière?*'

She frowned. His French was not very reliable. 'Yes,' she said.

'It shall be done.' Abstraction reclaimed him. 'Violin obbligato,' he murmured.

'Not for *The Triumphs of Oriana*!' He looked at her. 'Oh, very well, *Gloriana*. Though why it is necessary to change the name ... '

In his most magisterial way, he said, 'When you have been in the theatre as long as I, my child, you will recognize the need to have everything crystal clear for the audience. It is Gloriana, after all, who personifies England's defeat of the Spanish Armada. And who,' dismissively, 'was Oriana, in any case?'

'Well ... '

'No, no. Pray do not interrupt me. I know – you see? – I know she was a heroine of Spanish chivalry. And to sing of her triumphs in an Operatical Entertainment dedicated to the defeat of Spain could do nothing but confuse the gallery.' He thought for a moment. 'And the groundlings.'

She looked at him suspiciously. It sounded sensible enough, but Robert's arguments were noted for being slippery. Abandoning the problem, she said, 'Violin obbligato?'

'For the ghost scenes in *Hamlet*,' he replied, and turned away.

'Robert,' she called after him. 'Did you wish to talk to me?'

'Did I?' he wondered. 'Ah, yes. I have to warn you about the ships.'

'The ships?'

He said kindly, 'You know that you sing the madrigals while Drake plays bowls and so repels the Armada?'

'Ye-e-es,' she said.

'They roll.'

'The bowls?'

'No, no,' he said irritably. 'The ships. The wheeled ones we had left over from *The Siege of Rhodes*. The stage slopes a little to the footlights, and the ships are inclined to roll down into the orchestra. Ignore it,' he advised majestically. 'Just go on singing.'

'Very well.'

He waved an airy hand. 'Goodnight, sweet prince,' he intoned, and drifted off through the door again.

44

She looked after him. 'Prin *cess*,' she said acidly, and turned her attention back to the dressing glass.

Before leaving for the theatre, his lordship had taken the precaution of consulting one of the more recent reference works in his library. It was a book he had so far not found much occasion to use, the *Authentic Memoirs of the Green-Room, including Sketches, Biographical, Critical, & Characteristic, of the Performers of the Theatres Royal, Drury Lane, Covent Garden, and The Haymarket*. And so on. The editor, according to the preface, had 'admitted nothing but what he has been led to consider *as a fact*,' having formed a very low opinion of another work of the same kind issued twenty-four years earlier, which he claimed had been full of fabrications and had soon sunk into well-deserved oblivion. Briskly leafing through it, the earl decided this was certainly a book that would repay further study. The respectable John Philip Kemble, he discovered – Mrs Siddons' own brother – had once almost been prevented from appearing on stage because his laundress, too long unpaid, had refused to let him have his shirts back. And wild, truculent, drunken Edmund Kean had made his stage debut at the age of three as Sleeping Cupid. A commendable self-control carried the earl past other such tantalizing fragments until he found what he was looking for, the 'authentic memoir' of Signora Katarina, provisionally of Drury Lane. It stretched to two tightly-set pages.

'This young lady,' he read, 'already celebrated for her vocal abilities, was born in Shropshire of an extremely genteel family, in, we believe, about the year 1792. Her father having paid the debt of nature, our motherless heroine found herself, in consequence of some unfortunate speculations on the part of her deceased progenitor, deprived at one blow of parent, home, and fortune. Although possessed of some very respectable relations living in Hertfordshire, she disdained to cast herself upon their hospitality, and proposed instead to extricate herself from her difficulties by embracing a career as a concert singer, thus forfeiting the esteem of her relations, who wished to make a respectable provision for her in another sphere of life.'

As a governess, no doubt, thought his lordship savagely. Or

45

by marrying her off to some red-faced squire who was prepared to take her without a dowry.

'In deference to their sensibilities, however, our heroine chose to remain silent about her family name and to perform under the cognomen of Signora Katarina, a version of her Christian name. After a short but assiduous period of tuition under Mr Gesualdo Lanza, she collected as much courage as her natural diffidence would allow, and made her appearance at one of the concert rooms in this metropolis. Her success did not disappoint the expectations of her friends. Without any exuberance of ornament, and almost without effort, she threaded the mazes of the most difficult passages with admirable dexterity, and combined the most correct science with the most delightful brilliance of effect. She has since, for about three years, sung all the celebrated airs of Mandane in *Artaxerxes*, Polly in the *Beggar's Opera*, and Rosetta in *Love in a Village* with the greatest success in several Ladies' Concerts, public and private, at Bath, Bristol, Brighton, Dover, Deal, Chester, Hythe, Tunbridge Wells, &c. &c. and also appeared at the Pantheon, on its first opening, in the Italian Opera *Le Nozze di Figaro* of Mozart. Furthermore, she has often delighted the august patrons of the Philharmonic Society since that body was first established in 1813.'

His lordship decided to join the Society at once. He had only refrained, to date, because he had thought a regular programme consisting of not one symphony but two, not one overture but three, with the addition of at least one concerto, a number of vocal items, and a quartet or two as makeweight, was altogether more than his musical digestion could stand in a single evening.

'Desiring to expand her talents and become a candidate for Thespian honours, our heroine found an early place in the Olympic Theatre, now under the management of that noted luminary, Mr Elliston, where she has played a variety of roles with the greatest distinction during the last two years. We have seen her in some of the best characters of Mrs Siddons — somewhat distorted, it may be confessed, by the licensing provisions that forbid legitimate drama in its pure form to the lesser theatres — and despite all our veneration for that wonderful actress, dare to pronounce that the boldness of our heroine's attempts were justified by their success. She never forgets the woman in the actress, and never, in the midst of some sublime or pathetic passage, leads her auditors to suspect her of having made too close and recent a study of *Walker on Elocution*. On her recent application to the Managers of Drury Lane, she was tried and immediately engaged for the coming season. Whatever interest we might take in the success of her dramatic efforts has been increased and confirmed by the knowledge that she is not less entitled to praise and admiration in her private life than in her theatrical career. She is one of those who confer dignity and respectability on the profession by her refined appearance, correct behaviour, and purity of morals, and who are contributing to rescue the profession of the drama from the obloquy that has been cast upon it by prejudice and pride.'

What a splendid fellow! thought his lordship enthusiastically. His literary style might leave something to be desired, but his sentiments were quite unimpeachable.

When the earl presented himself at the house door of the Olympic soon after five o'clock, he did not know precisely what to expect. He had been backstage at Drury Lane on more than one occasion, for, like several dozen others among Sam Whitbread's friends, he had been persuaded to take £100 in shares to guarantee rebuilding costs after the fire in 1809 that had ruined not only the old theatre but its distinguished lessee, Richard Brinsley Sheridan. The earl could still see Sheridan watching the blaze, with a bottle clasped in his hand. When someone had suggested he should stand further back, he had said coolly, 'Cannot a man take a glass of wine by his own fireside?'

But the Olympic was not a 3,000-seat patent theatre, only a small pavilion built in 1806 mainly from timbers salvaged from a decrepit French warship, and licensed for music, pantomime, burlettas, and equestrian exhibitions. Philip Astley had sold it to Elliston in 1813, and he had hopefully rechristened it 'Little Drury Lane' until the Lord Chamberlain put his foot down.

The earl sniffed pleasurably. The backstage smells were the same, at any rate. With interest, he surveyed the room into which the doorkeeper directed him. It was clean enough, but incredibly untidy and urgently in need of refurbishing. There was little beyond a faint trace of colour in the ceiling coves to show that it had ever merited the name of green room. In a battered armchair in one corner sat an actor whom he recognized from the Norwich circuit. Blackett? No, Blanchard. His lordship bowed and sat down on a sofa that gave a tired twang of protest. Suppressing a grin, the earl bowed again in Mr Blanchard's direction and gingerly proceeded to re-adjust his limbs.

Five minutes passed, and then ten. Another actor entered the room, younger than Blanchard, and dashingly garbed in the ragged nether garments, striped jumper, and Liberty cap of the stage *sans-culotte*. The earl was just wondering, with interest, whose side Elliston thought the *sans-culottes* had been on at the time of the Armada, when the door opened again and Gloriana herself swept in.

She looked at the two players. 'William?' she said. 'Frederick?' They rose as one, bowed deeply, and departed.

The haughty gaze swivelled towards the earl. 'My Lord Moriston?' The voice was cool, commanding, faintly chiding, as if Majesty were consigning him, with the merest trace of regret, to the headsman.

The earl was already on his feet. But the sofa gave a valedictory groan and Gloriana's lashes flickered slightly. Compressing his lips against the surge of laughter welling in his throat, the earl replied with equal correctness, 'Miss Kenwood?' It clearly behoved him to hand her to a chair, and it was equally clear that the chair she had in mind was a straightbacked one that looked like the only piece of stable furniture in the room. Managing her stiff skirts and awkward ruff with the most perfect sang-froid, she sat down and looked at him composedly.

When he, too, had carefully seated himself, she said, 'You wished to speak to me?'

The soft, clear voice was as lovely as he had expected, the poise of the head as graceful, and the carriage as elegant. But the enormous dark eyes, so surprising with the honey-fair hair, the arched brows, the straight nose, the curving mouth, the faintly tinted, softly rounded cheeks that owed nothing to paint

48

or powder – all these had been dimmed by the barrier of the footlights. Miss Katharine Kenwood was an extremely beautiful young woman, even, he thought besottedly, when she chose to adopt a pose of regal indifference. He badly wanted to see her smile.

She said again, 'You wished to speak to me?'

With an unpleasant start, he remembered why he was here. Regardless of what he felt for her, Francis Mervyn's future was at the moment his primary concern, and in that matter Miss Kenwood was not his ally but his adversary. Reaction made his voice curt as he said, 'It is kind of you to receive me. I hope not to take up too much of your time.'

She hoped not, either. He was typical of the cool, controlled, and probably disapproving kind of man she had expected, and the fact that he was considerably younger than she had supposed, and strikingly good-looking into the bargain, irrationally increased her resentment. It had been impulse that had led her to talk to, and then employ John Townsend to investigate Imogen's murder, an impulse that had sprung as much from indignation over the Iredales' lack of initiative as from her own shock and anger. She did not regret it, but she did appreciate that to an unfriendly observer she might have been too quick to apportion blame. If she had been less positive with Townsend, she would probably not now have to justify herself to this formidable stranger. It was not as if she did not have problems enough already! Yet no matter how she looked at the question, everything Imogen had told her pointed to Francis Mervyn as the most likely murderer.

Unconsciously stiffening her spine, she looked at his lordship and said, 'Thank you. The curtain rises at six-thirty and *The Triumphs of Oriana* ... ' She corrected herself with invisible vexation. ' ... of *Gloriana* is the first work on the programme.'

'"Thus sang the shepherds and nymphs of Diana, Long live fair Oriana",' he quoted unexpectedly. 'Forgive me, but you are not singing all twenty-six of the madrigals, are you?'

'By no means,' she replied. 'That would leave insufficient time for the main entertainment of the evening, *The New Grand Serious Drama of Hamlet*.'

'With Mr Elliston as the Prince of Denmark?'

'The prince of Sweden,' she corrected him. 'This is not the Shakespearian tragedy of the same name, but an English translation of the French version made some years ago by Monsieur Ducis, who felt the original would benefit from redrafting in the style of Corneille.' The magnificent eyes defied him to comment.

He confined himself to a polite, 'Indeed?' Nerving himself to embark on the questions that had to be asked, he hoped to be able to phrase them in such a way as not to increase her resistance.

He said carefully, 'I imagine that Townsend has explained my involvement in the case of Miss Reece's murder. Francis Mervyn is my secretary, and I have the strongest regard for him. Nothing will induce me to believe that he is capable of killing a helpless young woman.' He paused. 'I did not know Miss Reece, just as you do not know Francis Mervyn.'

'I met him once,' she said austerely.

'Did you? Even so, I think you must agree that we both have our prejudices. I will be frank and admit that I have no proof that my secretary is innocent. On the other hand, Townsend has shown me no proof that he is guilty. Townsend's suspicions seem to be based largely on what you have told him. I wonder ...' he surveyed the luminous, unresponsive face before him, 'I wonder if you would be good enough to tell me why you are so sure that Miss Reece was murdered by Francis Mervyn?'

He had cut off her line of escape. If he had been hectoring, she would have felt justified in refusing to discuss the matter with him at all.

She said reluctantly, 'I have no proof either, of course. If I had, it would scarcely have been necessary to employ Townsend. But the circumstances...' Why, she wondered, was she hesitating? If he was going to tear her reasoning to shreds, he might as well tear it now as later. And the sooner she told him what he wanted to know, the sooner he would go away and leave her in peace.

He waited patiently.

She went on, 'As I said, I met your secretary once. He made me uneasy, with that extraordinary self-containment. I had the impression that if the lid blew off the effects would be quite frightening. Even then – and I am talking about six months ago

– I warned Imogen that nothing good would come of her relationship with him. What I said to Townsend, however, was based not only on my opinion of Mr Mervyn's personality. Imogen's murder led me to look for something more cogent...' She thought she saw scepticism in his face, and went on, her colour slightly heightened, 'And it was not difficult to find. Consider. The man who was keeping her had no reason to kill her, nor does he appear to have been the type of person who would have done so.'

His face changed slightly, and she read the question in it. 'No, I know almost nothing about him. I assume you are aware that he insisted on secrecy? I once asked Imogen why, but all she would say was that his reasons were good ones, and that for everyone's sake she proposed to respect them.'

'For *everyone*'s sake?'

Gloriana's mask slipped. An arrested look in her eye, Miss Kenwood said, 'Yes. Not "for his sake", or "for both our sakes". Quite definitely, "for everyone's sake". I attached no meaning to it at the time, but it *is* very suggestive, I suppose.'

'I interrupted. Please go on.'

Thoughtfully, she said, 'Yes. Well, from what Imogen told me, he was – is – the kind of person who would have disowned her without hesitation if she had displeased him. But no more than that. His style was cold realism, nothing as passionate as ...' She broke off. It was not scepticism in his face this time, but a hint of sympathetic amusement. An unwilling half smile curved her lips. 'Of course. How silly of me. I was going to say, "nothing as passionate as passion", but passion need not enter into it now, need it? You are thinking of blackmail?'

'Perhaps. The person, or persons, from whom the secret was being kept might have discovered it and taken independent action. That is one possibility. Another is that Imogen's protector, the mysterious "C.", might be the kind of man capable of murder in response to blackmail, even if he were not capable of it as an expression of passion.'

She considered this for a moment and then said, 'You are implying that *Imogen* might have been blackmailing him? And that's ridiculous!'

'Is it?'

The large dark eyes became, impossibly, larger. 'No,' she

said almost inaudibly. 'Strictly speaking, I suppose she was blackmailing Mr Mervyn.'

His lordship's brows snapped together.

Defensively, she said, 'But not in the way you think.'

'Tell me, please?'

'The thing was that the young woman to whom your secretary was hoping to become betrothed – I've forgotten her name – seems to have been a very innocent, conventional girl, and Mr Mervyn knew it would be the end of everything if she found out about Imogen. Imogen, of course,' she sighed, 'threatened to tell her. In fact, she was so desperately in love with him that she told him she was expecting a child, and that he was the father.'

The earl's eyes closed for an exasperated moment.

'It wasn't true, as a matter of fact. She wasn't expecting a child. But she would have said or done *anything* to persuade him to marry her. It was extraordinary, her feeling for him. Almost as if she were possessed.'

'I take it she was an emotional person?'

'No. *That's* what was so extraordinary. She was bright, vivid, amusing in some people's company; calm and restful with others. But although that might sound as if she had an unstable temperament, it was really just that she was unusually responsive to the mood of the people she was with. Perhaps she was too anxious to be liked, which made her adapt herself too readily to her company. But her feet were always firmly on the ground – until she met Francis Mervyn. Then, it was as if every commonsensical instinct had flown out of the window!'

'Have you any idea . . . how they . . . met?' His voice trailed off abstractedly, his eyes on the dark-breeched, white-shirted figure that had just materialized in the doorway. It was not a tall figure, nor a very athletic one – indeed, its waistline and stomach would have benefited from the discipline of a Cumberland corset – but its air of sublimity was something to behold. Wherever Robert William Elliston walked, or stood, or sat, there was the theatre. He carried his pits, boxes, and galleries invisibly around with him. On flintiest pavements, he would tread the boards still. Other actors might claim to be the same natural, easy creatures *on* the stage as they were off, but Elliston was precisely the same person *off* the stage as he was

52

on. The earl suspected that if he chose to address the actor at this moment – and he certainly expected to have to talk to him – he would find himself in converse not with Mr Elliston at all, but with Hamlet, Prince of Denmark. No, he remembered, not Denmark. Sweden.

The great man had a faraway look in his eye as the harassed menial behind him skipped forward and said, 'I beg pardon, sir?'

'Violin obbligato,' said Hamlet.

The menial turned and passed the words on to an underling in his train, who carefully noted them down.

'Oh, really!' exclaimed Miss Kenwood and, rising, swept towards them. 'Pay no attention, Cox. And if that man is the printer, for heaven's sake tell him to cross out what he has just written. Otherwise, you will find that next week's bill commits us to a hitherto unknown burletta calld *violin obbligato*. With one "b", no doubt. It is the conductor who needs to know. Mr Elliston wants a violin in the ghost scenes tonight.'

'Thank you, Miss Katarina,' said Cox gratefully, and grasping the bemused printer by the arm hustled him out just as a motley crowd of Spanish seamen, clowns, and gravediggers trooped into the room. One of the clowns tossed a skull on the earl's sofa. It bounced.

'Katharine, my dear,' said Hamlet in tones of pleased surprise, taking her hands in his and holding them wide. 'You look superb. And your voice? But when,' he answered himself, 'is it anything other than superb? The curtain rises in two minutes. Are you ready?'

'What?' she exclaimed, and turning to his lordship with a hasty, 'forgive me, I must go,' she vanished through the crowd.

The earl hesitated. To leave or stay? Postponing the decision, he nodded towards poor Yorick, and said to the clown, 'An acquaintance of yours?' The clown, who on closer inspection turned out to be Joe Munden, grinned and said, 'You've heard about our old friend Cooke, have you? No, as far as I know, his skull is still touring America with the troupe it was willed to. Did you ever meet ... '

He was interrupted by the entry of the harassed Mr Cox, who

cried anxiously, 'On stage, please. *Please*, gentlemen, on stage!'

'Don't mind if I leave our friend here, do you?' asked Joe Munden. 'I have to go and help push the Armada out to sea!' With another of his infectious grins, he burrowed off towards the door.

Like magic, the green room emptied. Almost at once, a neat little maid-servant appeared at his lordship's side. She curtseyed. 'My name's Betsy, sir. Miss Kate said to tell you you may wait if you wish. Or perhaps you'd prefer to suggest a time for tomorrow, if you have anything you're still desirous to talk to her about.'

She had a soft West-country voice, and the earl smiled at her. 'Tell me, Betsy, what will your mistress do when she comes off stage? Does she usually stay here, or go home? Has she had anything to eat?'

'Oh, no, sir!' Betsy exclaimed. 'She never eats until after the performance. Sometimes it's ever so late and she doesn't want to eat at all. But tonight she's only in *Gloriana*, so she'll be ready to go home about eight.'

He reflected. There was no question of taking a lady out to dine in a public place, and if he kept her here in the theatre she would starve, poor love. But he had a shrewd idea that even if he sent Betsy out to the finest chop house in the neighbourhood, the best she would be able to bring back would be a steak pudding or something of the sort, which, while no doubt sustaining, could hardly be considered romantic.

'Betsy,' he said. 'If I arrange for some food to be brought in, do you think your mistress and I might sit down to it somewhere reasonably quiet? We have not finished our talk, and this,' he looked round the green room, 'is scarcely the ideal place.'

'Ooh, sir!' she breathed. He was a lovely gentleman. 'I can lay it out for you in Miss Kate's dressing-room. Even with the door open, you'd be much more private.'

'Splendid!' he said, pleased with the suggestion. 'I will go and arrange the food, while you go and arrange the setting. I will be back very soon.'

54

Chapter 5

Something over an hour later, Miss Kenwood found her way back to her dressing-room, her beautiful eyes brimming with unshed tears.

'Inevitable!' she sobbed. 'Quite inevitable!' She sank down before her dressing glass, her shoulders quivering, and buried her face in her hands.

His lordship, who had been watching from the wings, said, 'You have my deepest sympathy. I do not remember when I have laughed so much. It must have been agony to have to go on singing!'

Her voice muffled by her hands, she said, 'And Elliston even warned me before the performance. *Me*, but not the conductor!' She moaned. 'I don't think I shall ever forget the orchestra's faces when they saw, not just one but two Spanish galleons thundering down on them. I thought they were all going to fling down their instruments and dive headfirst over the rail and into the pit.'

'While all the brave mariners leapt into the ocean and pushed the ships back through the swell ... '

'Tripping over the canvas waves!'

'And a couple of gravediggers and the ghost of Hamlet's father came rushing on from the wings to help ... '

She raised her face, alive with laughter, and his heart missed a beat. 'While, safe on Plymouth Hoe, I went on singing, and Rovedino mouthing, and de Giovanni whispering, and that idiot Fischer muttering "Mein Gott!" under his breath.'

'It went down very well with the audience,' said his lordship judicially. 'I shouldn't think there was a dry eye in the house.'

She suffered a slight relapse. 'That's what is so dreadful,' she

55

wailed. 'The galleries and the pit enjoyed themselves so much that Robert will insist on having it done that way *every time!*'

Belatedly, she became aware of him. He did not seem to be shocked or disapproving. Indeed, the half-light that was all that penetrated into the dressing-room at this time of the evening showed his eyes bright with amusement and the long, firm mouth creased at the corners. But she suspected it of being only a momentary aberration.

Sitting up, she dried her eyes with a wisp of white lawn and tried to collect herself. 'Alas for dignity!' she sighed, with a touch of deprecation. 'I assume you wish to continue our conversation, Lord Moriston? Perhaps you would be good enough to give me the opportunity to change my clothes and remove my make-up, and then ... ' For the first time, she noticed that the table in the corner had been set with linen, silver, glasses and covered dishes. There was a napkin-shrouded basket, too, and a chafing dish over a small flame, and a wine bottle beaded with condensation, and in the centre a vase of roses.

She looked at Betsy and then at his lordship. 'What ... ?'

'My conscience would not permit me to keep you talking when Betsy tells me you have not eaten since midday. So I sent my groom home for supplies. I hoped you would not take it amiss?'

She did, at first. Her housekeeper never prepared dinner for her until she had actually arrived home. The theatre was too unpunctual for any set routine. When she was very late, she sometimes did not eat at all, or went to the kitchen herself and found what she wanted. In truth, a quiet, civilized meal was an unlooked-for pleasure. But she thought he had been at best high-handed, and at worst condescending. She was not, it seemed, to be relieved of his company until he had discovered everything he wanted to know.

Coolly, she said, 'It was kind of you, but quite unnecessary. I am not accustomed to eat a great deal.'

But his lordship was learning every minute. 'How wise!' he said affably. 'Just think what *The Examiner* said of Madame Bertinotti – that she was too excessively well fed for a tragic

56

heroine, and clearly more skilful at wielding a knife and fork than a dagger.'

She giggled. 'No! Did it really? How splendid. And perfectly true. I never saw anyone look less as if she were wasting away in memory of a lost love, or being starved to death by some evil tyrant. For to sing in opera is to be doomed to an eternal round of sorrowing in semibreves and dying in diatonics. That is why *I* elected to vary my engagements. I felt I was about to expire from sheer melancholy.' She decided to resign herself to the inevitable. It would be ungracious, not to say ill bred, to refuse his hospitality. And besides, she had suddenly realized that she was remarkably hungry.

The impromptu supper was a notable success. From the direction of the stage came the constant murmur, sometimes rising to a roar, of the audience signifying its approval of Elliston, its idol, in time-honoured fashion. At one point, there was an earsplitting flourish of trumpets, followed by an eternity of morris-dance music. 'The king holding wassail,' Miss Kenwood remarked knowledgeably. Later came the tread of many feet. Fortinbras, and soldiers, marching? Or Laertes, followed by Danes (or Swedes)? As Miss Kenwood said cheerfully, one of the advantages of *Hamlet* was that it went on forever, so they need not worry about being disturbed for at least another three hours, especially with Betsy sitting on guard by the open door.

Surveying the gastronomic delights before her – the chilled Madeira consommé, the tiny, creamy, seafood *crêpes*, the *petits poussins* with their garnish of green, the fresh crisp rolls, still miraculously warm, the truffled ragout in the chafing dish, the cheese ramekins, the strawberry pastries and the raspberry creams – Miss Kenwood exclaimed, 'Your chef must be a marvel to pack all this into hampers at a moment's notice. Does he not object to preparing picnics when he has dinner to attend to?'

'My sister and brother are both dining out, I believe. But Alexandre will certainly have resigned by now, if he has been able to find anyone to resign *to*. He always does when his arrangements have been disrupted. However, I will talk to him sympathetically tomorrow, and he will agree – "jus' thees one

57

taime" – to withdraw his resignation, as a special concession. He always does. If the truth be told, nothing gives him more pleasure than an opportunity to top off his temperaments with a display of magnanimity.'

She accepted some seafood *crêpes.* 'Are his arrangements often disrupted?'

'About one day in four, when I am at home. I shudder to think how often when I am away. May I pour some wine for you?'

It was surprising how much they found to talk about, without touching on anything that might have been construed as personal. The earl did not even try to discover, as he might have done before reading the *Authentic Memoirs*, whether they had any acquaintance in common. He felt the name Kenwood ought to mean something to him in the context of Shropshire, but irritatingly it did not. And to ask would have been to invite the chilliest setdown. Miss Kenwood, he thought with loving exasperation, would regard her private life as very much her own concern.

In the end, they had to return to Francis Mervyn.

'You were asking me,' she said, 'how he and Imogen met. It was a very prolonged business, I may tell you, for they had been admiring each other from a distance for weeks. I remember when she first told me she had seen "*such* a man, a very god!" riding in the New Road. She saw him several times over a period of about two months and was increasingly attracted to him, not because he was dashing or gaily dressed (which he was not), or because he was handsome (which she thought he was), but because she was fascinated by what she called the "calm privacy" of his expression. She took to walking and riding along the New Road deliberately, and began to think of the younger men of her acquaintance as boisterous young puppies, and the older ones as staid and predictable. She became obsessed over the question of whether he had so much as noticed her existence. I remember her exclaiming once, "Better to be merely looked on by that fine, noble being, than adored by all the other men in creation!"

'I thought she was enacting a private drama for her own amusement, no more, and I laughed at her. But she paid no attention. If only she could see him once in company, she said, walking or riding with someone she had met before, she could at least discover his name.'

The earl smiled. 'I imagine she had no luck in that direction.'

'None. He was always alone. Occupied on business for you, I imagine?'

'Not at all. Francis has a consuming interest in architecture, and his idea of exercise is not a mild trot in the Park but a pilgrimage north to watch the progress of Nash's current enterprise by the New Road.'

'The Regent's Park scheme? But there's so little there at the moment!'

'True. The Circus is under way, though, even if – from what I hear – the whole plan is in danger of being watered down by the miserliness of the Treasury. I fear that Park Circus may diminish into a mere Park Crescent. But that's by the by. How did Miss Reece ultimately succeed in attracting the notice of my godlike secretary?'

'To be honest, I don't know. She was somewhat reticent about it, and I suspect that she was reduced to dropping her muff beneath his horse's hooves, or something equally un-subtle. However, one day she was quite ecstatic, for he had actually looked her in the eye, although he had not spoken. I told her she was in danger of making a complete fool of herself over a man who, for all she knew, might be vulgar, or ill-mannered, or downright criminal, but all she would say was that any of these faults would delight her, because she would become heart-whole again in a moment. "How many fine, elegant-looking young men have I seen about the streets," she said, "or at the theatre, who have not made the slightest impression on me? Yet if I could touch even his horse, I should be half wild with joy!"'

With a touch of self-mockery, the earl recognized that today he was able to understand Miss Reece's feelings a good deal better than he would have done yesterday.

Miss Kenwood went on, 'By this time it had ceased to be a laughing matter, and I told her she was being foolish beyond permission. It was useless. She said, "I know, but I cannot help myself!" Then one night she went to the Opera with Julia Johnstone. Do you know Mrs Johnstone?'

59

'I know *of* her, but very little. The "Mrs" is a courtesy title, I believe?'

She smiled. 'Only because there is no justice in the world. She has been a most dutiful and faithful wife to Colonel Cot . . . – no, I must preserve his *nom de guerre* – Colonel Johnstone for eight years now, and a loving mother to their eight children.'

'Good God!' exclaimed his lordship.

Miss Kenwood's eyes took on the melancholy look that he was beginning to recognize as a presage of one of her more sardonic observations. 'But alas!' she said. 'The Colonel has another wife, to whom he is legally married and with whom he lives on terms of the most perfect amity. They,' she paused, 'have *ten* children.'

The earl threw back his head and laughed. 'And to think I was about to ask you whether "Colonel Cot . . ." might possibly be Imogen's "Mr C." He could scarcely have had the time, I imagine.'

'Or the energy,' supplied Miss Kenwood before she could stop herself.

His lordship, delighted by this extremely improper remark, succeeded in concealing it at the expense of a slight constraint in his voice – which Miss Kenwood, regrettably if understandably, misinterpreted. He said, 'Mrs Julia Johnstone, however, scarcely lives the life of a recluse?'

She retreated into society manners. 'I believe she was accustomed to visit and entertain when the Colonel was not at home, for I know that Imogen made a number of acquaintances at her house. But to return to the evening at the Opera. Imogen was seated with Mrs Johnstone in her box when, in another box, she saw a man sitting alone. It turned out to be her adored stranger.'

'Oh dear!' said his lordship mildly. 'So the fault must lie at my door for giving Francis *carte blanche* to use my box whenever he wished.'

She smiled politely. 'By asking some friends who came to talk to her in one of the intervals, Imogen at last discovered who he was. But she was still no further on. Or so she thought. Because it later transpired that Mr Mervyn had seen her, too, and made it his business to ask about her. Even so, it took another two weeks – and very tedious weeks they were – before anything further occurred. Then, one evening, she happened to go to the window, and there, riding by with his face turned towards the house, was Mr Mervyn. Imogen's version of what ensued reminded me forcibly of one of the sicklier melodramas. Their eyes met. She clasped her hands to her bosom, and gazed passionately down at him. He changed colour, reined in, made as if to speak, and then suddenly put spurs to his horse and galloped off into the twilight. Imogen slept not a wink that night, but next morning she received her reward for all the weeks of yearning in the form of a letter from him. I don't recall the precise words, but it said something to the effect that he had long desired to make her acquaintance, and dared to hope that she felt the same. If so, would she write to him, for he was hers to command. And that was that. Unfortunately.'

His lordship hesitated. 'I know you were very much attached to Miss Reece, and I have no wish to offend you, but from what you have said she appears to have thrown herself at his head. She could scarcely have behaved more invitingly – short of going straight up to him and telling him how she felt.'

'Perfectly true,' she admitted. 'And I imagine few young men would have resisted the invitation. In fact, it seemed to me to be to Mr Mervyn's credit that he resisted it for so long. Imogen was an extremely pretty girl, and most young men would have come running at her very first smile. It was a pity that his reserve had the effect of increasing her infatuation. No, I have nothing to say against your secretary's behaviour at the beginning, but I do hold him very much at fault for what happened afterwards. He did not reciprocate her feelings, except perhaps in the early stages. He simply *used* her, until he decided he had no further need for her.'

The earl was in a difficult position. He knew from Townsend that Imogen's family and friends believed that, although it was necessity that had driven her to accept the offer of security from a rich man, the relationship was a stable one, a marriage in all but name, characterized by fidelity and a measure of affection. They saw it as almost, if not quite, respectable, just as it was almost, if not quite, a matter for understanding and sympathy that Imogen should have fallen passionately in love with someone else. Whereas the truth was that she had become a recognized demi-rep, with a small and select circle of clients, and that Francis had naturally – if regrettably – treated her as such.

If he told Miss Kenwood this, she would probably not believe him, and even if she did would dislike him for it. He had never known people think kindly of whoever was responsible for ridding them of their illusions.

Postponing the problem, he said, 'I wonder if you would assume for the moment that Francis Mervyn, despite his other misdeeds, did not murder Miss Reece. From what you know, does anyone else spring to mind?'

She shrugged her shoulders. 'The man who was keeping her. Who else?'

'And if not he?'

'Then whoever the secret of his relationship with her was being kept from.'

'And if not?' He paused. 'What about Elliston?'

She looked at him incredulously. *'Robert?'*

'Why not?'

'It's too ridiculous!' She giggled mischievously. 'Though I suppose if he had been playing Othello and was still in the mood ... !'

'What about the – er – casual acquaintances you met at Miss Reece's apartment?'

'Her court of young gallants, you mean? Quite harmless, all of them. She enjoyed company, and had ambitions to hold a salon. Her "evenings", as she called them, kept her up to date on gossip and fashions and so on.'

'No heavier artillery?'

'Not to my knowledge.'

He thought for a moment. 'Perhaps you could give me a few names?'

She frowned. She had no desire to drag a number of perfectly innocent young men into this unpleasant affair. On the other hand, she recognized that the earl had no alternative but to pursue every possibility. She said, 'I will try to set down a list tomorrow.'

'Thank you. And if by any chance you should happen to remember the name of the young lady who was Miss Reece's rival for my secretary's affections, it would be most helpful. As

Townsend may have told you, Francis is on holiday at the moment, quite legitimately. I hope to be in touch with him reasonably soon, but I would prefer not to be held up in the meantime for lack of information.'

The evening was at an end. The earl could discover no excuse for prolonging it, and Miss Kenwood, a little tired, had no wish to. She refused his escort home, politely. Her own arrangements, she said, were already made.

'I will send my groom up,' he remarked, 'to relieve you of all this clutter. Perhaps Betsy could ensure that he does not simply sweep it all into the cloth and tie up the corners, otherwise I fear Alexandre might well decide to let his resignation stand!'

She smiled again, politely.

As he bowed over her hand and opened his mouth to take a graceful farewell, there was a resounding series of crashes and a volley of acrid smoke surged into the backstage corridor. The earl closed his mouth abruptly, while Miss Kenwood, to some extent forewarned and protected by her position inside the door of her dressing-room, clamped her lips firmly together and tried very hard not to laugh. From the stage came an explanatory yell from Osric, ' . . . to the ambassadors of England gives, this warlike volley.' And then, over a background of splutters and coughs from the audience, the pained and reproving tones of Hamlet, Prince of Sweden. 'Horatio! Alack, I die! I die, I die, Horatio!'

The earl knew when he was beaten. With a last speechless glance at the afflicted face of his beloved, he bowed again and took his departure into the night.

Chapter 6

Just after eleven next morning, sombrely clad – as seemed fitting to the occasion – in black coat, grey silk waistcoat, and grey knitted pantaloons, the Earl of Moriston stepped into his town carriage and ordered his groom to drive him to the residence of the Reverend and Mrs Rowland Iredale, sole surviving relatives of the late Imogen Reece.

It was another brilliant day, and the streets were unusually full of people for the month of August. Affairs were still unsettled as a result of the recent upheavals on the Continent and the final defeat of the Little Corporal, and a great many gentlemen had sent their womenfolk off to the country or the sea while they themselves remained in town to keep an eye on things. With light hands, Fielding coaxed his lordship's highbred greys through the press of traffic in Piccadilly – bright yellow curricles; phaetons and carriages with blue, mulberry, crimson, or green bodies; and solitary horsemen returning from a morning ride in the Park. The earl noticed a couple of moustachioed Hussar officers languidly surveying the passing throng, and a Life Guard in his Grecian helm crossing the road towards St James's. Wellington, he knew, had been forced to relax the ban on home leave he had issued so uncompromisingly after Waterloo, when he had found his army beginning to melt away like snow in summer. As a result, London would soon be filled with dashing veterans of his greatest battle. The earl supposed that his brother Robert, next in age to him and a cavalry officer who had, he understood, been engaged at Ligny, would turn up on the doorstep soon. As the carriage crossed from Piccadilly into Coventry Street, he glanced down to the right and noted the flurry of building activity in the stretch leading down to Carlton House, the open space that

64

would ultimately be the starting point for the new royal mile that was destined to lead from Carlton House to the Regent's new Park.

On the carriage went down Coventry Street, then left and right into Gerrard Street, up Monmouth Street, and across St Giles's to the borders of the Bedford Estate. Fielding reined the horses in to a standstill outside a smallish terrace house in one of the unpretentious streets off Bedford Square. They were neat houses, stucco-faced on the ground or rustic floor, brick above, with railed areas and panelled front doors chastely free of ornament and surmounted by segmented fanlights.

With a brief word to his groom, the earl descended from the carriage and mounted the four shallow front steps. But even as he raised his hand to ply the knocker, the door opened to reveal, not a butler, nor, as he had half expected, a little maid of all work, but the black-garbed figure of a clergyman who was presumably the master of the house.

'She won't see you, you know,' said this gentleman without preamble. 'She doesn't want to see anyone.'

The earl was momentarily taken aback. In his experience, clergymen were never rude to a landowner who might have a comfortable parish to bestow. He suspected there might be some mistake.

'My name is Moriston,' he said.

'Yes, I know. I got your message. But she won't see you. Or anybody.'

For an astounded moment the earl thought the door was about to be slammed in his face. But the Reverend Rowland Iredale was clearly so shocked by his own temerity that he hesitated, allowing just sufficient time to elapse for the earl to say in his usual calm, unhurried tones, 'I quite understand. But I think she might be prepared to talk to me if I might have the opportunity to explain why.'

'She won't ...'

'Perhaps we could leave it to Mrs Iredale to decide?' His lordship's manner could scarcely have been more bland. 'It is important, I assure you. If she is still not prepared to talk to me after I have explained, I will not, of course, be so discourteous as to insist.'

Iredale stood there, worriedly chewing his lip. He was a slim

65

man of something above average height, with a mane of fair hair, steel-rimmed spectacles, and the now somewhat slack remnants of what must once have been boyish good looks. The earl knew that he was thirty-five years of age, but he could easily have been considerably younger or older.

'What do you want to talk to her about?'

The earl, weary of being kept on the doorstep, glanced to his right and left. An errand boy was whistling his way down the area steps of the house on the right, while the front door of that on the left was just opening to eject a middle-aged lady and two younger ones, obviously her daughters. Gratefully, his lordship heard her exclaim in piercing tones, 'Selina, I have forgotten the pattern for the new cushions. Pray run and fetch it from my dressing table. We will wait for you.'

He looked at Rowland Iredale and said, 'You wish me to tell you *here*?' The clergyman's expression changed, and, opening the door to its widest extent, he stepped to one side and declaimed in the carrying tones of a man trained to the pulpit, 'Do, pray, come in, *Lord* Moriston!' Then, as the earl strode thankfully past him into the hall, he poked his head outside, and with the mellow air of a bishop conferring a blessing, said, 'Why, good morning, Mrs Corder! *What* a delightful day! Off to make some purchases?'

His lordship waited amusedly in the narrow hall until Iredale turned and opened the first door on the left. 'Perhaps you would come in here for the moment, my lord?' His decision to allow the earl to cross his threshold had at least restored his manners, even if he was not as yet sure whether to give the earl access to the misanthropic Olivia.

Rarely had his lordship seen a room so full of books. It stretched right through from the front of the house to the back, and there were books not only on the shelves and tables, but on every piece of movable furniture, chairs included, as well as the window ledges and the floor. Towards the back of the room they appeared to be in neat piles, but at the front many of them were in the wildest disarray, lying open on top of each other in slipping, sliding profusion. It seemed a very cavalier way of treating books whose bindings showed them to be, almost without exception, old and valuable.

Following him in, Iredale closed the door with some care and said, 'You see me at work, I fear.' His eyes darted about the room, and then he scooped some books off a chair with practised hands, deposited them on the floor, and said, 'Would you care to sit down, my lord?'

The earl did so, while his host pushed a few volumes back from the edge of a large work table and leaned against it.

It was not an attractive room, everything that might have given it charm having been removed to make way for the books. There were no pictures on the walls, only dusty rectangles where they had been, and the floor was uncarpeted. The curtains, pulled fully back from the windows to let in maximum light, were marked and creased over their lower halves where dusty tomes had been piled against them.

'You are librarian to Lord Ballinton, I believe,' said his lordship, making conversation.

The clergyman was chewing his lip again. 'Only to the extent that he wanted his books catalogued.'

'I should have thought ... '

'Oh, yes. A *sort* of catalogue does exist, but it's no more than a list of titles. And with the prices old books are fetching at auction these days, his lordship is anxious to know whether he has anything saleable.'

'Such as a two thousand-guinea Valdarfar Boccaccio, or a one thousand-guinea Caxton's *Troy*?' the earl asked drily.

'Maybe. But I haven't found anything like that yet.' Iredale woke up slightly. 'You know something about books, my lord?'

'I'm not a collector, if that's what you mean. But I have an interest, and I remember the prices at the Roxburghe sale two or three years ago.'

'Who doesn't? They're what stimulated Lord Ballinton to look through his library. Not that I've found anything so rarefied – yet. There're a few oddities and collections. There was a scrapbook of twopenny portraits of criminals that fetched fifty-four pounds at the Roxburghe sale, and three volumes of half-penny ballads that reached one hundred and seventy-seven. That kind of thing is more in our line.'

The earl did not feel that he was making much headway. Iredale, obviously, was talking for the sake of talking, while he debated within himself whether to allow the earl to see his wife.

He did not appear to be a true bibliophile, prepared to relax his hostility in an atmosphere of bibliomaniacal gossip.

Changing his tactics, the earl said, 'Have you always specialized in this field?'

'In books? No. But impoverished parsons have to take what employment they can find.'

It sounded more promising. 'The situation in London is not easy, I know,' said his lordship. 'One of my brothers is in the Church, and considers himself very fortunate to have a town living, although "fortunate" is not a word I would choose, myself, to use in connection with a parish that borders on Seven Dials.'

A faint gleam of interest had come into the pale eyes. 'Nor I. A clergyman by choice, is he?' He exhaled a cynical breath, and answered his own question. 'But of course. A member of *your* family would not be forced to do what he didn't wish to.'

It was an extremely impolite remark, however true, but his lordship chose not to take offence. He raised his eyebrows mildly, and the other man shrugged and said, 'I apologize. That was uncalled for. But in my own case, when I had taken my degree my father refused me any further financial aid and told me I could be a college tutor or a parson. When I jibbed, he said, "Then you may go as a supercargo to China". So I went into the Church.'

'And your interest in books?'

'I had a small West-country living for three years, and then the squire asked me to become tutor to his elder son, who was supposed to be going to Weimar before he went up to Oxford. But Napoleon put an end to that, and we went to Edinburgh instead. After the first son had completed his education, I became tutor to the second. But when I married, my wife wished to be in London to be near her sister. Until a few years ago, I could have had a country parish and still been able to live in London, provided I could find a neighbouring curate to fulfil the majority of my parish duties. But the Act compelling clergy to reside in their parishes ruled that out. However, I have a few minor appointments. I preach at the Foundling Hospital sometimes, and take the morning service at St-George's-in-Bloomsbury. And I am occasionally asked to deputize for other clergymen. About a year ago, the squire heard of his lordship's project of cataloguing his library and recommended me for the task. His lordship is not, by nature, a scholarly gentleman, and was happy to be relieved of the prospect of finding someone for himself. So I became interested in books.'

From what the earl knew of Lord Ballinton, this sounded entirely plausible. Furthermore, an impoverished clergyman could be got, he supposed, for about £100 a year – rather less than half what the earl paid his chef. He felt sorry for Iredale, but at the same time considered him a spineless creature.

Perhaps aware of sounding ungracious, Iredale said, 'I do know something about them now, a good deal, in fact. I might even be able to build a career there, given time. Look at Dibdin. He is in orders, but who could have a more enjoyable life? Lord Spencer sends him all over the place, visiting libraries and shops and bookstalls, and now that Boney's been defeated he'll be off to France and Germany again, no doubt, bribing librarians and monks to part with their treasures.'

'Not everyone, however,' said his lordship gently, 'is quite as ready to pour out gold as Spencer is, for the sake of enriching the library at Althorp. But certainly, if you have no vocation for the pulpit, I imagine you are wise to look elsewhere.'

For the first time, Iredale's eyes focussed on him properly, and his mouth relaxed into something resembling a smile. 'Thank you, my lord,' he said. 'I am afraid I may not have been as respectful this morning as I should have been, but we have been somewhat disturbed here lately, as you may imagine. Perhaps you will forgive . . . '

The door crashed open, and framed in it stood a woman who, though still quite young, was dressed in a matronly, high-necked gown of dull buff and a frilled muslin cap tied firmly under her rounded chin. She bore a feather duster in one hand, and was obviously in a thoroughly bad temper.

She did not see his lordship at first, but addressed the clergyman as if she were continuing something she had been saying only a moment earlier. Her face flushed to an unbecoming dusky pink, she announced, 'And what is more, Mr Iredale, if he *should* come you will oblige me by ensuring that the door is not opened to him! Why should he wish to talk to me? None of this is any of his business!'

It could be no one other than Mrs Iredale. Her husband, who had stood silent during this speech, with his mouth slightly ajar, found his tongue again. Hurrying forward, he put his arm round her shoulders and said warningly, 'There, there, my dear! As you see, Lord Moriston has come to call on you. He has promised not to persist if you do not wish to speak to him.'

Swinging round, she saw his lordship for the first time. He bowed. But she was not in the least abashed. If anything, she became even angrier. Planting her fists on her hips, so that she inadvertently poked her husband in the stomach with the feather duster and left a patch of fluff on his waistcoat, she demanded, 'Why did I not hear the knocker? Who let you in? That maid must go, Mr Iredale! I gave her the clearest instructions!'

'Yes, yes, my dear. The blame is mine. I just happened to open the door – to see if the bread man was coming, you know? – when his lordship was mounting the steps.'

'Then why did you not send him away? You know I don't want to talk to him!'

'Hush, my dear! Hush! You will give his lordship a very odd impression of you.' He looked at the earl in embarrassment. 'My good lady is most upset by our recent bereavement, as you can see. Quite distracted.' His tone was almost pleading. 'She was very fond of her sister, very fond. We both were.' He went back to chewing his lip again.

Mrs Iredale ignored him. Continuing to stare at the earl, while still addressing her husband, she said, 'And why did you bring him in here? He will think you quite rag-mannered not to have taken him up to the drawing room.' Both men looked at her in surprise. 'Would you come this way, my lord, please?' She laid her duster down on a convenient pile of books, wiped her hands daintily on her skirt, gave a tweak to the muslin bow under her chin, and said conversationally as she led him up the narrow flight of stairs. 'We have only the one servant at the moment, so perhaps you will forgive everything not being done in proper form.'

With the Reverend Rowland Iredale hovering nervously

behind, they entered a rather meanly-proportioned but spotlessly clean room, furnished, the earl guessed, from the parental home, and marred only by the superabundance of ornaments, knick-knacks, tapestried cushions, mats, bellpulls, and footstools that filled every available space. Charitably, the earl assumed that some of them had had to be cleared out of the rooms downstairs to make way for Ballinton's books.

'May we offer you some refreshment?' Mrs Iredale said. She had lost her high colour, but his lordship still scented an inferior wine laced with rat poison. He said, 'Thank you, no,' and waited for his hostess to seat herself.

She said composedly, 'What did you wish to talk to me about?' She had a round, almost pretty face with regular features, and soft light brown hair, but her eyebrows were too thick and her blue eyes not sufficiently wide for beauty, and the sulky lips had developed the little folds of flesh at the corners that signal chronic discontent. Townsend had said that Imogen was somewhat on the plump side, and this was obviously a family characteristic.

The virago of a few minutes earlier had disappeared, so the earl risked going straight to the point. 'I wished to talk to you about my secretary,' he said. 'His name is Francis Mervyn, and Bow Street suspects that he killed your sister. May I offer you my condolences over that matter?'

Mrs Iredale inclined her head slightly.

His lordship continued, 'Francis Mervyn has worked for me for six years now, and I know him well. I do not believe he was responsible, and I am engaged in trying to prove it.' He hesitated. 'Now, although I am sure that you want your sister's murderer caught and punished, I cannot believe you would want Francis Mervyn to be condemned if he is, in fact, innocent?'

'I am afraid I have no information that will help you.' Her tone was final.

'But if an innocent man is convicted, Mrs Iredale, the guilty man goes free.'

'I can't help that.'

'But you wouldn't want it?'

'What I want is no concern of yours.'

The earl studied her thoughtfully. 'Mrs Iredale, I can assure you that anything you might choose to tell me would be a matter of confidence between us.' Her face had tightened again, and her resistance was almost tangible. What, he wondered, was the irritant factor? Parson's wife, or not, it seemed unlikely that she was Christian enough to *want* to turn the other cheek and let the murderer go free. An idea occurred to him. 'If you are anxious to prevent the fact that your sister was – er – being supported by a man who was not her husband from becoming public knowledge ... '

He had just enough warning to duck before first one knick-knack and then another went flying past his head, to end in a tinkling crash against the wall. He fielded the third one neatly just as Iredale made a grab for his wife's wrist and frustrated the despatch of a fourth. There was a moment's heavy-breathing silence. The earl glanced at the small china figurine in his hand and thought that it had perhaps been a mistake to save it. He had never cared much for Capo-di-Monte, even when genuine. Rising to his feet, he restored it politely to one of the empty spaces on the table beside his hostess. She might need it again.

As if nothing had happened, he said, 'I will be perfectly willing to keep it quiet, if that is at all possible.'

Her chest still heaving and her nostrils dilated, she said, 'Why did you *say* that?' Her husband gently unclamped her fingers and relieved her of a small glass paperweight.

'Say what, precisely?'

'Why did you lie about my sister?'

Momentarily nonplussed, he repeated, 'Lie?'

'Did you know her?'

'No.'

'Then how dare you talk about her like that?'

He waited, but she had finished. He said, 'Even if I had not been given the facts, it would have been obvious enough. A singer ... '

'An actress!'

'Very well, an actress. Who stops working, takes an expensive new apartment, employs servants, dresses well, buys what she wishes to. There's nothing very unusual in it, and it really isn't important. What I ... '

'It is to me.'

'I beg your pardon?'

'It is important to me. It is the most important thing in the world.'

The earl caught Rowland Iredale's eye, but it expressed nothing other than a kind of suspended interest.

'Now, now, my dear,' said the parson. He stroked his wife's hand limply. 'You know you should not agitate yourself.'

His lordship waited, and after what felt like a very long silence said, 'If it is as important as that, perhaps you would like to talk about it?'

Her eyes had dropped to her hands. Flatly, she said, 'She was twenty-one years old. When our mother died, she was seven and I was fourteen. That's why it's important. Our father had no idea of what mattered, and our aunt was stupid. She lived in a world of her own. Everything fell on *my* shoulders. I did my best.'

She removed her husband's hand and patted it absently. 'I was so tired of it all. And when she became a singer, despite all my protests, I made sure she was properly chaperoned and only sang at Ladies' Concerts. Then Mr Iredale asked me to marry him, and I agreed. I thought perhaps I deserved a life of my own.'

There was another silence. A good deal had become clear to his lordship. The motherly child with too many burdens for her slight shoulders, hoping to shift them. The handsome husband who turned out to be a broken reed. Her disappointment, disbelief, bitterness, as she shouldered not only the old burdens again, but new ones as well. And her sister's blithe disregard of the conventions that mattered so much to the girl who had raised her. The earl felt deeply sorry for her, while wondering whether she herself might have rained down the blows that had brought Imogen's life to an end.

Almost as if she had read his mind, she cried, 'I loved my sister very much. You said I would not want the man who killed her to go free, but I had rather he did than that there should be a trial where it would all come out. She was a good, virtuous girl, whatever you think, and if I had been here in London when she found herself in difficulties, none of it would have happened.'

It was a cry from the heart. Rowland Iredale recoiled a little, as if backing away from an accusation too long familiar. Was it his fault, the pale eyes behind their steel-rimmed glasses seemed to ask, that Olivia had been unable to save her sister from disgrace?

The earl said, 'I understand. You are afraid of *any* trial, for the sake of your sister's – and perhaps your own? – reputation. Whether it is the right man or the wrong one who is tried is of no interest to you.'

Her eyes lifted. 'I don't want a trial. No.'

'But, Mrs Iredale, there is almost bound to be one. And if it is the guilty man who is tried and the evidence is conclusive, there might be comparatively little fuss and publicity. Whereas if the man is innocent, as I know Francis Mervyn to be, every insignificant detail of your sister's life will be dragged out in his defence.' He did not enjoy making threats, and had no immediate intention of revealing the full scale of this one to its victim. Lacking other evidence, Francis's only defence would be the promiscuous history of Imogen Reece and a consequent diffusion of suspicion among several lovers, who might have several motives, any of them more urgent than his own. 'I can assure you, your sister's reputation will suffer much more if an innocent man is tried than a guilty one.'

She said nothing.

'Did your sister ever mention Francis Mervyn to you?'

'Once or twice.'

'Do you remember what she said?'

Olivia Iredale shrugged.

'As I have said, I am convinced he did not kill your sister, but I do not know a great deal about his relationship with her. He may even have been the man who was paying her rent...'

Had she shaken her head, or was it only a twitch of the nerves? He looked questioningly at her husband, who returned his gaze quite blankly.

The earl resumed, 'If Francis Mervyn is arrested for this, everything – I repeat, everything – that is known about your sister will come out in court.' Surely he had said it often enough by now for the idea to have penetrated? Yet she was still not responding. With distaste, he tried another tack. 'But if we can prove Mr Mervyn's innocence, now, and Bow Street fails to discover the man who *is* guilty, then you may have your wish and the case may never come to court at all.'

Mr Iredale was not a fool. He said, 'That sounds very convincing, but how do you prove your secretary's innocence without proving someone else guilty? I assume you have already failed to prove, for example, that he was somewhere else when the murder took place, otherwise you would not be here distressing my wife. I don't say I agree with Mrs Iredale that it makes no difference whether the right man or the wrong man is tried, but Miss Reece was *her* sister.'

The earl, firmly repressing his irritation with the reverend gentleman, said, 'All I need do is cast reasonable doubt on the matter. If I can show that someone else had a motive as good as Francis Mervyn's, or better, perhaps, that would be enough. If someone had threatened her, for example, and she had told someone about it – Mrs Iredale, say – it would suffice.' Although if Mrs Iredale were to turn up at Bow Street next day, having remembered Imogen mentioning that a certain Mr Jones had offered her violence, the earl, for one, would treat the information with a good deal of cynicism.

Iredale did not look convinced, but he turned to his wife and said, 'His lordship may be right, my dear. What he is saying is that, as things stand, Bow Street are going to charge some-one, and if they charge an innocent man everything will come out. If they do not have enough evidence to risk a charge, however, the murderer will go free, and Imogen's reputation will remain untarnished. I know how you feel on the subject, and you must do exactly as you wish.'

His wife ignored this speech, as it deserved. It was the earl's impression that she had given up listening to her husband soon after they were married, perhaps because he rarely said anything worth listening to, perhaps because he always said what he thought she wanted to hear – poor tactics with someone whom his lordship suspected was not unintelligent.

'You saw your sister often?' the earl asked.

'Yes.'

'Once or twice a week?'

'Not as often as that.'

'Once in two weeks?'

'Possibly.'

'When you went there last Friday, there was no reply when you knocked, and you asked the caretaker ... '

'The cleaning woman.'

' ... the cleaning woman to let you in?'

'Yes.'

'I don't wish to remind you of something that must have shocked you deeply, but please believe that I have my reasons. What was your first reaction when you saw your sister's body?'

Her features began to crumple, but she succeeded in bringing them under control again. 'Disbelief, then shock and nausea.'

'You didn't think, involuntarily, "He's killed her"?'

She was really trying, he saw with relief; projecting her mind back to the scene in Mecklenburgh Square that morning almost a week ago. 'No,' she said eventually. 'I remember nothing like that. I just felt sick and stunned.'

'Are you quite sure? The mind plays odd tricks at such times.'

She resented being pushed. The blue eyes snapped and her face muscles tightened as she said, 'Of course not. I did not think *he* has killed her, or *she* has killed her. All I thought was that Imogen was dead.'

He accepted it. 'Another question. For reasons that must be obvious, I should very much like to talk to the man who was paying the rent of your sister's apartment. Unfortunately, I don't know his name. Do you?'

'No.'

'You and your sister were close?'

'Yes.'

'But she did not tell you who had rescued her from her difficulties?'

'No. All I know is that he was a good, kind man, and they would have been married if it had been possible. And anyway, if she had not met him, she would have been perfectly capable of looking after herself! She didn't have to be rescued from her difficulties, as you call it. She had a lovely voice. She could have earned her own living very well!'

She had become progressively angrier, and anger had banished both logic and consistency from her mind.

76

His lordship, anticipating another hail of ornaments, risked a last question. 'You know he was good and kind, but do you really know *nothing* else about him?'

Her whole face disintegrated. 'No, no, no!' she screamed. 'Why ask me? Why should I know? Go away! Go away and ask someone else! Why should everyone always lean on *me*? Oh, God! I'm so *tired*!' And she burst into a fit of tearing, hysterical sobs.

Ineffectually, her husband patted her shoulder. 'There, there, my dear. It will be all right. You'll see.' His own eyes were moist as he looked up at the earl. 'It has all been too much for her,' he said. 'I'm sure you understand, my lord. She really cannot help you.'

The earl bowed slightly. 'Forgive me,' he said. 'I will see myself out.'

When he returned to St James's Square, feeling very much as if he had been first wrung out and then put through the mangle, his lordship discovered his sister seated in the garden with a sketch block in her lap and a general air of having her back to the wall.

'It is all very well,' she said in injured tones, 'to talk of keeping Francis's troubles from the servants, but I have been positively beleaguered in my attempts to prevent anyone from seeing what I am doing!'

Mildly puzzled, he said, 'I should have thought you would simply retire to your bedchamber or dressing-room?'

'When Lamotte is engaged on the most minute inspection of every item in my wardrobe, for marks, loose threads, or insecure buttons that she *might* not already have noticed?'

'The library, then.'

'I tried that, too. I told Brandon I was not on any account to be disturbed, and fifteen minutes later he tiptoed in with a tray. He explained that he was not disturbing me, but had thought I might care for a glass of chilled tea.'

'Damnation!' he said. 'Would they recognize whose portrait you were working on?'

She looked at him, offended.

He grinned. 'I apologize. Have you finished yet?'

'Yes. No. Just a minute.' She surveyed the drawing with

narrowed eyes, and then added two more short, feathery lines before turning the block towards him for inspection.

The likeness was extremely good, considering it was done from memory. The dark, slanting eyes and brows were right, and the long, slightly curled mouth with its deep corners. The set of the head was right, too, and the conservatively cut dark hair.

'Yes,' he said thoughtfully. 'It's very near. But I think you might emphasize the slightly Roman hook of his nose a little more, and although you have made the jawline sharp the cheekbones are not perhaps quite angular enough. Could you strengthen the shadow under them, do you think?'

She turned it back and looked at it, then picked up the charcoal and intensified the hollows of the cheeks and the bridge of the nose. 'Better?' she asked.

'Much. Yes, it will do very nicely. You must present it to Francis as a memento when he returns. In the meantime...'

'I know. A second copy.'

'Tomorrow would do.'

'Certainly not. Today, I am in the mood for being a martyr.' With a sigh, she removed the sketch, clipped it to the edge of the block, and began again on a fresh sheet. 'What did your visit to the Iredales produce?'

'Hysterics!' he said gloomily.

She looked up, her face alight with laughter. 'On whose part?'

Briefly, he told her what had happened, concluding, 'So I learned nothing very specific. But it was interesting in its way. Olivia Iredale did not want to talk to me, and in fact told me very little. I still have no idea whether she knew anything to tell, since I am not – thank God! – accustomed to hysterical women. But it occurred to me that her tantrums might very well have sent any man less dedicated than myself,' he smiled wryly, 'hurriedly about his business. It may, of course, have been coincidence that her first tantrum, which took the form of throwing things, failed to divert me, and that the second one took a different form – a storm of tears, which very successfully *did* divert me.'

'You mean you think the whole performance may have been put on for your benefit?'

78

'Not at all! I am sure Olivia Iredale is one of those women who are prey to easy emotion. The – er – facility with which she picked up and threw ornaments was quite impressive. If it had been acting, I would have expected a fractional hesitation while she decided which missiles were most readily expendable. But there was nothing like that, I assure you!'

'The profusion of knick-knacks, in fact, representing her own private arsenal?'

His eyes gleamed responsively. 'What really bothered me was a vague impression that somewhere, deep down, she was rather enjoying herself. Do you think it likely?'

She glanced up. 'Goodness, yes. She sounds like precisely the kind of woman who uses her nerves both to attract attention to herself, and to get her own way. The world is full of them. I shouldn't read anything particularly suspicious into it, if I were you.'

'Very well, I won't,' he said obligingly. 'Or not much. In any case, sororicide is a moderately rare crime, and I think Mrs Iredale really did love her sister. I merely wonder what, if anything, she was holding back, in her anxiety to protect Imogen's reputation.'

He began to turn away. 'I must go and change, and then do some serious thinking.' He had a sheet of paper in his hand, covered with a neat script that she did not recognize. Seeing her eyes on it, he said, 'Miss Kenwood has sent me a list of some of Imogen's male acquaintances. Oh, and the Christian name of the young lady of Francis's, which I fear does not help much – unless Letitia means something to you?'

She shook her head. 'I only know of one Letitia, and she is well past the age of consent.'

'A pity,' said her brother.

But after he had departed, Lady Susan cocked her head slightly and addressed the portrait in front of her. 'Though it might be more helpful than we think, Francis, my friend. For I have the beginnings of an idea.'

Chapter 7

Mademoiselle Lamotte was not pleased when, at five o'clock in the afternoon, her mistress discovered that she had run out of embroidery silk.

'And do make sure that you match it exactly,' said Lady Susan, 'otherwise it will be quite useless.'

' *Oui*, madame,' her dresser replied a little sourly. Herself a practical rather than a decorative needlewoman, she found little to choose between one white thread and another. But madame insisted that the thickness and the degree of silky sheen were perfectly crucial, and told her that she should not waste time in the haberdashers' nearby, but must go straight to one of the silk mercers in Artillery Lane or Bishopsgate. 'You may ask Fielding to take you in the coach,' said her ladyship kindly, 'since it is such a long way. But be sure he asks Lord Moriston's permission first.' Slightly mollified, Lamotte departed, and fifteen minutes later Lady Susan heard the distant sound of one of the carriages being driven out.

Within five minutes she had laid out her very plainest morning gown, with a gathered chemisette to fill in the neckline. There was a cottage mantle to go over it, which looked boringly plain when it had been turned wrong side out so that the appliquéd ribbon border did not show. And to complete the outfit an Oldenburg bonnet that was only too obviously last year's model and had never suited her anyway. As she ripped away the three ostrich feathers and replaced them with a modest knot of ribbons, she wondered why Lamotte had not thrown the thing away months ago. She dressed and looked at herself in the glass with a shudder. The pink of the dress and the pink of the cloak clashed slightly but nastily, and both disagreed with the peach shade of the bonnet. Should she wear a muslin cap as well, she wondered, and then made do with pushing her hair firmly back under the brim. Surveying herself again, critically, she decided that, as a lady's maid, she would probably pass. And decided, in future, to be kinder to Lamotte. How dreadful it must be to have to dress in one's mistress's cast-offs.

With extreme caution, she peered out of her bedchamber and then slipped down the back stairs that debouched into the corridor outside Francis Mervyn's private rooms. From there, she turned towards the back of the house and delicately pushed open the door that led under the glassed-over landing to the area that housed the stables. Another flight of stairs, and one of the horses whickered a welcome to her. She patted him on the nose, and tiptoed past. Since Anderson was still in Wiltshire, and Fielding had gone off on a quest for embroidery silks, no one came to investigate.

A few minutes later she emerged into Jermyn Street and imperiously summoned a hackney. The jarvey, having first looked her up and down and then heard her instructions, very much disconcerted her by saying, 'Yes, my lady,' in a tone that had nothing satirical about it. Not until they were half way up Bond Street did it occur to her that he had responded to her manner and her voice, rather than her clothes, and she beguiled the rest of the journey to Oxford Street by practising, under her breath, the unnaturally genteel accents of a certain Miss Bailey, who had served her for a short time before the advent of Mlle Lamotte.

She paid off the hackney about a hundred yards from the haberdasher's shop that was her goal, and made her way there at a speed that was not at all comfortable on a hot August evening, arriving – as she had intended – with a faint and inelegant sheen on her nose and unfashionably high colour in her cheeks. Conscious of a wisp or two of hair that had escaped from her *démodé* bonnet, she nobly refrained from tucking it back in again.

The shop, which she had never visited before, was astonishingly full of customers, and surprisingly large. But it was also well staffed. There must be at least a dozen assistants, she thought, perhaps more, all of them looking tired and downtrodden as they refolded, rewound, and stowed away the tossed and tumbled goods on the counters, or ran to produce others from the boxes that were stacked right up to the ceiling, so that they had to drag ladders along and climb up, candle in hand, to search out what was wanted. The atmosphere was unpleasantly stuffy, but Lady Susan consoled herself with the thought that it would help to keep up her high colour.

To begin with, she made no attempt to attract anyone's attention, but stood at the end of one of the counters turning over a collection of pretty little padded and embroidered buttons, and covertly surveying the assistants. It was not difficult to identify who were the seniors among them. Most were boys of about fifteen, but there were two considerably older men, one of whom, Lady Susan discovered with satisfaction, was the great Mr Smith himself. He was just the kind of man she had hoped, middle-aged, undeniably vulgar, and with small, twinkling eyes that were vivid with curiosity. She heard him greet three customers by name, and waited patiently as he bustled by with a fourth, bowing her and her equally stout friend out of the door with the most extravagant civility.

As he returned to his counter, Lady Susan waylaid him genteelly. 'Excuse me,' she murmured in the accent of the unregretted Miss Bailey. He gave her his attention, first summing up her clothes as Quality cast-offs, and then raising his eyes to her face. She had not expected his twinkle to take on quite such an appreciative gleam, and it was as much as she could do, for a moment, not to freeze him on the spot.

'And how can I help you, miss?' he enquired, popping his bald head towards her in a rather disconcerting way, and punctuating his question with a loud, 'Hey, hey!'

Valiantly entering into her role, she said mincingly, 'Shirt frills, please. Embroidered ones?'

'Ahhh! If you'd let me have knowed, I'd have laid some in special. Don't have much call this time of year, m' dear. Hey, hey!'

Intrigued by the thought of shirt frills as a seasonal delicacy, she addressed herself once more to the ear presented to her, and lisped, 'But surely you must have *some*. It's vehwy important!'

'Ahhh! Well, we'd better see, then, hadn't we. Mustn't disappoint a pretty lady like you, must we? Hey, hey!'

The deaf ear approached again, and unable to think of anything else to say, she murmured a feeble thank you.

'Just you wait there, and we'll look.'

Mildly irritated by her own lack of invention, and at the same time wondering whether she was going to be able to sustain her gravity long enough to get out of the shop, she awaited events. Mr Smith vanished into the upper darkness, reappearing down the step-ladder a few moments later with a large box that showed an uncontrollable tendency to flop at the corners, and appeared to be in imminent danger of precipitating its contents all over the floor. He succeeded, however, in reaching the counter with it, his pink and ruffled countenance somewhat at variance with the professional joviality of his speech.

'Not built for climbing ladders,' he puffed. 'Usually get the lads to do it. But not for you, miss. Hey, hey?'

She smiled winsomely, and he removed the lid from the box and displayed to her revolted gaze a frill that the Prince Regent would, no doubt, have been happy to sport in his salad days twenty years earlier, but which to the eye of 1815 was unquestionably *passé*. She shook her head. The pink-embroidered frill was laid aside, and replaced with one tastefully finished in blue. She shook her head again. The next was finished with a chaste edging in white, but it was altogether too chaste for this difficult customer's taste. By the time Mr Smith had unpacked half the box, without winning more than a weak smile of negation, his flirtatious twinkle was beginning to look a trifle fixed.

But at last the lady began to look more interested. 'Oh!' she exclaimed, and Mr Smith beamed happily. 'Is that more like it, my dear? Hey, hey?' he enquired, and Lady Susan, no longer reduced to complete speechlessness by his habit of presenting his deaf ear to her mouth before she had even opened it, replied creditably, 'Oo-ah, yes. Very neah-ly. But I should *so* laike one just laike the one Miss Letitia bought for . . . ' She stopped, her hand covering her lips in artistic confusion.

'Ho! Ho!' he exclaimed for a change. 'It was little Miss Letty who sent you here, was it?'

Not trusting herself to blush to order, she cast her eyes down in a maidenly fashion and said confusedly, 'Oh, deah! I should not have said. Her mama, you know!'

'Never fear, miss!' he told her reassuringly. 'Miss Letty and I understand each other very well. Always have done, hey, hey! You can tell her, pretty little creature that she is – oh, *such* a pretty little creature! – that I'd never let the cat out to her mama. Oh, no, never on my life. Hey, hey!'

Lady Susan, furiously trying to think of some way of extracting Letty's mama's name from the encroaching Mr Smith, looked at him doubtfully. By the greatest good fortune, he misread her expression.

'You think I'd tell? No, never.' He beamed at her. 'Mama would be annoyed if she knew I had aided and abetted – that's the word, I'll be bound! – her little puss, and I never like to offend good customers like Mrs Lang, you know. Not good business. Oh, no!'

He was rewarded with the most enchanting smile. 'Oh, deah!' said her ladyship conspiratorially. 'I suppose you must have to be so careful. If she comes in often, I mean.'

Mr Smith was rummaging in the bottom of the box. 'Ay, well, she does, being just round the corner, so to speak. But then I've known Miss Letty since she was ten – a real little rogue she was, too – so we have a kind of understanding. She don't tell her mama when Johnson in Bond Street has ribbons cheaper than me – though not so good, I do assure you – and I don't tell mama when Miss Letty wheedles something out of me she's not supposed to have.' He emerged triumphant. 'And there we are! That's the one, isn't it? Hey, hey?'

It was. It was the perfect twin of the evening shirt frill Francis had been wearing a few weeks ago, which he had laconically confessed to having received as a present.

'Oh, how splendid!' she exclaimed. 'How clev-ah of you to remember. That is exactly the one. Is it dreadfully expensive?' It was. She made a show of consulting her purse, and then haggled a little, but Mr Smith was one of the new breed of shopkeepers who operated on a fixed price and no credit basis. Even for such a charming young lady, with such excellent connections, as herself.

She was ushered out of the door with the greatest ceremony, and if she had not succeeded in appearing overburdened with her reticule and her package, would certainly have had her hands clasped in benevolent farewell. With his parting injunction ringing in her ears – 'Come and see me again soon, miss, whenever you want pretty things. Gloves and ribbons my speciality, hey, hey!' – she walked off feeling very pleased with herself indeed. So jubilant, in fact, at meeting success on her very first try, that without thinking she gave the hackney driver the correct address in St James's Square, and only realized her error when she saw Brandon's thunderstruck face at the open door.

Carrying things off with an air, she relinquished her cloak into his hands and said, 'Is my brother in the library, Brandon? Oh, good. I want to talk to him.'

'Yes, my lady. May I enquire whether you wish dinner put back, my lady?'

'Why? What time is it?'

'Almost seven, my lady.'

'Goodness, is it? Then we'd better put it back half an hour. Make my apologies to Alexandre, please.'

The earl was still at his desk, surrounded by reference books and sheets of notes. He did not look up when she strolled in, but merely said, 'Did you contrive to finish the second portrait?'

'I did.'

'Good. I shall need them both tomorrow, unless John is delayed.' His eyes travelled from one book to another, and he made a note, then looked at it for a moment, muttered, 'Impossible!' and crossed it out again.

He threw down his quill and sat back just as his sister spread out before him a crisp new shirt frill, edged with a white Greek key pattern.

'How kind!' he said, surprised. 'Is it my birthday?'

'No,' she replied, looking down at him in a very superior way. 'It is a Clue.'

His eyes gleamed appreciatively. 'Is it, indeed! To what, pray?'

'To the surname of Francis's respectable young lady.'

He sat forward again. 'I am impressed. Do you mean you have discovered it?'

'Her name is Miss Letitia Lang, and she lives with her

85

mother – and possibly even with her father! – somewhere not too far from Oxford Street. In the area between Manchester Square and Stratford Place, I would guess. They are probably Cits of the better sort.'

He shook a directory out from the midst of a pile of books that tottered and then collapsed. 'Damn!' he said. 'Lang! Lang, Lang, Lang, Lang, Lang. There's one here in Barrett Street. Does that sound right? It's the only one in the area.'

'It could be. They have lived there for eight or nine years, so you could check back in one of the older directories, couldn't you?'

He rose to his feet and went to the shelves. 'What a sensible notion. Let's try 1809. Yes, here they are. Mr Greville Lang, number seven.'

Sitting down again, he beamed at her extravagantly. 'So tell me. How did you do it?'

The smile brimming over her lashes, she said, 'I remembered last night a little incident that took place a few weeks ago, not long after Francis's birthday. He was coming to the Opera with John and myself, and I commented on his shirt frill, which I hadn't seen before.' She waved towards the frill on the desk. 'It's a striking design. All he said was, "A present," but there was an odd little smile on his face that made me think it had *not* been a present from one of his sisters.'

She perched herself on the edge of a chair, and began thoughtfully to draw off her gloves. 'Now, it occurred to me today that his young lady might have given it to him. If so, it was quite an improper thing for her to have done. After all, one does not give something so personal to a man who is officially no more than an acquaintance. I thought it unlikely that her mama would be so permissive as to allow it – so she could not have embroidered it herself. Therefore she must have bought it somewhere.'

Her brother's eyes were fixed on her frowningly. She said, annoyed, 'Well! It was a perfectly reasonable supposition.'

His brow cleared slightly. 'Oh, yes. I quite agree. I was just a little distracted. I am not used to seeing ... ' He sighed in a perplexed way. 'Susan, I feel that I would be failing in my duty as your elder brother, your guardian and guide, if I did not say that that bonnet gives you a very odd appearance. It is quite the most dreadful thing I have ever seen you wear! It is positively dowdy!'

She giggled, and said, 'It is, isn't it? Brandon almost had a fit when I came in just now.'

'Understandably.'

'Well, there are times when sacrifices have to be made. The thing was that if Miss Letty had purchased the frill, there were not too many places she could have gone to. She would not, I thought, choose somewhere dagger-cheap, nor a place where it would have to be specially ordered. I thought I could at least try Smith's in Oxford Street, which I had heard was the best place in town for ready made gloves, and moderately-priced ribbons and haberdashery. So, disguising myself as a lady's maid – since I could scarcely make ingenuous enquiries in my own person – I took myself off in a hackney ... '

'Susan!'

'Yes, I know. Not the thing at all, but such fun. I repeat, I took myself off in a hackney to Mr Smith's. As soon as I saw him, I knew he was *just* the kind of man who would remember a young girl buying embroidered shirt frills. And he did!' She rose to her feet again. 'I don't think I should have succeeded if I hadn't know Miss Lang's first name, but, with that, the whole thing worked like a charm.'

He shook his head smilingly. 'You were extraordinarily lucky, you know.'

'Of course. But luck, as you so frequently tell me, is no more than a by-product of enterprise.' Descending from her high horse, she confided, 'I am quite disappointed, if the truth be told. I was so looking forward to trying the Pantheon Bazaar tomorrow.'

This provocative remark fell on stony ground. She sighed. 'Oh, well! I am going to change for dinner. And I would advise you to do so too, unless you want Alexandre to resign for the second night in a row.'

Her hand was almost on the knob when the door opened to reveal John, looking as neglectful as only he knew how. She surveyed him for a moment and then closed her eyes in pain.

John said, 'Well, really! What a welcome for the returning traveller!' He took in her own appearance. 'And it's hardly for you to criticize, is it? What a quiz of a hat!'

Lady Susan inhaled deeply, but the earl intervened with a grin. 'Well done, John! I didn't expect you back so soon. You must have made very good time.'

'I had to break my journey last night, of course, but I reached Worthing just after nine this morning. I was only there for a couple of hours, and then started straight back.'

'You don't sound as if you were very successful?'

'I wasn't. Not that the Reverend Isaac was unhelpful, he just didn't know anything. It seems Francis wrote some weeks ago to say that if the weather looked settled he thought he would take a riding holiday, possibly around Kent, so that he could look at Canterbury, and then go along the south coast to spend his last day or two with the family at Worthing. And my saints! I don't blame him for wanting a peaceful break. I've never seen anything as chaotic as the Mervyn household. There must be at least a dozen children still living at home – well, maybe just six or seven, but it *felt* like a dozen. And all at the noisy age, from about ten up to seventeen or thereabouts.'

'Ummm,' said his lordship. 'Never mind, it wasn't a wasted journey. At least it explains Francis's disappearance. Why, by the way, did Mr Mervyn not tell Bow Street? It might have saved us all a good deal of trouble.'

John eased his neckcloth with an impatient forefinger and flopped into a chair. 'I could scarcely ask him straight out, since all I'd said was that you wanted Francis in a hurry because you had a problem on your hands and needed his help. But my impression was that the messenger from Bow Street had been not only vague but rude, and that the Reverend Isaac, who is pretty high in the instep, I may say, had told him in a very un-Christian way to go to the devil.'

Lady Susan gurgled. 'He sounds just like his son.' She had heard Francis take a very incisive tone with the lower orders. 'Do they look alike?'

'I suppose so, though papa is as thin as a thread, and very grey. I would say ... '

There was a discreet tap, and the double doors of the library were flung open in fine style to display Brandon, his basset-hound features refolded into what the family recognized as a delighted smile.

'A gentleman to see you, my lady,' he said, and stepped aside to make way for a tall, lightly built man with brown hair, tanned complexion, and humorous eyes.

'Adam!' cried his wife, her face transformed, and ran precipitately into his arms.

Brandon, still beaming fatuously, withdrew. Captain Gregory had said that he would find his own way to the library – he was, after all, a member of the family – but nothing would have deprived Brandon of the pleasure of officiating at the reunion. Robed in a warm satisfaction, he trod back to the hall with the intention of sending a message down to Alexandre in the kitchen, and only the sight of a dirty mark on one of the most junior footman's stockings wiped the smile off his face.

Over Lady Susan's head, Adam grinned at his two brothers-in-law, and then released his wife slightly so that he could look at her. He observed the light in her hazel eyes, and the smile that trembled slightly on her perfectly chiselled lips, but there was something disturbing on the margins of his vision. The faintest trace of doubt shadowed his brow, and he raised his eyes slightly and then looked over his wife's head at Moriston and John. They could see him carefully not saying anything.

They began to laugh. 'Adam!' gasped Lady Susan. 'You are splendid, and I adore you! Yes, it *is* a dreadful bonnet, and you will hear all about it presently. But why did you not let me know you were coming?'

Maliciously, his lordship interrupted. 'I think I hear the carriage returning. Your dresser back from her errand, perhaps?'

Her ladyship's eyes opened wide, and her hand flew to her mouth. 'Gracious heaven!' she exclaimed. 'If she sees me like this, she will leave on the instant!' And she fled through the door leading towards the family stairs.

Incontinently deserted, Captain Gregory surveyed his brothers-in-law with a resigned twinkle in his eye. 'How nice it is to be home,' he said.

Chapter 8

'If it wasn't infantry it was cavalry, and if it wasn't cavalry it was artillery,' complained Captain Gregory after dinner that evening, when they were all comfortably settled again with the candles lit against the falling dark.

'I thought the Duke was using hired transports to get the army over to Ostend?' the earl said.

'Mostly. But there was a nasty log jam in April and early May, and I found myself drafted. I should prefer not to have to repeat the experience of commanding a seventy-four-gun ship of the line loaded with enormous scarlet-and-gold Guardsmen and their even more enormous black chargers. I won't tell you how much holystone we had to use to get the decks back to normal again! The artillery was even more of a headache, for everything had to be lashed down. A few hundredweight of metal can cause real havoc if a gun breaks loose from its moorings. Nor is it pleasant to feel like a floating arsenal with all the extra powder aboard. I was always expecting one of Whinyates' beloved rockets to go off spontaneously, and send us all to kingdom come.'

The earl laughed. 'And I hear the Duke wouldn't have anything to do with them when they arrived! "Newfangled nonsense!" he said, and ordered the rockets put in store and the troop issued with good old-fashioned guns, instead.'

Adam stared at him. 'Is that true? Well, I'll be damned! I know they're chancy things. Though if they'd frightened the enemy as much as they frightened me, the battle of Waterloo would have been over in an hour.'

Lady Susan was listening wide-eyed. 'And to think that all your letters led me to believe that you were on a pleasure cruise, ferrying the faint-hearted from there to here!'

90

He grinned. 'Well, I *was* – on the way back. The Belgians began to evaporate from Brussels fairly early on, and a substantial number of the English visitors there, after having declared that all would be perfectly secure once the Duke arrived, began to think better of their heroics in the last two or three weeks and joined the general exodus. Some of the Belgians were pathetic, quite in despair when they learned that one of His Majesty's ships was unable to accommodate all their household goods as well as themselves. I had to rule that only one chest of possessions could be stowed for each family, so there was a good deal of unpacking and repacking on the quay. By the time we sailed, I suppose we must have carried as great a weight of valuables as a Spanish treasure ship, because every chest was crammed with silver, porcelain and glass, and silks and laces, and paintings, illuminated manuscripts and icons, and furs and ... '

'And jewels,' John contributed drowsily.

'No, *they* were mostly hung round their owners' necks, hidden – they thought! – by layer upon layer of mufflers. I fully expected them all to be robbed the minute they set foot on land. By sheer coincidence, I took a few of the same people back after Boney surrendered to the *Bellerophon* and released us all from patrolling off Rochefort, and very gloomy they were, poor souls. They hadn't been robbed in the direct sense, but because they needed ready cash so badly, they had been forced to sell their treasures at a price that was certainly very little short of robbery.'

'Which reminds me,' said his lordship. 'There was a truly scurrilous broadsheet circulating in Paris on the subject, showing the refugees departing for England with all their possessions, and returning with only their shirts. I brought a copy home, for I thought it might amuse you.' He paused. 'Now, where the devil did I put it? It's probably still upstairs. I'll go and look.'

Scarcely had the earl disappeared through one door when the other opened. There was a lady to see his lordship, Brandon announced.

Brandon was having a most enjoyable day. First, his lordship in mourning clothes, then her ladyship making sketches of Mr Mervyn and subsequently turning up outside the front door in a hackney carriage and a very odd bonnet. Then Mr John back from goodness knew where, and Captain Gregory home from sea, and now a most beautiful young lady come to see his lordship. And one whose face Brandon obscurely felt to be familiar.

'Miss Kenwood, my lady,' he said.

Lady Susan was not in the mood for a visitor, especially an elderly female whom she judged to be of a managing disposition, but since it was presumably important she merely said, 'Very well, Brandon. His lordship will be back in a moment. You had better bring Miss Kenwood through here.'

John, having had two very tiring days, levered himself to his feet with the intention of making himself scarce before the interfering old lady appeared. He did not hurry, since in his experience it took a tottering valetudinarian some time to negotiate the distance between the hall anteroom and the library. Adam also rose to his feet and waited with interest for his first sight of one of the dramatis personae in the case he had heard about at dinner.

Whatever any of them had expected, it was not the strikingly elegant figure in the buttermilk *gros de Naples* gown, with the swathe of honey-gold hair coiled from crown to nape, and the huge, dark, dramatic eyes. As Miss Kenwood paused on the threshold, they froze into a startled tableau – which slightly alarmed her. Professionally expert at making an entrance, she was not accustomed to reducing her audience to a state of paralysis. But almost at once Lady Susan came forward with a smile, Captain Gregory drew forward a chair, and a bedazzled John tried surreptitiously to straighten his neckcloth and smooth down his hair.

A few moments later, his lordship strolled back into the room, the broadsheet in his hand. The attention of both Adam and John was concentrated on Miss Kenwood, but Lady Susan, who had just realized why their visitor's face was familiar, glanced up as her brother entered and surprised the look in his eyes. It gave her a very severe shock.

His face was quite expressionless, however, as he went forward to greet Miss Kenwood. 'This is an unexpected pleasure,' he said coolly. 'Have you come from the theatre?'

'Yes. *Gloriana* again, so there was no need for me to stay

92

late.' She sounded distressingly businesslike. 'One or two things occurred to me in relation to what we were talking about yesterday. In the first case, I could simply have sent you a note. But the second is more complex . . . ' She stopped.

He smiled slightly, and his blue eyes glimmered. 'You need have no hesitation,' he said. 'You have met the rest of the household, and they know all there is to know about the business. In fact, you will be doing me a favour if you tell me in their presence, otherwise I will be forced to repeat it all afterwards.'

She nodded and settled back in her chair.

Lady Susan said, 'We usually have tea about this time. Would you care for some?'

Five minutes later, cup in hand, Miss Kenwood said, 'It seemed to me that you might wish to talk to Julia Johnstone?'

'Undoubtedly.'

'You will have no luck there, I fear. Colonel – er – Johnstone is with the Army of Occupation, and his wife having declined to accompany him to foreign parts, he took Julia instead. They have been away for several weeks now.'

'How very unhelpful of them. But at least we can rule them out of the list of suspects,' added the earl.

'Were they on it?'

'Not seriously,' he admitted.

Miss Kenwood sipped her tea. 'On the second matter . . . It is curious that I should not have remembered the incident before. Perhaps I even chose to forget it because it was the kind of crude transaction I prefer not to associate with Imogen. But I know it is important. The thing is, Imogen met Mr C. through a woman I now realize must have been a professional procuress. And furthermore, Mr C. knew even then that Imogen was in Robert Elliston's keeping – *and* that their association was very nearly at an end.'

The earl crossed one knee over the other and, resting his chin on forefinger and thumb, said in a voice of considerable interest, 'Did he, indeed!'

'Yes.' She gazed reflectively into her cup. 'I have been trying to fit it all together from odd, unrelated remarks Imogen let out from time to time. And what I think must have happened was this. One evening in the late summer of 1812, Mr C. had his coachman set him down at the White Horse Cellar in Piccadilly, and went from there on foot to one of the houses in Berkeley Street. If I remember correctly, it was one of the low numbers – two, or three.'

'Oh-oh!' said Adam, who had not been married long enough to know better. His wife looked at him, and John grinned. The earl closed his eyes.

Miss Kenwood was amused to discover that the address, which had at first meant nothing to her, was obviously familiar to the gentlemen present, if not to Lady Susan.

'It was a house inhabited by a certain Mrs Porter,' she went on, 'who was an old acquaintance of his.'

There was a smothered choke from John, which brought a wary look to his sister's eye, but Captain Gregory and the earl had recovered themselves and their faces now expressed nothing more than courteous interest.

Miss Kenwood resumed drily. 'The long and the short of it was that Mr C. asked Mrs Porter to approach Imogen on his behalf, assuring her that he knew Imogen to be in financial difficulties because of the unreliability of a certain famous actor, and believed she might therefore prove amenable. He said that for personal reasons he did not wish to approach Imogen directly until he knew how she would respond. Nor did he wish to make any firm arrangement until he had had the opportunity of meeting her, and assessing her for himself.

'Mrs Porter went to see Imogen next day and told her ... Now, let me remember the *exact* words, for they seemed to me extravagant, even at the time! Yes. She said Imogen had "made a conquest of a very fine, noble, and quite unimpeachable man." Imogen, looking perfectly innocent and angelic, I have no doubt, waited to hear more. "I dare not tell you his name," Mrs Porter went on, "but you may be quite assured that he is a man of fashion, rank, and fortune." Thinking that this sounded very promising, Imogen nevertheless said, "No one needs a good, kind friend more than I do, but I *cannot* meet a stranger as a lover!" In the end, however, she agreed to meet Mr C. and was very much surprised to find that he was not only a man of rank, as Mrs Porter had said, but kind and generous into the bargain. Since she had no understanding of economy,

94

and was frightened to death of debts, she decided she had no alternative but to enter into the arrangement he suggested. And, of course, it worked very well – until Mr Mervyn came along.'

There was a moment's silence, then, 'Well!' said John portentously. 'That certainly tells us something!' He was wide awake again.

'Such as?' enquired his brother.

Adam caught his wife's eye in private amusement.

'You can find out about him from Mrs Porter!'

'I can *ask* Mrs Porter, and receive a very uncivil answer! Confidentiality is the procuress's stock in trade. Townsend might be able to force something out of her, though. We'll bear it in mind. Miss Kenwood, may I congratulate you on reconstructing such a coherent story from what you say were mere fragments of conversation? Most impressive!'

She chuckled deliciously. 'One of the hazards of appearing on the stage is that there is sometimes very little time to study a script. So one soon becomes accustomed to fleshing out the bones of a play with whatever is necessary to make it acceptable to the audience.'

'Is that true?' said John curiously, if not very politely.

'Yes, of course. Did you never hear about Sheridan's *Pizarro*? He wrote it in – 1799, I think – and on the opening night, until the end of the fourth act, neither Mrs Siddons, nor Charles Kemble, nor Barrymore had all their speeches for the fifth, for Sherry was still working on them. The delays between the acts were so long that the after-piece did not start till about midnight, to an audience consisting of seventeen people in the dress circle and twenty-two in the pit.'

'My God! That can't have made him very popular with the cast!'

'I don't believe so. What Mrs Siddons had to say about it is not recorded, but Sheridan on a later occasion remarked that he would as soon make love to the Archbishop of Canterbury as he would to Mrs Siddons, which may give you some idea of how they felt about each other.'

With some reluctance, the earl intervened to bring the conversation back to the point. The fact that he was fighting

95

an overmastering desire just to sit and look at Miss Kenwood made his manner abrupt.

'The valuable thing is that Mr C. knew about Elliston. Miss Kenwood, can you think of anyone in the theatre who might fit the bill?'

Miss Kenwood, who felt she had been put in her place, replied satirically, 'With *that* kind of money? No!'

'Does Elliston have a wide acquaintance outside the theatre?'

'I shouldn't think so.'

'Can you suggest any way in which we might find out?'

To her own considerable surprise, she heard herself say, 'I suppose *I* could try.'

The earl dropped his eyes. Oh, blessed Kate! Who had come round, quite unaware, to Francis Mervyn's side.

She was not unaware at all. She said, 'You must not think, my lord, that you have convinced me of your secretary's innocence. But since there is an intelligent investigation afoot, and a possibility of finding out more about Imogen's protector, I am prepared to accept that the cause of truth would be better served by my help than my hindrance.'

Lady Susan was completely fascinated. A glimpse of her brother's face and half an hour of Miss Kenwood's acquaintance had served to convince her that here, at long and improbable last, was the perfect wife for him. No two people – with the exception of herself and Adam – could have been more ideally suited. For years she had watched hopeful mothers throw their daughters at his head – docile innocents or spoilt little ninnies, most of them. For years she herself had cast a critical and hopeful eye over the brighter ones, only to find them mercenary, or humourless, or intolerably self-satisfied. And Charles had simply gone on his way, amusing himself with well born flirts and less respectable but equally lively ladies of whom his sister was supposed to know nothing. She had almost begun to despair for him. But now! Yet there was something wrong. Was it just that they were on opposing sides? She thought not. Was Miss Kenwood frightened by Charles? Not that, either, she thought. She felt Adam's eye upon her, sympathetic, faintly humorous, unmistakably expressive, and immediately forgot everything but her need to be alone with him.

It was not to be. As she opened her mouth preparatory to uttering a delicate reminder that it was getting late, Brandon, who seemed to have been ubiquitous today, materialized at the door yet again, ushering Matthew Somerville into the room. Nobly suppressing a desire to see him at Jericho, she exclaimed, 'Gracious, Matthew, how late you are! Have you been travelling all day? More tea, I think, Brandon. Or would you prefer something stronger?'

Matthew, who could have done with a very stiff brandy, stammered, 'Tea would be splendid, thank you. I feel quite dry after ... ' His voice tailed off in characteristic fashion.

' ... your long drive,' supplied the earl helpfully. 'Miss Kenwood, may I introduce my cousin Matthew Somerville, who manages my estate in Wiltshire?'

Matthew bowed, and Kate smiled and began to go through the motions of being about to leave.

The earl could not bear it. 'No, pray stay, Miss Kenwood. For a little, anyway. You are as much involved in this case as we are, and I hope Matthew may have something to tell us about it.'

Gracefully, she subsided again and submitted to having fresh tea poured for her. She was enjoying herself enormously, and would have been very much disappointed to have been allowed to leave. She liked people, and loved meeting new ones, a rare pleasure these days when her evenings were usually circumscribed by the demands of the theatre. The majority of her acquaintances were actors and actresses, whose talk was mostly of the stage, entertaining enough but sadly limited.

She was intrigued by his lordship's household, who did not appear to be in the least awed by him, even if the young man who had just come in, fair-haired, pink-complexioned, and exuding an almost tangible aura of nervousness, could scarcely have been said to be at ease. A state, she suspected, that was natural to him in any company. Among the three Dornays, there was a strong family resemblance. Despite Lady Susan's difference in colouring, she had the same patrician bones, the same set to the eyes and mouth, and the same long, shapely hands. At the moment, Kate sensed that she was somewhat on edge, but thought that her more usual style might be humour and a perhaps startling candour. She was clearly very much in love with her husband, a nice man, with lean, weathered good looks and extraordinarily kind eyes. It would be pleasant to know them better, Kate thought. John, a slighter edition of the earl, had a most engaging grin, which reminded her irresistibly of her own brother, whose death early in the Peninsular War – when he had been about John's age – had helped to put a merciful period to her mother's long invalidism and reduced her father to the reckless indifference that had ultimately killed him. She saw that John's eyes were on her and, brushing memories aside, twinkled at him conspiratorially.

'You are not too tired, are you, Matthew?' his lordship was saying.

Matthew blinked slightly. It would have taken a stronger personality than his to give an affirmative to a question so phrased. So he said, 'Oh, no! I – er ... '

'That's fine, then. Sit down.' The earl looked at him intently. 'And concentrate, Matthew!'

The open, boyish face dutifully took on a fixed expression, and Miss Kenwood suppressed a smile. This, she could see, was a scene that had been played before.

'Now. What do you know about Francis Mervyn's private life?'

Matthew's eyes dilated. 'I ... I ... Ab-bout Francis's private ...?'

' ... life,' concluded his lordship. 'Yes.'

'Don't bully him, Charles,' her ladyship said. 'It's most unfair. Matthew, Francis is in trouble, and we believe you might be able to help.'

Matthew, still wearing a hunted look, said, 'I?'

Exasperated, the earl replied, 'Yes, you. I suppose I had better tell you what it's all about, otherwise we shall get nowhere.' Crisply and lucidly, he summarized the history of Francis, Imogen Reece, and Letitia Lang, explained Townsend's interest in the affair, and Miss Kenwood's, and described the attitude of Imogen's sister towards the search for the murderer.

Miss Kenwood listened quite as attentively as Matthew, for there was a good deal that was new to her. It took almost superhuman self-control to refrain from interrupting when his lordship, forgetfully, related the tale of Imogen's conversion into an accredited demi-rep, but as he continued – privately cursing himself for the slip – she saw the inevitability of the whole thing. There was a kind of natural logic to it that invited belief. She was sufficiently convinced to find herself thinking irritably, 'How *like* Imogen!'

'Now,' said the earl in conclusion. 'It seems to me – to us – that it is of the first importance to discover the identity of the mysterious Mr C. We know the names of a few of Imogen's other gentlemen friends, thanks to Miss Kenwood, but I am acquainted with most of them and I frankly cannot see any in the role of murderer. Darius Thornton, for example. And young Tom Gaydon!'

John gave a shout of laughter. 'I didn't know *their* names were on the list. How I shall roast them!'

'You will have the opportunity tomorrow,' his brother assured him briskly. 'For you are going to spend the day putting them through an interrogation.' Cutting John's protests short, he returned to the matter in hand. 'The only person who might possibly know the identity of Mr C. – leaving the undesirable Mrs Porter aside for the moment – is Francis. So I need to find him. I won't ask again how much you know about his private life. In fact, Susan has succeeded in answering the most important question I had intended to ask you, about Letitia Lang.'

Lady Susan interrupted. '*Did* you know about her, by the way?'

'Er, yes,' Matthew confessed.

'Pooh!' said her ladyship. 'So I could have saved myself all that trouble this afternoon.' No one except her husband displayed the least sign of sympathy. 'Oh, well, I suppose it was an adventure,' she concluded in a small voice.

'Have you finished?' her brother asked. 'The vital question now, Matthew, is, when you saw Francis a few days before he left London, did he tell you where he was going?'

'No.'

The earl bit his lip. 'You are quite sure? He said nothing that might have given you a hint?'

'No.'

Captain Gregory, his eyes on Matthew's scarlet face, intervened for the first time. Out of his wide experience of subordinates, from lieutenants down to loblolly boys, who thought they could evade the purpose of a question by clinging to the literal truth, he said, 'But you *know* where he is.' It was a statement, not a question.

Matthew gulped. 'Er, yes,' he admitted.

'Thank you, Adam,' said his lordship. 'How nice to have you home!' There was a rueful gleam in his eye. 'Well, that's something to be thankful for, at all events. But Matthew, why didn't you say so before, instead of having to have it dragged out of you?'

'Francis told me not to, until I discovered what you knew, and how you felt about everything.'

The colour fled from his cheeks as he became aware that every eye was fixed accusingly on him. 'Well, er ... ' he stammered.

'Do you mean,' said his lordship bodingly, 'do you mean you have *seen* Francis in the last few days? Where the devil is he, then?'

'At Atherton.'

The earl sank his head in his hands, and groaned. 'Go on. When did he arrive?'

'He just turned up, late on Saturday, saying he had decided to have a peaceful holiday away from his family, and take the opportunity at the same time to reorganize his office, which he never has the leisure to do ordinarily.'

'And that was all? He told you nothing about all this?'

'Well, you know Francis. He never ... It was only on Wednesday ... '

'Yesterday.'

'Was Wednesday only yesterday? It seems longer.'

Lady Susan made a small sound of sympathy. 'Poor Matthew,' she said. 'You must be worn out. Brandy is what you need, not tea.'

Gratefully, Matthew accepted the drink John poured out for him. 'Yes. Well,' Matthew began. 'Anderson arrived with your message yesterday noon, and by the time I'd packed my traps, and talked to Francis, and got on the road, it was after six. So I *am* a bit saddle-sore. And the bed I slept on last night was

100

rather lumpy. And by the way, Charles, I told Anderson to take a day's rest before he followed me back.'

'Yes. Fine. But *what happened yesterday*?!'

Miss Kenwood was enchanted to discover that the earl was human after all.

Matthew swallowed a mouthful of brandy and said, 'Well, when Anderson told me to come up here immediately, if not sooner, it was clear that something was up. Since I didn't know how long you wanted me for, I thought I should tidy up a few loose ends before I left.' He paused enquiringly.

'Very proper,' said his lordship, containing himself with difficulty.

'Francis came into my office while I was doing so, with a letter he thought you might like to have.'

The earl closed his eyes for a moment and held out his hand.

'Oh,' said Matthew, and produced it from his pocket after a struggle.

The earl looked at the superscription. *Confidential* was written in large letters across one corner. He balanced it thoughtfully on his palms, but did not open it. 'Go on,' he said.

'He also told me what I was to tell you, since he didn't have time to write it all down. He began with his relationship with Miss Reece, but I needn't bother with that since you know all about it. However, it seems that last Friday morning, before he left town, he went to see her. He had decided that this would be the best time to make the final break. Miss Reece had known it was bound to come, although she fought against it, but he said he had the feeling that if he remained in town she would be quite capable of turning up on the doorstep and making a fuss, whereas if she knew he was away and realized there was very little she could do, she might have calmed down a bit by the time two weeks had passed.'

'That makes sense,' Lady Susan remarked.

Kate said nothing, though secretly she thought that two weeks would scarcely have taken the edge off Imogen's grief.

'Well, *I* thought so,' Matthew agreed conversationally. 'In fact, I ... '

'Matthew!' exclaimed the earl ominously.

101

'Yes. Er . . . He reached her apartment at about eleven in the morning, but there was no answer, which he thought odd, as she never went out before midday. He tried the handle, in case she had gone out for a few minutes and left it unlocked. Thinking, you see, he might wait for her inside, or write a note if she were very long, though he hoped not to have to do that. Anyway, the door was unlocked and he went in – and found her dead. It must have been a terrible experience for him, though he didn't say much about it.' Matthew shook his head mournfully. 'He says he couldn't think what to do, and sat there for quite an hour, just considering. He knew the servants would find her when they came back later in the day, and despite looking at it from every angle could see no reason why he should be involved at all.

'He said that if you had been here, instead of in Paris, he would have come straight back and told you everything, and asked your advice. But since you weren't here, he thought the sensible thing was to go away as he had intended. There was always the possibility that his name might never come up in the matter, and he knew nothing that might help to identify the murderer – or nothing that other people didn't know, too. By going to Atherton, he was bound to hear as soon as you returned to London, and he thought he could *then* decide – depending on what, if anything, had happened in the meantime – what to do.'

His lordship was beginning to look a good deal happier, and Lady Susan's brow had lightened, too. Kate suddenly realized that, despite everything, they had both been uneasy over Francis's disappearance, however reasonably it had been explained away.

Stretching the truth a little, John said triumphantly, 'There you are! I told you that you were worrying unnecessarily.'

'So you did!' his sister replied melodiously.

Captain Gregory said, 'It sounds to me as if Francis behaved quite responsibly, on the whole. I'm damned if I know what *I'd* do under similar circumstances.' His wife flicked him a mock scandalized glance, and he grinned at her.

'Yes,' the earl agreed pensively. 'Though if he had left a letter here for me, he might have saved us all a good deal of the trouble we've taken in the last three days.'

'Come along, Charles!' the captain exclaimed. 'He could hardly have been expected to produce a rational letter covering all that territory in just a few minutes, especially in the state of mind he must have been in at the time. And he was probably still hoping none of it would have to come out at all.'

'True enough,' his lordship agreed after a moment. 'Go on, Matthew.'

'Well, when Anderson arrived with your message, it was fairly clear that something was up, and Francis decided to give me an outline of what had happened, and a letter for you, just in case ... Well, *you* know ... He said I was not to trouble you with the affair at all, if you didn't already know about it. And I think, deep down, he was terrified that you *might* know about it and think him guilty. That was why I was so incoherent to begin with, you see ... ?'

'Not at all, Matthew. Not at all,' said his lordship magnanimously.

'And of course that's partly why he didn't come back with me. He thought that if the whole affair *had* blown up, you might prefer him to stay out of the way.'

Captain Gregory looked at the earl consideringly. 'An awkward point, Charles!'

'It is, isn't it?' His eyes lifted to Miss Kenwood's. 'My own feeling is that he should. If he returns here, Townsend will pounce on him, and I would really prefer not to have my secretary arrested for a murder he did not commit. Besides which, it would put pressure on us, and to hurry an investigation rarely produces the best results. It's up to you, though, Miss Kenwood.'

She had been so interested that, for a moment, she could not think *why* it should be up to her. 'Oh!' she exclaimed rather weakly. 'You mean it's open to me to tell Townsend where he is? I should, of course.' Her mind raced over what she had heard that evening. Almost insensibly, she had come round to the opinion that Francis Mervyn was, after all, innocent, and that if anyone was going to discover who was really guilty, it was going to be the earl, not Townsend. 'I should,' she said again. 'It was I who called him in. And I can't very well call him off, can I?'

'Not without very good reason indeed.'

She thought again, and then directed a pained look at his lordship. 'I am going to be in an extremely embarrassing position if he discovers that I know where Mr Mervyn is.'

He smiled at her, and her heart, with absolute and astonishing precision, skipped a beat. 'We will all swear on oath that you know nothing!'

She made a quick recover. 'That's all very fine,' she said, in rallying tones. 'But "ignorance is the curse of God!"'

He capped it. 'And "knowledge the wing wherewith we fly to heaven." So you see, you win both ways.'

Lady Susan felt there was a flaw in the argument somewhere, but could not quite put her finger on it. She contented herself with asking amusedly, 'Shakespeare?'

'*Henry VI* Part 2,' replied her brother, and Kate added blithely, 'Act IV Scene 7.'

'I suppose you can do that with almost anything from Shakespeare?' said John, impressed.

She smiled at him lightheartedly. 'What? Supply chapter and verse? Gracious, no. Try me with *King John*, for example, or *Timon of Athens*, and I'd be in desperate straits.' She turned to the earl again. Since no one else seemed to be saying it, she said, 'You don't think your letter might perhaps contain something of interest?'

Oblivious of his sister's perceptive regard, he forced himself to concentrate. 'It might,' he said with an effort. 'Indeed, it might!' and turned his attention to it.

His eyes glanced down the page, noting phrases here and there.

' *... hoped you need not be troubled at all ... my own foolishness ... but I think you know me, and I hope you will believe ... but who? ... one realizes how little one really knows of people ... '* And here was something more solid. *'Miss Reece was extremely scrupulous. She had made an arrangement and was determined to see it through. But by piecing together unguarded remarks and apparently innocent references, I began to think that the man she referred to as C. might have been – and I only say might – Sir Julius Considine. I cannot now remember how I reached this conclusion. As I say, it was a sum of casual details. I cannot think that such a man could* *have killed Miss Reece. But I repeat – how little one knows of people!'*

Carefully, the earl placed the letter on his lap. 'Considine,' he said flatly. 'Sir Julius Considine. What do we know about him?'

Miss Kenwood, John, and Captain Gregory all looked blank. But Lady Susan cast a startled glance at her brother. He raised his eyebrows.

'You know about his wife,' she said. 'Surely? I thought everyone did.'

'Yes,' said the earl slowly. 'I do remember something. She was very young, wasn't she?'

'They were married about four years ago, when she was sixteen. You must have seen her – the sweetest, prettiest, most angelic thing.'

'There was some unfortunate history, wasn't there?'

'Goodness, yes. When she was about fifteen she had the most violent attack of scarlet fever, and her life was despaired of. Then, when she recovered, she was quite deaf. Her mama was in despair. But Considine had always been fond of her, and was so horrified lest such a fragile, delicate little thing be married off to someone quite unsuited to taking care of her that he offered for her himself. Although he was over forty, her mama welcomed the alliance, and so – it seems – did the child herself.' She stopped.

'And?' her brother prompted.

She shrugged. 'Whether it was the fever or not, I have no idea. But her understanding is – less than moderate. She is still only a child. But he is quite charming with her. He adores and cherishes her as if she were a piece of fine porcelain.'

'Or his daughter. Yes, I remember there was some gossip in very poor taste when he married her. But it died down quite quickly.'

'It could hardly do anything else! When you see them together, you see at once that their relationship is – there's no other word for it – quite beautiful.'

'Even so, it must be something of a strain for him. It sounds as if he might need a companion, a woman, an adult, as well as his little porcelain shepherdess.'

105

Adam said, 'Do you know what she is like, Susan? Other than exquisite, I mean?'

'I scarcely have more than a nodding acquaintance with her, but I should imagine she is as possessive as any pampered child towards the adult who pampers her. She has the most enchanting way of commanding him to do this, or do that.'

'My God,' said his lordship. 'It all sounds too hideously probable, doesn't it? You can quite see why he should need Imogen, and why secrecy should be so important to him.'

'Certainly it would be dreadful to hurt such an innocent, trusting little creature,' his sister remarked.

'Are you not acquainted with him at all?' Adam asked.

The earl shook his head. 'We nod at each other if we meet in White's, but no more. He is older than I and has never been seen much in society. I'm told he has a scholarly turn of mind. I know he has estates in Leicestershire. He has a country house not far out of London. But that's about the sum of my knowledge of him.'

John roused himself. 'You'll have to go and see him, won't you?'

'How can I? I can scarcely start talking about murder to him just because my secretary thinks he *might* have been keeping a demi-rep. I need one incontrovertible fact to start off with. Just one would do. But without it he would be perfectly justified in telling me to go to the devil.'

'You mean we're no further forward?' John asked sleepily.

Miss Kenwood, who was beginning to feel quite one of the family, said in a voice of honey, 'You are forgetting about our friend Robert William, are you not?'

She was quite right. Matthew's disclosures had temporarily cast her own in the shade.

His lordship's eyes came to rest on her again. 'If we could establish that Considine knew Elliston and Imogen to be on the brink of parting ... '

She looked guilelessly back at him, her eyes twin pools of darkness. 'Yes,' she said. 'I will talk to Robert tomorrow.'

Chapter 9

Searching next afternoon for Robert William Elliston, Miss Kenwood found him enthroned in the green room, frowning heavily upon a small, tawdry figure who stood twisting her hands before him. Kate recognized her as a very junior member of the cast of last night's after-piece, a spectacle entitled *Caravan*, in which Persians, Arabians, Christians, Camels, Palanquins and Cars wound a picturesque and vociferous way across The Desert, with the commendable object of filling in the last half hour of the programme.

Elliston was in a majestic rage. King Lear, Kate noted automatically. 'And how dared you, how *dared* you, I say, withdraw yourself without notice from your theatrical duties?'

The girl said nothing.

'Nothing will come of nothing,' he pointed out. 'Speak! Tell me! How dared you?'

Kate turned to Cox, who was standing just inside the door. 'What did the poor child do?' she murmured.

He flashed her a worried look and, leaning over, confided in a strangled mutter, 'She flounced off the stage *during the performance*!'

Kate rounded her mouth into a horrified 'Oh!' and turned back to the *divertissement* currently being enacted.

'They hissed me,' the girl said sullenly.

'And you have the presumption – I say again, the presumption! – to disagree with the judgement of *my* audiences? Better thou hadst not been born than not to have pleased them better!' Definitely King Lear.

'I don't know that, sir, but I will not stand to be hissed.' Draggle-tailed she might be, but she had her pride.

Elliston drew himself up royally in his chair, nostrils flaring, curly mouth compressed, eyes staring. His voice a direful blend of horror, wonder and pity, he pronounced, 'They – have – hissed – *me*!'

So might the son of Peleus have said, 'I too am mortal!' Kate stifled an admiring giggle.

'Well, maybe you deserved it!' said the girl, unimpressed.

If Elliston had been considering giving her another chance, he changed his mind on the instant. 'Hear me, recreant!' he thundered, and then stopped. Kate could see him mentally running through Act I Scene 1, selecting and discarding. 'Five days we do allot thee' might have done at a pinch, she thought, if he was going to give her a week's notice. But he settled in the end for a pithy summing up of her failings and a fluent lecture on the moral fibre required of any young person who hoped to grace the boards of the Olympic. Instant dismissal was the verdict, and he concluded, 'Away! By Jupiter, this shall not be revoked!'

From the torrent of words, the girl selected the only ones she understood and marched off towards the door, her head held high. Reaching it, she turned for a moment, looked the Great Manager up and down, sniffed, and said, 'Well, I hope they hiss you again. So there!'

Indulgently, Elliston surveyed the closed door. 'A spirited little thing,' he remarked. 'Cox, you may pay her.'

Cox hurried off in pursuit of the girl and Kate advanced towards the throne.

'Robert,' she began, 'I would like to speak to you privately.'

'Of course, my dear!' He rose, and handed her graciously to a chair.

'About Imogen.'

After a moment's pause, he repeated, 'Imogen?' and then added slowly, 'Ye-e-es. A harrowing tale.'

'You don't mind talking about it?'

'Why should I?' His furry eyebrows rose in surprise.

It was not quite the reaction she had expected, but the fact that he knew made things easier. 'Very well,' she said. 'Then would you mind if I asked you ...'

He raised his hand. 'Say no more, my dear Katharine. Say

108

no more. I have had it in mind these several weeks to mount a new production of *Cymbeline*, and I believe you are right. As Imogen, you would be superb.' He added politely, 'As in everything you do.'

'Robert!' she exclaimed. 'You are quite impossible! Why will you always ignore the fact that there are *people* in the world, as well as characters?'

'But the characters are so much more interesting,' he said simply.

She let it pass. 'I was talking about Imogen Reece,' she said. 'Did you not see *The Times* last Saturday?'

'Last Saturday?' he repeated. 'Saturday? No, I believe I did not have the requisite sevenpence about me at the time. What has the dear child done to merit the attention of Mr Walter?'

Irritated by the condescension, she said more bluntly than she intended, 'She was murdered.'

Half braced for a rendition of Lear mourning over the body of Cordelia, she waited. But he gazed at her perfectly blankly for a moment, and then closed his eyes and placed a spread thumb and forefinger over the lids. It was several seconds before he looked at her again, and when he did there were tears sparkling on the lashes. 'Poor child,' he said softly. 'What happened?'

If it was a performance, it beat to flinders any other she had ever seen him give. Briefly, she told him the circumstances, and concluded, a little touched by his emotion, 'So I went to see John Townsend at Bow Street. I am surprised he has not been to call on you.'

With impeccable timing, the door opened and Townsend himself pattered in, an innocent beam wreathing his prim little mouth. 'Hallo!' he said happily.

Elliston, who had been on the point of exclaiming, 'To call on *me*?' gazed at him with residual astonishment, while Kate had the unpleasant feeling that she herself must look a picture of guilt.

Townsend did not appear to notice. After a conventional exchange of greetings, however, he remarked sapiently, 'Ay, well. To judge by the looks on your faces, you must have been talking about me when I came in?'

Elliston, restored to normal, announced in throbbing

accents, 'Miss Kenwood has just broken the news to me of the sad – nay, tragic – death of Imogen Reece, with whom you may know that I was acquainted. Some years ago, of course. Alas, how one loses touch with those one once loved so dearly!'

The Runner, beady little eyes dancing, pushed his hat towards the back of his head and vigorously scratched his brow. 'Ay,' he agreed. 'Very sad. You wouldn't care to tell me when you saw her last?'

The expressive gaze shifted. 'I? When *I* saw her last?' He looked at Kate. 'When was it, Katharine, when was that ill-omened day when she chose to abandon my protection for that of Another?'

She restrained herself with difficulty from telling him he was overdoing it. Briefly, she said, 'Two years ago.'

He sighed. 'In the spring.'

'July, as a matter of fact,' she corrected him frostily.

'Was it? If you say so, my dear.'

Townsend cocked his head. 'Not since?'

'No.'

'Quite sure?'

'Of course.'

Townsend knew his man. 'Not even from a distance?'

Elliston hesitated. 'Possibly,' he conceded.

'Possibly?'

'My good fellow,' Elliston replied, as if he had not been acquainted with the Runner any time these last ten years. 'An actor may see his audience, but he does not *see* them. I believe I noticed Miss Reece once or twice in one of the boxes during a performance. Not as herself, but simply as the occupant of a box.'

This was a little beyond Townsend, but he persevered. 'But still, you have seen her more recently than two years ago.'

Elliston shrugged pettishly. 'Oh, well! If you wish to be pedantic about it ... '

Kate thought it was time to intervene. 'Did you notice any of the other occupants of her box?'

The Runner turned. 'Miss Katharine,' he said reprovingly. 'Do you mind?'

It was the excuse she had been looking for. Offendedly, she said, 'Oh, very well! If you had rather I left, I will do so on the instant. I was only trying to be helpful.' Rising, she stalked towards the door, uncomfortably aware of Townsend's eyes boring into her back. 'No doubt you will inform me if my presence should be required?'

As she closed the door behind her, she heard Townsend's placid voice say in a peculiarly irritating way, 'Dear me, the ladies! I seem to have offended her.' With something between a snap of annoyance and a sigh of relief, she took herself off to her dressing-room. What a blessing it was that Townsend had turned up before she had had the opportunity to tell Robert anything about the earl's investigations!

Rather more than half an hour later, Betsy popped her head round the door and said breathlessly, 'He's gone, miss!' and for the second time that afternoon Kate set out to talk to Robert William Elliston.

She found him still in the green room, this time confronted by the theatre dresser, who was complaining volubly at being expected to garb thirty-six Roman senators, when there was only sufficient material to make togas for two.

'Bed sheets,' said Elliston dismissively. 'And dyed borders.'

'But indigo's too dear, Mr Elliston'

'Did I say indigo? Certainly not. Ink.'

The oracle had spoken, and the dresser departed, muttering.

Elliston turned to Kate, Townsend's visit still occupying his mind. 'Who is this man – this earl fellow – whose secretary murdered Imogen?'

Swallowing a giggle at the thought of his lordship as an 'earl fellow', she said, 'It is not, I fear, quite as simple as that. Lord Moriston believes that it was not his secretary who was at fault, and I am inclined to think he may be right.'

'But I understood it was you who first told Townsend whom to look for!'

'Oh, drat the man!' she thought. 'It was,' she confessed, 'but I think now I may have been overly hasty.'

'Townsend doesn't think so.' With unexpected shrewdness, he added, 'He only came to see me as routine. His heart wasn't

111

in it. All his suspicions are directed against this man – er – Mervyn, so you had better tell me more, had you not?'

She said, 'Well, no one could suspect *you*, Robert. Of course not.'

Since late last night, she had been perplexing her brain with the problem of how to handle the conversation, and had reached no satisfactory conclusion. She suspected it would be unproductive to ask him for a list of Imogen's acquaintances, because in all probability he had been too wrapped up in himself and his own affairs even to be aware that Imogen had any acquaintances at all. No other line had suggested itself, however, so she opened her mouth and said, 'But I wonder if . . . '

He silenced her with a raised forefinger. 'I know what you wonder,' he said. 'You wonder if I know the name of the man who was keeping her after she left me!' Wagging the finger in an odiously chiding way, he went on, 'Really, my dear, you must not permit yourself to become involved in such sordid matters. Townsend has already asked me that question, and I was able to tell him nothing. You, I know, are moved only by an innocent feminine curiosity, but it does not sound well. Not at all well. Leave the question to those whose business it is to penetrate humanity's darker mysteries.'

A little more, she thought, and she would undoubtedly go off with a pop. There were times when she almost began to sympathize with the late Mrs Godwin's overheated views on the subject of women's rights. By exercising the most impressive self-control, however, she contrived to smile sweetly and say, 'I know you are right, Robert.'

Suddenly, she recognized that he had given her an opening, and took advantage of it in the most unprincipled way. After all, she told herself, paraphrasing what she had hitherto regarded as one of *Henry V*'s more specious arguments, her cause was just and her purpose honourable. 'It is simply that I understood from Imogen that he was a very kind man, and there were some books in her apartment that I think must have belonged to him. It occurred to me that he might like to have them back.' She added winsomely, 'For sentimental reasons, you understand.'

It worked. 'Of course. And you would send them back quite

anonymously, as if to prove that his desire for secrecy would still be honoured. What sensibility!'

Demonstrating sensibility was no problem; she had played Ophelia often enough. 'You understand so well, Robert.'

It intrigued him to think that he might succeed where Bow Street had failed. He said, 'Do you know no more than Townsend about this man? What about his background, his habits?'

She had already decided not to mention the man's initial if Townsend had not done so. This was partly because she did not wish to put words into his mouth. But she also hoped to be able to extract the name from him without unduly emphasizing it, so that he himself would not realize which, if any, of the people he mentioned had taken over his role as Imogen's protector. For the time being, there seemed no good reason to breach the secret that had been kept with such pains.

She said mendaciously, 'All that I know – or think – from something Imogen once said to me, is that he knew of your association with her, and that he also knew it was coming to an end. I had the impression that it was someone unconnected with the theatre.'

His eyes took on a faraway look, and she waited patiently while a whole gamut of expressions chased each other across his face. He had adopted the classic pose of the thinker, elbow on knee, chin on gracefully clenched fist, but it was marred by an increasingly heavy frown. Eventually, he swivelled his head round towards her, and said in an injured tone, 'There was no one.'

Bracingly, she told him, 'There *must* have been, Robert! Even if only the ... ' Just in time, she succeeded in changing 'pawnbroker' to 'mantuamaker.'

'Oh, *that* class of person, you think?'

'Well, Imogen did incline to chatter to people.' Anything to start him off.

'Yes.'

It took twenty wearisome minutes to work through Elliston's recollections of tradesmen, casual lady visitors, and the smitten young musician who had continued to give Imogen singing lessons long after he had stopped being paid for it. Only the tea

113

merchant had a name beginning with C. Suddenly, Kate was struck by the appalling thought that the initial might refer to the protector's first name, rather than his second. She firmly suppressed it. Imogen would never have used a man's Christian name right from the start.

'What about neighbours?' she asked, after Elliston had run dry.

'None would have been sufficiently plump in the pocket, I think.'

'But some might have had rich relations.'

'I suppose so. There was a youth who lived upstairs, with ambitions to be a poet. He might have been possible. But his name? Rowley? Rumsey? Ruthven?'

'Russell? Rutherglen?'

'Rutherford! That was it! I believe he lived on a small allowance from his father, who disapproved of him. An odd young man,' Elliston remembered. 'He replied to me quite offensively when I assured him that a period of deprivation in one's salad days was an invaluable aid to artistic development.'

She could imagine. 'And who lived below?'

'A doctor. A medical gentleman. He was most amiable when Imogen suffered from a feverish cold. He had a short, vulgar name, I recall. Glugg, or something of the sort.'

Kate chuckled. 'Surely not!'

'Well, perhaps it was Glubb. But he was not the type of man to have money to burn, or to know anyone who had.'

'Not even a patient?'

He shook his head disdainfully. 'He was not a fashionable fellow.'

Beginning to feel a trifle exhausted, Kate said, 'Was there a housekeeper?'

'Only a cleaning woman. The house was managed,' his voice trembled, 'by a man without feeling, a heartless, callous *brute*, a very Shylock for his pound of flesh, ignorant of the bowels of compassion ... '

Kate winced.

' ... a stranger to all the softer impulses of humanity, who would have thrown my sweet Imogen out into the street without so much as a thought – and *laughed* while doing it!'

114

'Yes, Robert,' Kate said soothingly. 'And what was *his* name?'

'Thurlow. He was agent for a fellow called Considine, who owned the property. I took him to task afterwards,' he went on virtuously, 'for his misdeeds. "Base villain", I said. "You were aware of the unfortunate position of that poor girl! How could you ... "'

Wondering where precisely one drew the line between self-delusion and hypocrisy, Kate said prosaically, 'I am sure you did, Robert. But Mr Thurlow does not sound to me the kind of man we are looking for. Are you sure you can think of no one else?'

By a merciful dispensation of heaven, he could not. She said, 'Oh, dear! So it could be any or none of the people you mentioned.' She looked discouraged.

He rose and patted her benignly on the shoulder. 'There, there, my dear! It was a kindly – nay, a generous – thought, but you must reconcile yourself to remaining ignorant. Keep the books yourself, as I am sure Imogen would have wished. Perhaps you might spare just one for me, as a memento.'

Feeling slightly ill, she looked up at him but said nothing.

Observing the melancholy look in her great dark eyes, he said, 'You are tired and overwrought. You must rest now, for *The Beggar's Opera* tonight. And I will see if I can arrange for you to have a day or two at home, in perfect quiet, next week.'

Aware that she was not on the bill for either Monday or Wednesday of the following week, she looked even more melancholy.

Elliston cogitated, and said at last, 'I believe, I *do* believe that I might be able to arrange for you to have – let me see – next Monday and Wednesday free. Would you like that?'

'How *kind* you are, Robert!' she said feelingly.

Chapter 10

The members of the Dornay family were having a notably less successful day than Miss Kenwood.

The earl had despatched John and Matthew to talk to all the young men on the list of Imogen's clients – even Darius Thornton and the Honourable Thomas Gaydon – and it proved to be a singularly frustrating task. Although summer arrangements had been much disrupted by the suspense of the weeks before and after Waterloo, so that London was less thin of company than usual in August, the majority of young gentlemen who had not taken themselves off to the country, or to Brighton or some other watering place, were out driving, or riding, or picnicking in such rural havens as Richmond Park and Hampton Court.

The same reply was forthcoming at each of the first five houses John and Matthew tried, although better fortune attended them at the sixth, where they discovered their quarry laid up on a sofa with his right arm reposing interestingly in a sling. A broken wrist, he told them wanly, the result of a toss he had taken – in Hyde Park, if you please, and in full view of everyone! – three weeks ago. He could only attribute it to his having been slightly bosky at the time, and had resolved never to fall into the same error again. Or not during daylight hours. He was happy enough to have someone to gossip with, even about Imogen Reece, when John introduced her name artlessly into the conversation, but all they left with was three further names to add to their list in place of the one they were able to cross off.

As they proceeded to the next address on their itinerary, John observed gloomily that this was going to take the devil's own time, and he wished he thought it would prove worthwhile in the end.

Adam had been enrolled to assist his lordship in finding out as much as possible about Sir Julius Considine, including where he was likely to be found at this particular season. They spent a large portion of the morning immersed in reference books, and after luncheon the earl went to visit his man of business, then his banker, and then Sir Andrew Cowan, a friend of his who had a hunting box in Considine's home county of Leicestershire. Adam was dispatched to Brooks's and White's clubs, to both of which Sir Julius was reputed to belong, and thereafter to gossip with an acquaintance at the Royal Academy. Considine, it appeared, was something of a collector, and well known in a quiet way as a patron of the arts.

By the time the two men met again in the library at St James's Square, it was well into the evening. Adam could only nod wearily when the earl remarked, 'And the lowering thing is that I have no doubt Francis would have gathered just as much information as the two of us put together, in half the time and with far less expenditure of energy. It is only when he is not here that I realize how much I depend on him. He must be the most efficient thing in nature.'

Lady Susan, who was equally weary, remarked, 'I wish he were more efficient about the girls he falls in love with! Goodness knows, London is full of agreeable girls, and yet he has to fix his hopes on someone like Miss Lang!'

The earl had decided that his sister should be allotted the task of seeing Letitia Lang. When she protested, he said, 'Only you can do it. If I went along myself, I would have to talk to her with a chaperone present, probably her mama, and there would be no possibility of keeping the matter quiet. Which I think we should try to do, in deference to Miss Lang as well as to Francis. It is up to her to decide whether to tell her parents that the man she – presumably – wishes to marry is suspected of murder. The trouble is that, however wrong the suspicion, parents in such a situation are only too quick to think in terms of no smoke without fire.' Lady Susan had seen the force of this argument, but had approached her task with misgivings that, in the event, had proved to be justified.

She had sent round a message in the morning, to say that she would like to call on Miss Lang at four o'clock, if that was convenient, and had received a polite, colourless little note in reply. Five minutes after the appointed hour, the carriage set her down outside a tall, narrow terrace house whose windows, paintwork and brass all proclaimed the supervision of some perfectionist within. The front door had been opened before her footman even reached it, and she was ushered straight through the hall and upstairs without delay, gaining no more than an overall impression of conventional decorations and blinding cleanliness before she found herself on the threshold of the drawing room, with a dainty, fair-haired girl with large grey-blue eyes coming forward to greet her.

'Would you care for some refreshment, your ladyship?' the girl said in a soft little voice, and when Lady Susan declined dismissed the butler with a nod.

How, Lady Susan had asked her brother a little tartly that morning, did he recommend she should phrase her question as to whether Miss Lang had murdered her future husband's mistress? Infuriatingly, he had grinned and remarked that that was a matter in which he would trust her judgement more than his own. But he could see no way of avoiding mention of the fact that Francis was suspected of murder, and they must just hope that the girl loved him enough to have faith in him. Assuming, that was, that she had not herself killed Imogen.

When the two ladies were seated, Lady Susan said, 'I have no doubt you are wondering who I am, and why I wish to talk to you.'

'Oh, no,' said Miss Lang naïvely. 'I looked you up. You are the sister of the gentleman who employs Mr Mervyn as his secretary.'

'Well, that makes things easier,' replied Lady Susan. 'It was about Mr Mervyn that I wished to speak to you.'

'So I supposed.'

'You know him quite well, I understand?'

Miss Lang said breathlessly, 'We hope to be married next spring, if all goes well. If my father approves, and if you approve.'

'If *I* approve?' exclaimed her ladyship, considerably taken aback.

'I thought that was why you were here? Mr Mervyn is most concerned that Lord Moriston should favour the match, and I assumed you had come to – what is the expression? – look me over on his behalf.'

It was not quite the expression Lady Susan would have used. Rallying, she said, 'Good gracious, Miss Lang. Neither my brother nor I would dream of interfering in Mr Mervyn's private affairs in such a way!'

'Would you not? I don't know about the *ton*, you see. My father is only a manufacturer, though a very gentlemanly one, of course.'

'Yes,' said her ladyship, rapidly revising her strategy. 'And how does he feel about the match?'

'He had hoped I might do better,' Miss Lang said composedly. 'He is not one of the great ironmasters, you understand, who could buy a peer for me. But Mr Mervyn is very well-bred, and when we became attached my father thought he might be able to help him improve his position in the world. Being a secretary is not very distinguished, you know, but one is forever seeing advertisements in the newspapers.' She rose to her feet. 'Do you know the kind I mean?'

Wordlessly, Lady Susan shook her head, and Miss Lang went to a stand in the corner of the room and returned with a copy of the *Morning Post*. 'Like this,' she said, and read aloud, '*A Premium of One Thousand Pounds will be presented to any Person who can procure to the Advertiser a Permanent Situation in the Exchequer or any other office under Government where not more than six hours daily employment is required. Strict secrecy may be relied on if requisite. Letters should be addressed to Mr Mason at 4 Salisbury Street, Strand, and none but principals will be treated with.* That kind of thing, you know? I am sure that if Mr Mervyn had government employment he would advance quite rapidly. I have the greatest faith in him, and so has my papa, or he would not be prepared to buy an appointment for him.'

Her ladyship was feeling slightly faint. 'Does Mr Mervyn know of this plan?'

The heart-shaped face smiled sunnily at her. 'Oh, no! It is to be a surprise.' The smile clouded a little. 'But if you did

119

not want to see whether I was suitable, I don't quite understand ... '

Lady Susan took a deep breath. 'Well, the situation is this. Through no fault of his own ... ' She stopped and tried again. 'The thing is that a gentleman from Bow Street is anxious...' She was making a mull of it. 'Mr Mervyn,' she said decisively, 'as I have no doubt you know, is away on holiday. Unfortunately, something has cropped up, a matter in which Bow Street believes Mr Mervyn might be able to help them. I wondered if you might have any idea.'

'Bow Street?' Miss Lang's soft little voice was shocked. 'Papa would not like that at all!'

'I assure you there is nothing reprehensible about it. It is simply a question of assisting them.'

'It sounds dreadful! Oh, no! I don't like that at all. I don't think I even want to know.' She sounded panic-stricken.

Lady Susan's qualms had begun to evaporate. She said sharply, 'Miss Lang! If you have any feeling for Mr Mervyn, you can scarcely take such an attitude!'

'Yes. No. I suppose not. Oh, dear, what shall I do? Perhaps you had better tell me?'

'Have you ever heard of a lady called Imogen Reece?'

The helpless look died before her eyes. 'No,' said Miss Lang. 'Who is she?' The grey-blue gaze had become the colour of ice water.

Despairingly, Lady Susan thought, 'And that *has* torn it! Poor Francis!' Aloud, she said, 'A lady who was found dead last Friday in unhappy circumstances. Bow Street are anxious to talk to everyone she knew.'

'And where does Mr Mervyn come into it?'

'He was acquainted with her, apparently. Did he never mention her to you?'

'No.'

'You don't know whether he knew her?'

'No.'

'Have you any idea where Mr Mervyn might have been last Friday morning?'

'No.'

'Did he not come to see you before he left town? I should have thought he might.'

'No. Besides, I was out.' She caught herself. 'Why should you want to know where *I* was?'

'I don't,' Lady Susan assured her untruthfully.

'Why are you asking me these questions? I don't understand.'

But she did. Lady Susan said, 'I am afraid Bow Street wish to see Mr Mervyn, not because they think he might know something about the lady's death, but because they think he was responsible for it.'

The girl's rosebud mouth was slightly open. Her centre front teeth were just neat enough and pointed enough to give her the look of a vicious little rabbit. Lady Susan did not like her.

'I don't believe it,' Miss Lang said, just a little too late to be convincing.

'Neither do I, and neither does my brother. He intends to prove it. But he might need your help.'

'Why should they think he killed her? Why *should* he kill her? He must have had a motive!' There was clearly only one motive that she could think of, and the fact that it was the right one, near enough, did not endear Miss Lang to her visitor. 'I don't wish to have anything to do with it.'

Her ladyship was quite unable to resist. She said coolly, 'Bow Street Runners also have a limited imagination. It might lead them no further than the assumption that you held Miss Reece down while Mr Mervyn picked up the candlestand that killed her. Possibly you could prove them wrong. But I would recommend you to be honest, Miss Lang, for your own sake – though to be frank, that concerns me very little – and also for Mr Mervyn's, which concerns me a good deal. *He* has nothing to fear from honesty.'

'Neither have I!' exclaimed the girl, her soft little face quite transformed. 'And I will thank you to leave, right now! I never want to see you, or Mr Mervyn again. And you may tell him so!'

She jumped to her feet, preparatory to opening the door, but it opened at that moment to reveal a thickset man of middle height, impeccably dressed and groomed, wearing a benevolent expression that was wiped clear at the first sight of his daughter's face.

'What's amiss, my pet?' he asked in a deep, faintly hoarse

voice that retained traces of a Yorkshire accent under the London veneer.

His daughter ran to him and took his arm. 'Papa,' she exclaimed, her face as plaintive as that of an indignant kitten. 'Her ladyship says Mr Mervyn is suspected of having murdered someone. A lady. You never liked him, and now I know you were right. There must be something wrong, must there not, if Bow Street wants him? I should have heeded you, indeed I should!'

Mr Lang patted her hand. 'You should always listen to your da, my pet. So it's murder, is it? Too many airs for my taste, he had, but I wouldn't have thought he'd go so far. Aye, but the quiet ones are always the worst.'

'You leap to conclusions, sir,' her ladyship said tersely. 'Mr Mervyn may be suspected, but he is most certainly not guilty.'

'That's as may be. But no smoke without fire, is what I always say.' He was *quite* as unattractive as his daughter. 'Even to be suspected means he ain't respectable. No, I'll not be spending brass on him, I can tell 'ee. Not after this. I'm glad your eyes have been opened, puss.' He patted his daughter's hand again, looking the while at her ladyship with eyes as matt and expressionless as grey pebbles.

'I see,' she said, picking up her reticule. 'Forgive me for wasting your time, Miss Lang. And yours, sir. I imagine there is nothing I can say to convince you, so I will take my leave.'

They escorted her downstairs and out to the front step.

She cast a final look at them as she drove away, the square man and the slight girl, standing arm in arm like effigies on some ancient Egyptian tomb.

'And with just about as much good red blood in their veins!' she concluded disgustedly to her brother and Adam.

'You sound as if you were a little rough with her,' her brother said.

She glared at him. 'I kept a rein on my temper until there was no bearing it any longer. And then I spoke out because it seemed to me that it might, just *might*, be possible to shock something out of her. As, in a way, it did. Pray don't criticize! You should have gone yourself if you think you might have done better!'

His lordship, preferring discretion to valour, regarded her quizzically and said nothing. For Susan to lose her temper was practically unheard of.

Adam, however, went over and perched on the arm of her chair, putting an arm round her shoulder. 'Calm down, my love!' he said. 'It must have been excessively unpleasant. Don't think we don't know! And now you're feeling conscience-stricken about wrecking Francis's relationship with the girl. But by the sound of it, you've saved him from a fate worse than death.'

She smiled reluctantly. 'Yes,' she admitted. 'It was horrid. What put me in such a rage was the thought of poor Francis being cozened by such an artful little minx. You or Charles *would* probably have done much better, because, unless I am much mistaken, Miss Letitia Lang is one of those girls who is never anything but enchanting with gentlemen. It is women who bring out the vixen in her.'

'Especially beautiful ones,' said her husband coaxingly.

'Liar!' She was beginning to feel better.

His lordship said, 'If I may intrude on this idyll, would a pretty rival bring out the vixen in her? Or the murderess?'

'It could. But unless she is a better dissembler than I give her credit for, I don't think she knew about all this. Her father, however ... ? There,' she said thoughtfully, 'I wouldn't wager a farthing either way.'

Chapter 11

At the unprecedentedly early hour of ten next morning, the Earl of Moriston brought his magnificent pair of match greys to a standstill outside one of the smaller houses in Cavendish Square. But even as he was handing the reins to Fielding, preparatory to descending from the curricle, the front door opened and Miss Kenwood appeared, bewitchingly attired in a highwaisted, highnecked carriage dress with a white skirt and a bodice of deep rose pink. Perched on her elegant head was a nonsensical hat composed entirely of tiny pink rosebuds. She looked ravishing. Betsy, curtseying to his lordship, handed her mistress a frothy white parasol and a silky white shawl, and Miss Kenwood descended the steps gracefully, saying with a smile, 'You see? I promised I would not keep you waiting.'

Handing her up into the curricle, he smiled back. 'I cannot tell you how grateful I am. My eldest sister Verona is a neighbour of yours, and Cavendish Square is a place in which I prefer not to linger.'

'Is she so alarming?'

He took the reins, and Fielding swung nimbly up behind. 'Quite terrifying! She is something of a bluestocking, and has the lowest possible opinion of the rest of the family. We meet ceremonially now and then, but even Gavin – who is a parson and the only truly respectable one among us – finds her as much as he can stomach.'

'Are you a large family?'

'Large enough. Verona is the eldest, and shares her house with two other, equally intellectual ladies. Then there is Charlotte, now Lady Rothbury, who lives in Yorkshire to John's great relief. He can never see eye to eye with her about anything, and unfailingly ends up in her black books through his total inability to remember even the number of her children, far less their names. I never remember myself,' he said, 'but I am cleverer at disguising it. After Charlotte – eight years after, to be exact – there is myself. Then Susan. Then Robert, who is a cavalry officer and very dashing. He survived Ligny and Waterloo with a few minor cuts and grazes, and we expect him home at any moment.

'Gavin,' he went on thoughtfully as they turned into Hyde Park, 'is undoubtedly a changeling. There is no other way of accounting for his saintliness. As I said, he is a parson, and not in any fat country parish but in one of the least salubrious quarters of London, bordering on Seven Dials. And last, of course, there is John. He came down from Oxford last year and has not yet discovered his mission in life.'

The sun was shining and the river sparkling. It was a beautiful day. He risked a question. 'Do you come of a large family yourself?'

'No.'

He thought that was the end of it, but after a moment she went on, 'I had one brother, but he died in the Peninsula. At Talavera. It killed my mother and destroyed my father. I have thought since that perhaps larger families do have something to recommend them.' She caught his expression and exclaimed, 'Gracious heaven! You look as if I had been enacting a Greek tragedy. I assure you, it is all in the past now, and I scarcely think of it. It was simply that Mr John Dornay reminded me very much of my brother David, who had rather the same volatile attitude to life, and very much the same engaging manner.'

'Volatile,' said his lordship, amused. 'What a very well chosen word.'

They were driving west along the river, skirting its banks as far as the crossing over the old Fulham Bridge. The water was improbably clear, skimmed by a faint, cleansing breeze that whisked away the smells of slime and sludge and left only a delicious freshness.

'What a perfect day!' Miss Kenwood exclaimed. 'This is what I miss about the theatre. There is no such thing as morning!'

She was in a carefree mood, her guard down, and the earl

would have given almost anything to be able to encourage her to talk. There was so much he wanted to know. But with Fielding sitting rigidly up behind, arms folded and ears agog, there was nothing he could do about it.

They crossed the bridge and headed for Richmond, where lay the country house of Sir Julius Considine.

The earl had ask Miss Kenwood to go with him, not only because any excuse for her company would have sufficed, but because the presence of a lady lent an innocent and social air to a visit that was not innocent at all. His lordship had succeeded in hitting on only one excuse for calling on Sir Julius – an urgent desire to see his unique collection of medieval and Renaissance paintings. He had thought briefly that he ought to take Susan, who was at least distantly acquainted with Lady Considine and might take the opportunity to talk to her while he was engaged with Sir Julius. But Susan had flatly refused, for more reasons than she vouchsafed to him. 'I had Mr Smith on Thursday, and Miss Lang on Friday,' was all she had said. 'I will *not* have Lady Considine on Saturday.' Catching Adam's eye, his lordship had yielded. He had even dispatched a protesting John and Matthew on their rounds again, so that Susan and Adam might have a few hours of privacy and calm. He would have been very much surprised to know that his sister's primary object had been to ensure *him* a few hours of privacy and calm with Miss Kenwood.

'I imagine,' he said conversationally, 'that Lady Considine will be happy to show you the gardens while Sir Julius and I are indoors. I believe there is a charming rose arbour.'

'You mean you would like me to lose myself?' she said pathetically.

He missed it, for a moment. Enquiringly he turned towards her, looking down on the exquisite face, crowned by its outrageous rose-decked hat . . .

When they descended at the door of the manor, both were laughing. Sir Julius, who happened to be on the terrace, thought what a charming couple they made and envied them the companionable freedom that contrasted so strongly with the careful solicitude that marked his own relationships. He was surprised to discover that they were no more than acquaintances.

Only initiates knew of Sir Julius's art collection, so he welcomed the earl on terms of equality and offered his guests some refreshment before taking them to the picture gallery that had been added to the north side of the house. It was not a particularly large room, but the windows and skylights, the bare polished floor, and the paucity of furniture gave it an appearance of space and peace. On the walls hung about thirty paintings, which caused Miss Kenwood to draw in her breath. She did not know what she had expected, but it was not these rich colours, these sunlit landscapes, these milky-fleshed women, gorgeously robed men, fat little pink-and-white children naked under gilded haloes.

A faint smile touched Sir Julius's weary mouth. 'As you can see, I have a particular interest in the fifteenth century, and since one cannot collect at random I have made the Virgin and Child my special study. This Mantegna is, I suppose, the jewel of my collection.' He led them over to a canvas more than nine feet tall that filled the wall between two windows. Enthroned in the centre sat the Virgin, red-robed, with the Child standing in a curiously adult pose on her lap. An infant John the Baptist was at her feet, and all round, erect or kneeling, were other figures of saints, and worshippers, and donors. Even the saints were armour-clad. Above the throne hung a branch of coral. 'A protection against evil,' Sir Julius explained. 'Quite pagan. The picture is full of symbolism, but one can only guess how much of it was intentional. Mantegna was saturated with the ideas of classical antiquity.'

He moved on. 'There is a panel here by Fra Angelico which might interest Miss Kenwood.' The weary smile appeared again. 'I find it nearly always attracts admiration from ladies like yourself.'

Miss Kenwood's hackles rose.

'Perhaps it is the colours,' he went on, oblivious. 'The pinks and blues and golds are charming, don't you think?'

They reminded her of nothing so much as sugared almonds. But she was saved by the earl from the need to find a tactful evasion.

'I imagine the recent disturbed state of Europe must have brought a number of paintings on to the market that would otherwise have been quite inaccessible to collectors,' he said. 'Have you found it so?'

'Undoubtedly. The Fra Angelico used to be in one of the religious houses of Tuscany, until they were suppressed in 1806. And the Mantegna was looted in 1797. Over here, there is a Van Eyck that the revolutionaries confiscated from a private collection in Burgundy, and that Van der Weyden over there was smuggled out of France before anyone had the opportunity to confiscate it.'

They studied each of the paintings with interest, tempered in Katharine's case with a slight resistance to their artificiality. It was not the artificiality itself that troubled her, but the attempt to combine it with reality. One or the other, she felt, but not both.

But her resistance collapsed when, after touring the walls, Sir Julius led them over to a specially constructed cabinet which held works of art that could not be hung up on display, handwritten books from the days before printing – copies of psalters, gospels, the book of the Apocalypse, canticles, bestiaries, and Books of Hours. The margins of the texts were decorated with the most enchanting miniatures, exquisite little paintings in which the colours looked as if they had been polished and the gold gleamed out, flaky but brilliant, from coronets and haloes and thrones and borders.

'I have only one manuscript that is complete,' Sir Julius said. 'At the time of the Reformation, many of the books were destroyed, with the exception of the pages containing the paintings. So it is more usual to find stray sheets than complete manuscripts. This complete psalter, you see, has twenty-four calendar illuminations in colour and gold, twelve of them showing country occupations for the months of the year, and twelve the signs of the zodiac. But when other such volumes were broken up, each of the twenty-four paintings from the calendar may well have found a different owner.'

He drew a single sheet of vellum from a folder. 'This, for example, obviously comes from a series of paintings intended to illustrate the life, death and miracles of the Virgin Mary.'

It was a masterpiece in miniature, a small and perfect representation of the Madonna, seated in solitude in a medieval garden starred and spangled with tiny, gem-like flowers and leaves. She wore draperies of dark blue, and the long fair hair fell loose to her shoulders. Her hands were clasped in her lap, and in each tender sorrowing eye had gathered a large and luminous tear. It was one of the most beautiful things Kate had ever seen.

Considine said, 'There are probably more than fifty other paintings in the same series. And here is a Saint Sebastian from the litany pages. I should think there must be fourteen or fifteen other saints' portraits in the manuscript *he* originated from.'

At last, the treasure chest was exhausted. His lordship, who had not been enjoying himself at all, requested the favour of a private word with his host. Sir Julius, agreeing with mild but courteous surprise, suggested that Miss Kenwood might care to join Lady Considine in the garden. 'We entertain very rarely,' he said, 'but I know she would be delighted to show you our rose arbour. Her hearing, I should tell you, is somewhat impaired, but she has learned to read lips.' The ghost of a smile just touched his eyes. 'And no doubt she would be happy to be apprised of the latest gossip from the outside world.'

Miss Kenwood had reservations on that score, but she followed the stout and fatherly-looking butler out through some French doors on to a terrace, and then down to a charming little green bower, framed in a canopy of cloudy white blossom. Lady Considine sat there alone, a fragile figure clad all in white, long flaxen hair tossed back from a slender neck, and her pale, slim fingers occupied in fashioning a garland of white columbine. Oh, no! Kate thought, depressed. Not Ophelia!

Wide, pale eyes looked up at her, startled under their thin brows, eyes of a strange bistre colour, like shallow water flowing over sand. The soft pink mouth curved into a tentative smile, and she rose to her feet with insubstantial grace. The earl, who had visited Italy the previous year, would unerringly have recognized a Botticelli. Kate, less widely travelled, identified her as a lovely child trapped in a woman's body. Exaggerating the movement of her lips, she said, 'Good morning! I hope I am not disturbing you?'

Her ladyship could not hear other people. Nor could she hear herself. There was something peculiarly shocking about it when a shrill, discordant voice whinnied out from between the perfect lips. 'Hallo!' she said. 'Have you come to see my garden?'

Meanwhile, in one of the rooms adjoining the picture gallery, the earl was broaching the subject of his visit to Sir Julius.

The older man listened with a face of stone, his customary pallor tinged with grey. Every muscle was inflexible in the tired countenance, with its heavy eyes, deep double creases bracketing the mouth, and high lined forehead under the receding dark hair. He was not a man to break down and confess all. Indeed, when the earl had finished, he said bitingly, 'No doubt you have learned your manners through consorting with criminals. No gentleman would gain entry into my house on such a pretext as you have used, in order to insult his host in such a fashion.'

The earl, his own jaw tightening, said, 'Would you have admitted me at all, if I had told you why I wished to see you?'

'Certainly not.'

'Yet this is a matter of murder, Sir Julius. The brutal murder of a harmless young woman. However important the social courtesies may be, they are nothing compared with the importance of bringing a murderer to justice.'

Considine looked at him without expression. 'I refuse to be involved.'

'You can scarcely do that. You *are* involved, and nothing you can say will change it.'

'I repeat, I refuse to be involved. I know nothing whatever about the murder of this girl.'

The earl said reasonably, 'What concerns you is whether your two-year association with Miss Reece can be prevented from becoming public knowledge. What concerns me is whether you killed her. If you did, I will prove it. If you did not, then I have no wish to wreak havoc in your private life. In fact, if you choose to be candid with me, I am prepared to do everything in my power to prevent the story from coming out.' He hesitated. 'I have, I believe, some idea of what such a disclosure would mean to you.'

Considine's face did not change, but after a moment he gestured the earl to a chair and sat down himself, facing him across a small table on which reposed something that looked like, but his lordship decided could not be, a genuine Cellini cup. 'I am prepared to listen,' he said tonelessly, folding his arms.

'As I told you, my secretary Francis Mervyn is suspected of having murdered Miss Reece. I don't know whether you were aware that he had been on intimate terms with her since early this year?'

'I said I was prepared to listen, not comment.' But in a nervous gesture that the earl thought was probably habitual, he was flicking the nail of his left thumb unceasingly against the tip of his forefinger.

'Miss Reece told Mr Mervyn a good deal about you, but not your name. She kept a diary, however, which is in the possession of Bow Street. In it, she referred to you by the initial C. Have you been visited by any of the Runners?'

Considine said nothing.

'I'm afraid that won't do. You are not committing yourself by answering such a question as that. Have you had a visit?'

'No.'

'Or has anything else occurred to make you think your name may have cropped up in relation to Miss Reece?'

The thumbnail continued to flick. 'No.'

'Then they have not yet connected you with the mysterious C. Frankly, I hope to discover the murderer before Bow Street lays hands on Mr Mervyn, who is out of London at present. But if I fail, the Runners will be bound to make the most concentrated attempt to establish who was paying Miss Reece's bills before they risk bringing him up for trial. And if *I* can find out, so can they.'

Sir Julius rose to his feet and strolled towards the window. He stood looking out, hands clasped behind his back. After a moment, the tiny movement of thumb and forefinger began again.

Addressing his back, the earl said, 'And let me be blunt. If I fail so badly that Mr Mervyn does have to stand trial, your name is bound to come out during the course of it, whatever promises Bow Street may make to you beforehand. In his own defence, Mr Mervyn will have no option but to try to fix suspicion on someone else, and that someone else can be no one

131

but you. On the other hand ... ' Irritated at being unable to see Considine's face, the earl rose to his feet and walked, more heavily than was his custom, towards him. As he had hoped, the other man automatically swung round to see what he was doing.

'On the other hand,' his lordship repeated, 'it is quite probable that the real murderer – assuming he is someone other than yourself – may not know who you are. Furthermore, if the murder should prove to have been unconnected with Miss Reece's intimate affairs, even the fact of your existence could be irrelevant. So it is in your interest that Francis Mervyn should not be brought to trial. If he is, *you* will inevitably lose. If not, there is a very good chance that you might come through it all unscathed.' He waited and then added, 'So far, I have been talking in terms of your own self-interest. But I would have hoped that, if you felt any affection for Miss Reece, you would also feel a compulsion to help me identify the man who killed her.' He allowed another pause to develop. 'And I must of course point out, however distastefully, that if you refuse me your cooperation, I shall be forced to draw my own conclusions from it.'

Considine's face was still perfectly schooled. He said nothing. Then, 'What does this man Mervyn look like?'

The earl produced one of Susan's sketches from an inner pocket of his olive green coat.

Considine took it and turned once again to the light. The earl could see him only in quarter profile. Was he contrasting Francis's spare and stylish looks with his own worn and seamed countenance?

'Yes,' he said at last, and handed the paper back. 'I see. You have made your point clear.' Which point? About the murderer, or about the fact that neither Imogen nor Francis could be altogether condemned for the attraction that had drawn them together?

'It appears to me,' Considine said, reseating himself and slotting his fingers together, 'that I have no way of confirming or disproving what you have said. I suppose you must have spoken the truth as you see it, for I can think of nothing you could gain by distorting the facts. Would you answer me a question? When did – Francis? – Mervyn first discover my name?'

'I have no idea. And he deduced it, in effect, rather than discovered it. But I could find out, if it is important?'

'Could it have been as much as two months ago?'

'I imagine so.'

'It's not important, but I would like to know.' He contemplated his interlaced fingers. 'I did not, of course, kill Miss Reece, though I suppose I might have difficulty in proving it. All I can say is that the very idea is nonsensical. You want me to help you identify the man who did kill her. To that, I must say yes!'

He had an odd trick of raising his eyebrows and dropping his lids without making any real change in his expression. With anyone else, the effect would have been quizzical, or sardonic, or supercilious. In Considine's face, it merely produced a readjustment of the planes. 'Miss Reece was one of those rare people who lives for the moment. She was a well bred girl. She was honest and kindly. She was even intelligent. And she was a realist, who knew what the world was about. I did not love her. I made use of her, with her own consent. I was generous with my money, and she was generous with herself.' His eyebrows and lids returned to their usual latitude. 'No, I did not love her. But I did like her. And for that reason – for that reason alone – I am prepared to help you.'

The two men regarded each other measuringly.

The earl broke the silence of conditional truce. 'Where were you last Saturday morning?'

Considine raised his brows, more expressively this time. 'Bearing in mind the distance between here and Mecklenburgh Square, I think I could provide sufficient evidence, even if only from the servants, to free me from suspicion.'

'What about your wife?'

Considine's face became very still, and then his eyes opened wide and he said in a grating voice, 'Oh, no!' His cleft chin came up. 'You go too far.'

The earl inclined his head. 'I accept that. But are you quite sure she knew nothing of your association with Miss Reece?'

'Quite.'

'She has brothers, however, who might have felt the need to take action on her behalf.'

'They would have come to me. They know nothing.'

'Very well. If none of your family was involved, who was? You spent many hours with Miss Reece over a long period. You talked. She must have told you about people she knew, places she went. In all that time she must have said *some*thing. Perhaps if you were to take your mind right back to that very first day when you went to see Mrs Porter ... '

It jarred Considine to realize just how much the earl knew.

' ... and proceed from there. Do you keep a diary or engagements book?'

The sigh was a confession of defeat, of regret – of who knew what. 'Yes,' he said heavily. 'But you must give me time to think.'

'There is very little time.'

Considine made an impatient movement. 'I wonder if you *really* understand. My wife means everything to me, but there are a few things, a very few, that she cannot give me. The kind of conversation that an adult man and woman can enjoy, free and uncircumscribed, about everyday things. And a certain – physical relationship, a kind of mechanical relief, a fulfilment of needs that have very little to do with the spirit. To reduce it all to one word, a sense of relaxation. Imogen was very well attuned to my requirements. If anyone gossiped, it was I. If anyone reminisced, it was I. If anyone talked about the latest books, or poems, or plays, or discussed the political situation, or Wellington's tactics, or Brougham's antics, or Castlereagh's unreliability, it was always I. Imogen was the perfect mistress. After two years, I suppose I knew very little more about her own opinions, her likes and dislikes, her acquaintances and tastes, than I did at the beginning.' His voice, pitched low, changed slightly. 'Looking back, I am ashamed and embarrassed. Any human being deserves more than that from a relationship. But I hope it explains why I do not think I will be able to tell you anything.'

'Perhaps you will try, nevertheless. It is surprising what one can remember with a little prompting. Did she ever mention her sister, for example?'

'Not that I recall. Casually, perhaps.'

'Did she never say that her sister had a fetish about respectability, and disapproved most strongly of her way of life?'

'I have no recollection of it.'

'Did she ever mention a woman friend who sang at the Opera?'

'No.'

'Or the young men who danced attendance on her when you were not there?'

A muscle in Considine's jaw twitched. 'No.'

'Did she tell you about her interest in the progress of Nash's building works along the New Road?'

'No.'

The earl rose to his feet. 'Sir Julius,' he said, 'I cannot believe that a man so intelligent, so observant, so – forgive me – sensitive as yourself can have spent so many hours in the company of one person and learned nothing at all about her. Why, by the way, did you wonder when Francis Mervyn learned your name?'

'Curiosity.' But there had been a momentary hesitation.

'You said it was not important, but you asked, just the same. There may be a number of other things that seem unimportant to you, or seemed so at the time. Would you make a concentrated attempt to remember, please? Anything, or everything, might matter.'

Considine also rose, and faced his lordship across three feet of carpet. 'The only thing that matters to me,' he said, 'the only thing in the whole world' – the earl had a fleeting memory of Olivia Iredale using almost exactly the same words – 'is that my wife should be protected. I have no doubt,' the creases at one side of his mouth deepened wryly, 'that you know something about our marriage. Who does not? But if my wife should discover *through you* that I have failed her, I swear by all I hold sacred that you will regret it until your dying day.'

His lordship, profoundly unimpressed, said, 'I see no need for these heroics. The problem that concerns you was, after all, of your own contriving, and you have not the smallest right to demand the assistance of anyone else in resolving it. As I have said, however, I will help you if I can. But *whether* I can may very well depend on how much help you choose to give me.'

135

He held out his hand and said formally, 'I will bid you good day now, Sir Julius, and hope to hear from you soon.'

Soon after they entered Richmond Park on their way home, the earl slowed his horses to a walk and asked, 'Have you had enough of trees and flowers for today, Miss Kenwood, or would you care to stroll on the grass for a little?'

'That would be very pleasant,' she replied sedately.

But as soon as the curricle was out of earshot, she exclaimed, 'What a relief! I could not think how I was going to contain my curiosity until we got back to town.'

He smiled. 'Do you really want to walk, or would you rather sit on one of those benches over there?'

'Certainly not. We must preserve the fiction. Besides, a pleasant stroll is one of the most calming pursuits I know.'

'That, I confess, was my primary reason for suggesting it. I have the most urgent desire to wipe the dust of that dreadful house from my feet.'

She was surprised. 'You felt it too?'

'Oh, yes. Even a man can be sensitive to atmosphere, you know. Not just "ladies like yourself"!' he added wickedly.

She giggled. 'Your interruption was deliberate, then? I wondered about that. Nothing, really nothing, irritates me more than being treated as a mere female. As if women weren't people, too!'

'Especially when you so disliked the painting!'

'You *are* observant. But even if I had liked it, I would have been forced to revise my opinion on the instant. The illuminated manuscripts, on the other hand ... '

'Very beautiful. Have you not seen any before?'

'Nothing of that quality. If I ever find myself with a great deal of money, I shall know how to spend it.'

'Do you expect to find yourself with a great deal of money?' He gave her his hand to steady her over the edging of the path, and the faintest vibration ran up her arm.

'Of course,' she replied jauntily. 'Mrs Siddons has retired from the theatre, and Madame Catalani from the Opera. I propose to replace *both* of them. Just think how profitable it will be! The Opera used to pay Catalani more than two thousand pounds for the season, and by the time benefits and

136

private engagements had been added she never made less than five thousand in the year, usually a good deal more. I am not quite so sure how much Sarah Siddons earned, but on provincial appearances she frequently ended the week five or six hundred pounds richer than when she began. I can scarcely lose. In another year or two I shall be able to buy illuminated manuscripts by the score.'

'I hesitate to point out that, although your voice seems to me to be superior to Catalani's and I am sure that, in comedy at least, you must certainly outshine Mrs Siddons, no theatre will be able to afford you if you cost as much as both ladies put together.'

'There is that,' she admitted. 'So I have accepted a mere forty pounds a week for my first season at Drury Lane, in order not to frighten them off too soon.'

He laughed. 'Are you looking forward to it?'

'Yes, and no. Obviously, it will be a genuine pleasure to have the opportunity of acting in plays produced as the playwright intended them to be, rather than adapted and musicalized. But Drury Lane is so enormous that it is impossible to convey emotions without exaggerating dreadfully.'

'Too large to act in and too small for a bullfight, in fact. Like Covent Garden.'

'Nicely put. And my other doubt is about acting with Kean.'

'Really? I should have thought it would be quite stimulating to appear with someone so – er – distinguished.'

The large and melancholy eyes gazed up at him. 'Stimulating, certainly. I played *Othello* with him two years ago in Dorchester, and every time he laid hold of me he pinched me black and blue! And since his performances spring from his instincts of the moment, he growls and prowls and roams and foams about the stage, like a caged tiger, so that one never knows whether he is about to appear on one's right or one's left, or let out the most fearsome roar from just behind one's ear. He even prowled right off stage when I was on my knees, addressing my most touching pleas to him! No, I don't very much care for Kean, and I fear he may feel the same about me, since I am coming from the Olympic, and he and Elliston detest each other.'

She stopped suddenly, and consulted her little fob watch. 'Gracious heavens! Elliston will detest me, too, if I am not back at the theatre soon. You should not have encouraged me to prose on. Are you going to satisfy my curiosity about Sir Julius before we go?'

He wondered, when he had delivered her at the stage door of the theatre some little time later, why she had found it necessary to point out to him that she was capable of keeping herself in perfect comfort by her own exertions. Seated before the glass in her dressing-room, Kate was wondering precisely the same thing.

Chapter 12

Less than an hour after the earl arrived home, Brandon came to inform him that there was a gentleman who wished to see him.

'Sir Julius Considine, my lord.'

It was the first time Brandon had ever seen his master look startled, and he returned to the hall anteroom to look with new interest at the unimportant seeming gentleman responsible for this aberration. But he was no more striking on closer inspection than at first sight. Middle-aged, of middling height, accustomed to patronize a better-than-middling tailor, and to employ a poorer-than-middling valet. There was a long blonde hair adhering to one shoulder of his claret-coloured coat, and faint but unmistakable grass stains on the knees of his knitted buff pantaloons.

Brandon, disappointed, said, 'If you will please to follow me, sir?'

The earl was not alone, and Considine halted on the threshold, his right hand going to the large, flat, loosely wrapped package under his other arm.

His lordship said, 'I had not expected us to meet again so soon. May I introduce Captain Gregory, who is a member of my family?'

Considine bowed slightly. 'I hoped to find you alone.'

'Captain Gregory will, of course, leave if you wish. But I should tell you that he is aware of the matter we were discussing earlier, and that I value his judgement and advice.'

Sir Julius frowned. 'If he knows all about it, I suppose there is no purpose in his leaving,' he said grudgingly. 'But I should like to know how many other people have been regaled with the details of my private life?'

His lordship's mouth deepened at the corners. 'Other than Miss Kenwood, no one outside my family, I can assure you.'

'Hmmm,' said Considine, seating himself and placing his package, with a slight thud, on the earl's desk.

His manner was subtly different. Earlier, he had been concerned. Now, he was worried. The earl suspected he might be one of those people whose brains, though quick to understand a situation, were slow to transmit its full implications to their nerves.

Without preamble, Considine said, 'You told me you could find out when Mervyn discovered who I was.'

'Deduced.'

'Very well, deduced. I will tell you why I asked. As you know, I took the greatest precautions whenever I visited Miss Reece. I made sure that she sent the servants away. I took a hackney carriage to her address. I wore a ridiculous slouch hat and a bulky greatcoat when I entered or left the building. I gave her cash to pay for everything. I had impressed on her how much it all mattered, and I trusted her and placed every reliance on her discretion. I was completely certain that no one other than the two of us knew what there was between us.'

The earl said, 'But any secret can be discovered if someone cares enough.'

He nodded. 'I now know there were things I should have seen, but did not see. Things I should have understood, but did not understand. It should certainly have occurred to me that Miss Reece would not expect our arrangement to last forever. Though it might have done. But I ought also to have foreseen that she might have,' he shrugged intolerantly, 'other fish to fry.'

'That is unjust,' his lordship said decisively. 'From what I have been able to discover, Miss Reece observed your bargain with her quite as conscientiously as you had any right to expect.'

'Nevertheless, she became involved with your secretary. And, if I understood you correctly, more than involved with him. She was in love with him?'

The earl nodded.

Adam, sitting quietly in the background, was remarkably interested. Once before, he had been witness to a confrontation

140

between Charles and someone who was deeply involved in a case of murder and blackmail. Then, the man concerned had been wholly self-centred and not very intelligent. Considine was a very different proposition from Sir Augustus Home.

'That explains a good deal, I suppose,' Considine said.

No one spoke.

'I should have foreseen it,' he said again. 'However discreet she was, she would not be discreet with him. You agree?'

'With reservations,' his lordship said.

'Loose talk. Pillow talk. Enough to allow him to "deduce" my name, which no one else knew. I am afraid you are wrong, Lord Moriston. For your secretary *is* probably the murderer, and certainly a blackmailer. In the last two months I have paid him the sum of two thousand pounds.'

The earl's blue eyes met Adam's brown ones.

His lordship turned back to Sir Julius. 'Blackmail!' he exclaimed irritably. 'Why the devil didn't you say so before?'

Considine bridled. 'I didn't have the opportunity to think it out until after you left. I had never heard of the man before, and you were so definite about the fact he hadn't killed her. But now I think he did. He is the only one who could have known. And I'm here to make a bargain with you. You threatened that if Mervyn came to trial my affairs would be dragged out in court. Now, *I* say to *you* that, if he should come to trial for murder, I will say publicly that he was responsible for blackmailing me to a very loud tune. Once the thing is exposed, you see, it will matter to me no longer. And I will supply the evidence that hangs him!'

The silence this time was thick. Opaque. None of the three faces gave anything away.

The earl said crisply, 'Describe the man to whom you paid the money.'

Considine's mouth constricted in a sardonic grimace. 'That won't help you. I never saw him – did you think I would? I received a letter in the hand that every schoolchild writes. It didn't even say, "Pay up or I will tell your wife", nothing so blatant. It merely implied that I had a choice between paying, or discontinuing my visits to Miss Reece. The money was to be sent to the Receiving Office at Lombard Street, and although I thought very deeply about it, there seemed no

141

possible way of discovering who collected the letter from there. If you know Lombard Street, you will know what I mean.'

'The name?'

'Spencer. Obviously assumed.'

'Spencer?' the earl repeated in a very odd tone. Adam looked at him, but his face was perfectly still.

His lordship said, 'Did you tell Miss Reece about this?'

'Yes. I asked her if she had told anyone, anyone at all, my name. She denied it utterly. I asked her if she had told anyone about me in more general terms, my personal habits, my tastes, my interests. Well, she denied that, too, with even more conviction. Too much, looking back.'

The earl said, 'You're not good enough, Sir Julius. First you wanted to know when Francis Mervyn identified you. Now you talk of "my tastes, my interests". Why?'

Considine was not attending. 'Of course,' he said. 'Of course. She knew it had to be Mervyn, obviously. So she told him to stop, and he killed her.'

'Pay attention, please, Sir Julius. What do your tastes have to do with it?'

The other man was still lost in his own thoughts.

Sharply, his lordship said what Adam, too, was thinking. 'Do you have unconventional sexual tastes, Sir Julius?'

That caught his attention. 'What?'

'What did your tastes have to do with the blackmail?'

Sir Julius looked at him with dislike. He turned to the desk, and began to strip the outer wrappings from his package. There was a folder inside that the earl had seen before. From it, Considine drew a sheet of vellum, and placed it flat on the mahogany top. He said nothing.

Adam, rising and approaching, gasped. Part of the sheet was filled with black-letter script in old French, but two-thirds of it consisted of a rich, exquisite little painting in colour and gold, showing the Virgin Mary seated alone in a medieval garden, surrounded by a delicate tapestry of tiny, jewel-like flowers and leaves. In the centre of this enamelled brilliance, the Madonna's long fair hair fell loose to her shoulders, and in each of the sorrowful blue eyes was a large and luminous tear.

The earl looked at the painting, and then at Considine. There was something close to a smile on his face.

Considine said, 'What *is* blackmail? Money with menaces? Money in return for silence? Money in exchange for nothing? Then I have not been blackmailed. I have paid out two thousand pounds in the last two months for something I would willingly have paid considerably more for on the open market. I have sent four packages of five hundred pounds in bills to Mr Spencer at the Receiving Office in Lombard Street, and in return I have received four pages from an illuminated manuscript that any collector would give his eyeteeth for.' He produced three more sheets of vellum.

One showed the Virgin seated by an empty crib in a stable. At her feet were the beasts of farm and countryside, a charming curly lamb, a little goat with sleek tresses and twisty horns, a baby rabbit with upstanding ears, a fox cub with a vivid brush and mischievous look in his eye, a nest of mice with inquisitive noses and twitching whiskers. On the second sheet, the Madonna stood on a hilltop, looking down over a city of gleaming turrets and profiled bastions and drawbridges portrayed in the most meticulous detail. And on the third, she was one of a crowd, watching her son's Easter entry into Jerusalem, a spectator surrounded by people and palm leaves, unobserved, unregarded as all eyes were directed towards the man on the ass.

They were breathtaking, though none as breathtaking as the first. The Melancholy Virgin in the garden.

His lordship said carefully, 'I imagine that, as a collector, you are fairly well acquainted with manuscripts in the possession of other collectors?'

'Of course.'

'On the Continent, as well as here?' Adam looked at him.

'Of course.'

'Have you ever seen this one before? I take it all four paintings are from the same source?'

'Yes, they are. And no, I have never seen anything from this manuscript before.'

'And you submitted, quite willingly, to what you knew to be blackmail because you hoped that every – what, two weeks? – you would come into the possession of another such treasure?'

Considine, lips compressed, said, 'Yes.'

Sombrely, his lordship remarked, 'I can't say I blame you. You estimate that there are probably fifty paintings in this series? Did you hope to be offered them all?'

'Naturally. A vain hope, perhaps. To think of one man possessing *and parting* with fifty such miniatures is almost beyond belief.'

The earl planted his elbows on the desk. His face drowned in his hands, he said, 'And what do you think will happen now?'

'Even if the blackmailer is the murderer, as I believe he must be, I would expect him to go on tapping my purse until he is caught. If he is caught.'

Adam said, 'But they must be stolen!'

'Of course,' Considine replied coolly. 'Otherwise there would be no need for the man to sell them to me in such a way. Their legitimate owner could have approached me privately if he wished to sell without publicity. He could even have approached someone a good deal wealthier than I, and received more for them.'

The earl rose abruptly to his feet, and strode to the far end of the room and then back, his hands gripped behind him and his face set. 'And if the blackmailer is the murderer, and is caught, what then?'

'Then the theft is likely to come out. I accept that. But if my name is kept out of the affair ... '

The earl swung round to face him. 'Then you will be able to keep the four miniatures you already have, and continue to enjoy them in private?'

'Why not?'

Adam whistled incredulously under his breath.

'Why not?' Considine repeated. 'The thief will have been discovered, thanks to me. And the owner will presumably have all but four of the miniatures restored to him. Four miniatures seems a small enough return in the circumstances.'

The earl sat down again at his desk and regarded Sir Julius with something akin to awe. 'Certainly, it is a question guaranteed to keep several moral philosophers of my acquaintance engaged for the next ten years or so. Perhaps we would be wise to ignore it for the time being. Now, let me be sure I have this right, Sir Julius. You believe that Francis Mervyn,

144

having discovered your identity, promised to remain silent about it if you would buy from him, one by one, a hypothetical number of stolen miniatures – probably fifty at least. By selling them to you in this way, he more or less guarantees that you will not default for at least two years. If he had tried to sell them to you all at once, you might not have been able to raise the money, or you might have paid up, and then by some means exposed him while denying the whole transaction. Is that right?'

'More or less.'

'And you have no idea where Mr Mervyn might have acquired the miniatures?'

'None. I admit that it puzzles me. The theft of paintings of this quality should undoubtedly have created a stir.'

'Yes,' said his lordship noncommittally. 'If,' he went on, 'I told you that I knew Francis Mervyn not to be the blackmailer, what would you say?'

Considine sighed impatiently. 'I would place no more reliance on that statement than on your former assurance that he was not the murderer.'

'You would be making a mistake. There are several people who might have murdered Miss Reece, yourself among them. But there is only one who could have blackmailed you in this way.'

Considine stared at him. 'Do you mean that?'

'Of course.'

'Who?'

The earl smiled, without humour. 'Oh, no, Sir Julius. The blackmailer, for one thing, is not necessarily the murderer, although the motive you suggested might indeed end in murder. If Miss Reece had told the blackmailer to desist, I mean. May I ask you something? What made you decide to bring this to me? You must have left Richmond less than two hours after I did.'

The weary face creased sardonically. 'Your Parthian shot, I suppose, to the effect that my troubles were of my own making, and that I had no *right* to demand help. Followed by a quiet half-hour with my wife in the garden, when I realized how much I needed it. It seemed clear to me that the blackmail must be an important factor, and I decided to tell you about it before I had time to change my mind.'

'You realize that you have placed yourself completely in my hands?'

'I suppose so.'

'And that if I went to Bow Street and told them who the blackmailer was, they would almost certainly cross Francis Mervyn off their list of murder suspects? And that you would then suffer almost as much as the murderer?' He stopped. 'But since you have been open with me, I have to find another way. So now I have two problems instead of one. To clear Francis Mervyn, and to keep you out of it.'

Watching him, Adam recognized that he had simply withdrawn from the conversation. Considine looked at the earl doubtfully, and then at Captain Gregory. 'Should I leave the paintings here?'

Adam said, 'If it would not trouble you too much, perhaps it would be a good idea. Or if you would prefer to leave only one?'

He left the Melancholy Virgin lying on the desk, and pushed the other three sheets back in his folder. He was clumsy with the wrappings, and Adam, who had a sailor's deftness, went to his aid.

Rejecting an offer of refreshment, Considine gathered up his package and made to leave. 'Goodbye for the present, then, Moriston,' he said.

The earl looked up and then rose. 'Yes. Goodbye, Considine. I am obliged to you for coming. I assure you that I will do my best.' Returning to the present, he smiled brilliantly. 'I mean that.'

For the first time, something like an answering smile touched Considine's weary face. It took ten years off his age, and hinted at the kind of careworn charm that Adam supposed must govern his relations with his child-wife. 'Thank you,' he said, and turned away.

Returning from escorting him out, Adam exploded, 'Charles! What in the name of all that's wonderful are you talking about? How can you know the name of the blackmailer – which I assume is not Spencer! – when you didn't even know Considine

146

was being blackmailed until half an hour ago? Or were you just trying to pressure him, or reassure him? A risky game, I should have thought.'

'Calm down, Adam! Who do you know by the name of Spencer?'

'No one.'

'Surely! You have not been out of the country *all* of the last ten years.'

'You mean Earl Spencer?'

'Yes.'

'What the devil does he have to do with it?'

'What do you know about him?'

'Hell and the devil, Charles! Oh, yes ... He's a bibliophile. One of those fanatics who spends as much on a single book – provided it was published before 1500 – as would keep a whole family for twenty years!'

'*Incunabula* is the technical term,' said his lordship kindly. 'And where have you been hearing about rare books and private libraries recently?'

'Iredale? But he's a parson.'

'Damn,' said his lordship to himself, dissatisfied. 'Adam, do you know where Matthew is?'

'Out with John, pursuing suspects.'

'Damn,' said the earl again. 'But they should be nearing the end of the list by now.'

He summoned Brandon, who appeared almost at once. 'Brandon, I am leaving for Atherton in about an hour, and I expect Mr Matthew will want to accompany me. Would you tell Fielding to go in search of him at once, please? He should try – let me see – Mr Smyth's lodging in Brook Street first of all, then Lord Heffort's in Berkeley Square, and then Massey's in Hill Street. If he is at none of those places, one of them may know where he is to be found. And when Fielding returns, I shall want the phaeton. He can harness up the bays.'

'Yes, my lord.'

'Also, please ask Sanderson to pack some shirts and neckcloths for me, and lay out my riding-dress. I expect to reach Atherton tomorrow night, and to be back here on Tuesday. He will know what I need. Oh, and tell him I shall not be taking him with me. Or Fielding.'

Brandon bowed and withdrew.

'You're not taking a groom?' Adam asked.

'There's no necessity. You know I keep horses stabled along the way, so there's no problem about getting changes, and we'll make better speed with only Matthew and myself. Also, I will probably bring Francis back with me, and I should really prefer not to have someone listening to every word we say.'

'My God, no,' Adam said reverently. 'But why take Matthew if you want to travel fast?'

The earl shook his head. 'You disappoint me. I want two people to leave here in the phaeton today, and the same two to return in it on Tuesday.'

The captain looked at him austerely.

His brother-in-law laughed. 'You must have noticed that a new gardener has just appeared in St James's Square – one who is so attentive to his duties that he remains until dusk and reappears at dawn? I suspect he sleeps in the shrubbery. And at the back of the house I see there is a crossing sweeper whose face is unfamiliar. He, too, is unusually conscientious about his hours of work.'

'You mean ... You mean Townsend is having the house watched?'

'That's what it looks like. It would be a natural enough precaution. He is looking for Francis, who might very well turn up here – if he is not already lurking in the wine cellar. Townsend suspects, not without reason, that I might fail to deliver Francis up to him as a good citizen should, and is proceeding accordingly.'

'And I suppose poor Miss Kenwood is having the foot the bill!'

'Hell!' said his lordship. 'I hadn't thought of that! Oh, well, there's nothing I can do at the moment. The point is that I want to discover what, if anything, Francis knows about Iredale. Also, I should like to have him to hand, tucked away in the house somewhere. It's inconvenient not to be able to ask him questions when I need to.'

'Must you go yourself?'

'I can hardly send a servant to bring him back bundled up in Matthew's clothes, and I can't quite trust John to do it.'

'I suppose not. Would you like me to go? It seems a pity for

148

you to waste time dashing about the countryside when you could be more productively employed here.'

'How thoughtful of you. But has it occurred to you what Susan might have to say to that? After all, you've only been home for two days.'

The captain grinned. 'All in a good cause.'

'You think saving me effort would qualify as a good cause in Susan's eyes? Thank you, no.'

'If you put it like that! Is there anything I can do to help otherwise?'

'Not really. You can tell Susan and John what has been happening today, and where I have gone, of course.'

'And if you were to enlighten me about Iredale,' said the captain hopefully, 'I could tell them about that, too.'

'You could, indeed,' said the earl cordially.

'Anyway – why Iredale? Books are books. Manuscripts are art.'

'Nowadays, yes. But when they were written and illuminated, they *were* books, the only kind that existed before printing was invented. It was the text that was important. The pictures were only a bonus. And as a result, illuminated manuscripts are usually classified as books rather than paintings.'

'I follow you. So far.'

'Now, the important factor in this case is that Lord Ballinton's library has never been properly catalogued. Presumably some ancestor picked up a few things that appealed to him, and another added to them, and so on until, by the time there were enough to be worth cataloguing, there were too many to make it an easy job. Recent generations of the family seem to have been scarcely literate, and it was only the Roxburghe sale a couple of years ago that suggested to the present man that he might have an untapped goldmine on his hands. He employed Iredale to find out. And Iredale is doing the job on the basis of a list of titles which he is checking against the books themselves.' He sighed. 'Ballinton, of course, is the world's own fool. Not wanting to have a parson cluttering up the house, he simply instructs his coachman to bring up a few assorted armfuls to Iredale whenever he is coming to town. It's a perfect recipe for fraud.'

149

'But the list of titles must act as some form of insurance!'

'Only superficially. To collectors, it's the edition that's the important thing. One sixteenth-century Bible might fetch a mere ten pounds but the Ximenes Polyglot edition from the same period would attract nearer two hundred. If Iredale could lay hands on a comparatively valueless edition of something, he would have no difficulty in substituting it for a worthwhile one, leaving Ballinton none the wiser. The real snag would be how to dispose of the valuable copy. He might get away with it once or twice, for rare books sometimes do turn up unexpectedly, but he would never dare make a habit of it. Quite apart from anything else, collectors like to know the provenance of what they're buying – who owned it before, and that kind of thing. Another snag, except in extreme cases like that of the Valdarfar Boccaccio – which only made so much because it was up at auction – is that it would be a rare book indeed that produced enough profit to retire on. For real money, Iredale would have to steal at least a hundred middling rare books *and* find substitute editions for them all.'

'So?'

'So illuminated manuscripts are in a different class.' He ran his hands through his hair, and then stretched expansively. 'That's as far as I've got in my thinking, so bear with me. Assume that Iredale discovers that his employer, quite unknowingly, is possessed of a superb medieval psalter.'

Adam interrupted. 'Unknowingly? But weren't they specially bound. Covered in ivory and jewels and that kind of thing?'

The earl looked at him accusingly. 'I thought you didn't know anything about this. But it's a good point.' He meditated, biting his lower lip. 'Exotic bindings also attract collectors. Suppose some long-dead Ballinton sold the binding or even just prised the jewels out of it? Then he might reasonably have had the manuscript rebound in contemporary boards. It would be about the size of one of the topographical folios they were so fond of a hundred years ago, and I imagine might be mistaken from the outside for some traveller's-eye-view of Palmyra or Thebes or some place of the sort. Leave it at that for the moment. *Now*,' he went on trenchantly, 'Iredale has found a psalter that represents thousands of pounds going begging. But it is listed in the title catalogue as something like "medieval manuscript psalter with pictures in colour and gold". *What does he do about it?*'

Adam did not answer.

'He has to find another cheap and probably nasty psalter to substitute for it. But there are very few illuminated manuscripts, even bad ones, wandering around looking for an owner.'

He was looking directly at Adam as he spoke, and his whole face suddenly became relaxed. He took a deep breath, then placed his palms together with a slap and rested his fingertips against his pursed lips. When he spoke, his voice was satirical.

'You can answer that one, can't you?'

Adam looked at him without comprehension.

'Where have you seen illuminated manuscripts recently?' He sounded as if he had known the answer since the beginning of time.

His mouth very slightly open, Adam said, 'My Belgian refugees?'

'Or if not yours, someone else's.' He slammed his hands down on the desk. 'You see, it's perfect!' he exclaimed impatiently. 'Even the timing is right! I should be prepared to wager that Imogen told her sister who Considine was a year – or more – ago. And Olivia told her husband. But nothing happened. And then a steady stream of refugees began to arrive in London, burdened with family treasures which they were forced to sell. In May, most of them. And in June the blackmail started.' He stopped. 'Am I being too clever?'

'No,' Adam said slowly. 'I don't think so. My Belgians, from what I saw of their treasures, can't have got much for them. A few hundreds, maybe.' He glanced at the Melancholy Virgin, gleaming peacefully on the desk. 'The ones I was shown were nothing to compare with that.'

'In other words, Iredale's problems were solved. For a couple of hundred pounds, perhaps ... ' He paused, a speculative glint in his eye. 'Which he may even have borrowed from Imogen – I wouldn't put it past him – he could become the legitimate possessor of a poor or mediocre medieval psalter. Which he then substituted for the masterpiece in Ballinton's library. Which, in turn, he sold to a willing customer who did not dare to ask questions. It's really very clever,' he said appreciatively. 'No way of proving the theft, and nothing that the legal mind could legitimately define as blackmail.'

They both thought about it for a few moments.

'No,' Adam said at last. 'There's too much coincidence.'

'I don't agree. Given the original substitution idea, the only real coincidence was that a choice of suitable substitutes became available. And with the disturbed state of Europe in the last few years, even *that* wasn't as much of a coincidence as it looks. It might just as well have been silver, glass, or paintings. Considine would have been forced to buy whatever was offered. The fact that he was offered something he badly wanted to buy was merely an additional incentive to pay up. What looks like coincidence in fact represents the ingenuity of a rather fine criminal mind.'

'And that's another thing!' Adam said. 'A parson?'

'Why should you think parsons are exempt from human weakness? I should be very much surprised to hear that even half the clergymen in this country went into the Church from choice. Damn it, Adam, what else can an educated younger son – or an impoverished elder one, come to that – do in the present state of our society? We've scarcely progressed beyond the Middle Ages. I read the other day that, in thirteenth-century England, one adult male *in every twelve* was a cleric. Can you believe that every twelfth man had a true vocation? I can't. And things have not changed very much. No, Iredale himself told me that he was forced into it, and I can't imagine that the trials of an underpaid parson's life have helped to foster a sanctity that he never possessed, even to begin with.'

There was another silence. Then Adam volunteered hesitantly, 'I don't see how you can prove the blackmail, or even the theft.'

'Nor do I.'

'Unless you could find the refugee who sold him the manuscript – the one that now, presumably, reposes in Ballinton's library in place of the original.'

'We may be reduced to that.' His lordship revived. 'Now, *there's* something you can do while I am away. Produce me a list of your own passengers, and see if you can find out from

152

the Admiralty who else arrived on others of the King's ships.'

'Not to mention on hired transports and casual fishing vessels. Thank you very much. You're sure you wouldn't rather *I* went to Atherton?'

His lordship grinned, and became serious again. 'You're right, of course. How do we prove it? Theft, blackmail, and possibly murder. *Probably* murder, in fact. It all hangs together too neatly, and I cannot see two out-and-out villains of such calibre operating within the restricted circle of Imogen Reece's acquaintance. There must be evidence somewhere. But where do we find it? If only we could think of some way to flush him out.'

'You couldn't break him down? See him, I mean, and tell him you know all. In that calm, sword-of-justice manner of yours?'

The earl regarded him without enthusiasm. 'You mean, "Flee! All is revealed. The truth about your breeches buttons is known!" Either he would deny everything and summon up the Bedlam wagon to take me away, or else he would confess everything including Considine's involvement in the affair.' He shrugged. 'Oh, well. Let us hope that Francis may have something useful to contribute.'

The door opened to admit Matthew, anxious as ever, and John, who was not in the sweetest of tempers. 'What's all this?' he demanded indignantly. 'Why are you dragging Matthew off to Atherton? Do you mean me to continue this wild goose chase all on my own? Because if so, I tell you I won't do it!'

He glared at his brother, who said with one of his most disarming smiles, 'But John! It is for Francis!'

John was not appeased. 'That's all very well, but I don't believe we are being of any use at all. No one is at home. All we are doing is trotting from one house to another and back again. It's all fudge, I tell you!'

Matthew was murmuring hopefully in the background, and the earl smiled at him and said, encouragingly, 'Yes, Matthew?'

'I just wondered ... How long are we ... ? Should I pack everything? Will I ... ? Had I better go now and ... ?'

'The sooner you are ready, the better. I anticipate that you will remain at Atherton, so you had better pack accordingly. We will spend tonight at the Fox and Garter, I should think. Does that answer your questions?'

Matthew hesitated. 'Bustle about, Matt,' his lordship said kindly, and as his cousin turned dutifully to go, added, 'and by the way, if you have a caped coat and some kind of large, slouch hat, I'd be obliged if you'd wear them.'

'But ... ' began Matthew, and then catching his employer's eye vanished hurriedly in the direction of the house stairs.

The earl turned to his brother again. 'I may bring Francis back with me,' he said, 'and I shall want to smuggle him in. I leave the arrangements with you. Assume that we will arrive Tuesday mid-afternoon.'

Adam made as if to speak.

'Yes,' the earl said. 'I know it is hardly a secretive time. But there should be enough general activity to provide more cover than when it is quiet in the evening. Darkness, in itself, is suspicious. Broad daylight is not. We'll use the stable entrance.'

John was looking extremely confused. His brother said, 'Adam will tell you about it. Also, I want you to talk to Brandon. When Francis is back in this house, I do not want the servants disclosing the fact to all and sundry. Despite our precautions, I imagine Brandon has a shrewd idea that there is something havey-cavey going on, so I leave it to you to think up some satisfactory explanation.' He paused, and then added severely, 'There must be *some* respectable reason for my secretary to go to ground in my own house!'

John's mouth was still slightly ajar. Adam said, 'Don't think I wish to criticize, but wouldn't Susan be a better person to deal with that particular problem?' John's mouth closed with a snap.

The earl said, 'That's true. You can discuss the matter between you.' John opened his mouth again. 'No, don't interrupt,' said his lordship infuriatingly. 'You can ease up on your round of visits for the time being, though if you should happen to see any of the people on the list you should, of course, talk to them. And one other thing ... '

Giving up, John plumped himself down in a chair and leaned

his elbow on the desk. 'Yes?' he said, with an unconvincing air of absorption.

'You may go and call on Miss Kenwood and make my apologies to her. I promised to visit her on Monday to report progress.' John began to look much happier. 'And you may pass on to her all that Adam will tell you this evening, and ask her if she could try to remember anything Imogen ever said about her sister's husband, Rowland Iredale.'

'Iredale?'

'Yes.'

'But you can't suspect him. He's a parson!'

The earl looked at his brother-in-law obliquely.

Adam said, 'Goodbye, Charles. I'll attend to it. Have a good trip.'

'Yes,' said his lordship faintly. 'Two hundred miles in three days begins to look like a rest cure, doesn't it?'

Chapter 13

Next afternoon, looking tidier than Lady Susan had seen him for some time, the Honourable John Dornay took himself off to visit Miss Kenwood.

Happening to glance out of a window just as he bowled up to the front door, Miss Kenwood was very much amused to see him cast a furtive look at a house on the other side of the square before he tossed the reins to his groom, and then descended hastily from the curricle and ran up the steps to ply the knocker.

When he entered the drawing room, he said formally, 'I wondered whether you would care to take a turn in the Park, Miss Kenwood?' and then spoiled the effect by adding, 'though I have rather a lot to say, and it might be more private here.'

'Then let us by all means remain here.'

'Oh, good!' He went to the window and signalled. Almost at once, the curricle rolled past the window and then out of sight.

'My sister lives over there,' John explained, 'and I don't care to keep the carriage hanging around where she can see it! Otherwise, I am likely to be waylaid and called to account for all my shortcomings over the past year.'

She laughed. 'Your brother said much the same yesterday. Does Lady Verona know how anxiously you avoid her?'

'Doesn't she, by Jove!' He grinned. 'I have always thought she proses on at us the way she does for the very sufficient reason that she has no more desire to see us than we have to see her. To give you some idea, *even Charles* isn't intellectual enough for her! So you can imagine the opinion she holds of the rest of us.'

Miss Kenwood was suitably shocked.

Just as John was about to sit down, he recalled the courtesies and leapt to his feet again. 'I do hope I haven't interrupted you in something important?'

She waved him to his chair. 'Nothing that I am not happy to leave. I was studying the first act of a new music-play we are putting on this coming Tuesday.'

'Is it good? Should I come and see it?'

'I can't really tell, yet. It's not easy to judge from only the first act.'

'You mean you haven't seen the rest? It sounds like that Sheridan episode you were telling us about. Can you memorize it all by Tuesday? When will you rehearse?'

'Goodness, we don't rehearse! We have no time for that kind of nonsense. And at least I am more fortunate than Mrs Siddons. I know what the music is to be, even if I don't have the words to go with it.'

John sighed. 'It must be fascinating. I had no idea the theatre was so exciting.'

Miss Kenwood's curiosity was beginning to overcome her, and she had the feeling that, left to himself, he would never come to the purpose of his visit. 'Only sometimes, Mr Dornay,' she said dampingly. 'You mentioned that you had ... '

'Please!' he begged. 'Don't call me Mr Dornay. My name is John.'

He reminded her irresistibly of her brother. She smiled. 'Very well. You said you had a lot to tell me. What conclusions did Lord Moriston reach after his interview with Sir Julius Considine yesterday? He said he was going home to think about it.'

'Yes! But you don't know that Considine was hard on your heels all the way from Richmond. What happened was this.'

'Well!' Kate exclaimed half an hour later. 'What an extraordinary story! Do you need tea, John? I know I do.' She rang the bell.

He said, 'Charles is quite sure that Iredale is the villain. Well, it stands to reason! But he sees no way of proving it at the moment. The man has been much too clever. Unless we can find the refugee who owned the substituted manuscript, Iredale is perfectly safe.'

'It's appallingly ingenious,' she said.

'Did you ever meet Iredale?'

'Once. But I am not very much attracted by that kind of ageing Apollo.' She giggled. 'Olivia kept a very stern eye on me all the while. It was really quite funny.'

'Did she keep an eye on Imogen, too?'

'How astute of you,' she said, arrested. 'I had never thought about it before, but she did.'

The door opened and the butler appeared with the tea tray. When he had gone again and Kate had begun dispensing tea, she said, 'Olivia, from what little I know of her, is a very difficult person, but she adored Imogen. I think she may well have been torn in two directions. She desperately wanted Imogen to marry and become respectable, and yet recognized that she was probably better off on all counts – emotionally and financially – living in sin. Better off than Olivia herself, perhaps.' She broke off. 'No, I *cannot* believe in Iredale as the villain! He seemed such a weak vessel.'

Remnants of his brother's table talk sprang to John's mind. 'But a weak man with his back against the wall can be more dangerous than a strong one. The strong man knows he can probably save himself to fight another day, but the weak one suspects he can't.'

She thought she could recognize the turn of phrase, but considerately refrained from saying so. She put her cup down with a tinkle. 'What a coil!' she exclaimed. 'What happens next?'

'Well, Charles has gone haring off to Atherton to see Francis, in case he can shed some light on Imogen's relations with Iredale. If we can't prove the man is a thief and a blackmailer, we're back to the original problem of having to prove he is a murderer. Charles keeps saying that to be one isn't necessarily to be the other, but I don't think he believes it any more than I do. Essentially, of course, it doesn't matter which crime we nail him for, since the penalty is the same in all cases.'

He had lost her attention. She said, 'He *has* covered his tracks well, hasn't he! Even if one went to him and said, "We know everything", he could safely laugh in everyone's face. Proof. Proof, proof. What constitutes proof?' She looked at

John. 'If the rest of the psalter were discovered in his possession? Would that do it?'

'He could claim to have bought it. And unless we could produce the man who sold him the other one, that would be the end of it.'

'What about the money, then? Where would an impecunious parson find two thousand pounds in a matter of a few weeks?'

'That's more promising!' Then he shook his head. 'But we'd have to find the money first, and then he could simply claim to have sold something. And if pushed, he would say who he'd sold it *to* – which would drag Considine's name into it.'

The huge dark eyes gazed through him. 'Even so, the money still seems the best approach. Could Sir Julius not make some little private mark on the next lot of bills, so that they could be identified? Assuming Iredale does not give the whole scheme up.'

'I don't know Charles's view, but Adam doesn't think he will give up, only that there may be a break of a few weeks before he resumes his demands.'

'That sounds probable.'

'And besides, marking the bills would still involve Considine.'

'Oh, bother! So it would.'

They both sat immersed in thought. After a while, Kate said, 'More tea?' and poured some out. The silence continued.

Suddenly, Kate exclaimed, 'Of course! It's so obvious. Why didn't I think of it before? We must blackmail the blackmailer.'

'What?' John said.

Kate sat forward. 'Suppose we threatened to reveal all, unless *he* paid up. What would he do? He might decide it was safer to pay, and if he did we'd have our proof. If he submits to blackmail, it virtually proves the truth of what he is being blackmailed about!'

John said doubtfully, 'I'm not so sure. Besides, it would never work. He'd spot it right off. He must know Charles already has far more money than he knows what to do with. I suppose we might just manage to persuade him that Charles is a fanatical manuscript collector, and wants the rest of the miniatures ... ' His voice trailed off, unconvinced.

'But it wouldn't be Charles who was asking,' said Miss Kenwood triumphantly. 'It would be me!'

'What?' John said again.

'Just think. I am an actress, so Iredale is bound to assume that I am short of money – not to mention immoral! I was a friend of Imogen's, so he might easily expect that she had mentioned the matter to me. He *doesn't* know that it was I who called in Townsend, and he *doesn't* know that I am acquainted with Char ... I mean Lord Moriston. I don't believe he would find it strange at all if I sent a message saying,' she surveyed the ceiling for inspiration, 'oh, something like this: Imogen and I were friends and told each other everything. She told me all about "Spencer", and where you were getting so much money, and how she disapproved. She thought the best way to stop you was by threatening to tell her sister. And now, of course, after what happened to her, I wonder if that might have had anything to do with it. As her friend, I feel as she did. You should not be allowed ... '

'To keep the money,' John joined in. 'It's absolutely right! It would be bound to hook him.'

'Don't interrupt,' she said, sounding exactly like Susan. 'So I think you should hand it over to me, and I will give it to a deserving charity.' She brooded. 'Which charity? Indigent Actors? Or Fallen Women?'

'You don't have to say.'

'No, I suppose not.' Her gaze returned to John's face. 'I can't see a flaw, can you?'

Nervously, John made a snatch at sanity. 'No, I can't,' he said, 'but I don't think Charles would like it, you know. And after all, he's in charge.'

It was a disastrous remark. 'He's not having any great success, is he?' said Miss Kenwood rather unfairly. 'Besides,' and her slender brows rose, 'it was *I* who started the whole thing. Why shouldn't *I* finish it?'

It was not a very good argument, but John, dazzled both by Kate herself and the prospect of teaching his brother that there were other members of the family who were perfectly capable of managing things on their own initiative, began to be tempted. With increasing assurance, he said, 'I think it *would* work. But Charles is going to be absolutely furious.'

'Pooh!' said Miss Kenwood, slightly above herself. 'He can scarcely complain if he comes home to find the case settled and Francis Mervyn cleared of suspicion. Now can he? Besides, I suspect he may need to be taught that women and,' she added percipiently, 'younger brothers, are not as poor creatures as he thinks them!'

John exhaled silently, and then gulped. 'You don't think we should wait until he gets back before we try it?'

'Certainly not. That would spoil all the fun!'

He looked at her and convinced himself that she was going to do it anyway, regardless of anything he might say.

'Come along, John. You admit that it could work. And no one else seems to have any ideas.'

'I suppose if you posted the letter tomorrow, we might have some response on Tuesday,' he said carefully.

'By which time your brother will be home? Don't be such a coward, John. No, I will send a note round by hand, today.'

With unexpected sharpness, he said, 'You won't! He might arrive on your doorstep this very evening, and where should we be then? You mustn't see him alone – he might be dangerous.'

She laughed at him. 'What? With a houseful of servants?'

'And what help would they be if he slipped quietly in by a window? Don't you have a companion living with you?'

It was a sore point with Kate, the convention decreeing that a young woman should not live alone, but must share her days with a genteel companion. She considered that anyone truly respectable had no need of constant chaperonage, and that anyone unrespectable was not going to be held to the paths of righteousness by the mild remonstrances of some elderly dependant. 'I had,' she said, 'but she spent more time being a companion to the cat than to me. To chaperone an actress is almost impossible, and it all became very tiresome. So I decided to dispense with her services. Do you really think he might be dangerous? Then I'll make sure all the windows are bolted.'

'No, I'll tell you what. You send a note round first thing tomorrow morning, and I'll arrange to be here at nine o'clock.

161

Then I can be a witness, and at the same time make sure he doesn't try any tricks.'

It made sense, whichever way she looked at it.

John left St James's Square promptly next morning, precipitating a crisis in the kitchen by demanding breakfast at the unheard-of hour of eight o'clock, and another in the stables by ordering the curricle for 8.45. He had taken the greatest care not to let slip any hint of the plan to Lady Susan or Captain Gregory, suspecting – rightly, as it turned out – that they would unequivocally disapprove.

He arrived to find Miss Kenwood peaceably consuming coffee, toast, and peach conserve. Her footman, she said, had been despatched ten minutes earlier with the fateful note, and would John care for some breakfast? Perfectly willing to top off his recent collation, he sat down and joined her. They crunched companionably for a few moments, until John began to laugh and promptly choked on a crumb.

Miss Kenwood watched him quizzically as he strove to recover himself. 'My apologies,' he gasped at last. 'But I was just sitting here thinking how enjoyable it was to be sharing breakfast with a famous actress ... '

She interrupted him. 'You flatter me!'

' ... when I remembered Ben Haydon – the artist, you know? – telling me about an occasion when he went to a society tea, where Mrs Siddons was giving some readings.'

'One of her most profitable sidelines.'

'Is it? Well, Haydon said that after her first reading all the men retired to the refreshment table, but while they were eating toast and tinkling cups and saucers, she began again. It was like the effect of a Mass bell at Madrid. All noise ceased, and they slunk back to their seats like boors, two or three of the most distinguished artists of the day, with the toast still in their mouths, afraid to bite. Haydon could scarcely take his eyes off Tom Lawrence, who kept trying to bite by degrees, and then stopped for fear of making too much crackle, his eyes full of tears from the strain. And all the time Mrs Siddons intoning "eye of newt and toe of frog"! And Lawrence taking a sly bite and looking awed and pretending to be listening!'

162

She laughed. 'Poor Sir Thomas, always a martyr to the Siddons family!'

'Is he?'

'Didn't you know? It was a long time ago now, but there was a spell when he was in love with Sarah, and her daughter Sally, and her daughter Maria, all at the same time. He asked permission to marry Sally, and then discovered he preferred Maria. But then Maria died, and I have no doubt that if, on her deathbed, she had not extracted Sally's promise never to marry Lawrence, he would have transferred his affections back again. As it was, Sally died, too, poor girl, very soon after. Both the daughters were delicate, unlike their mama.'

'Do you know her? She must be a very tough lady.'

The morning passed pleasantly enough, despite the undercurrent of tension. Kate had instructed her footman to wait for a reply, but an hour went by, and then another, and still he did not return. When breakfast had been cleared, Kate said she must practise her music for the following night's opening, and John offered to play for her. He proved but a poor accompanist, however, for he was used to a piano with the sonorous English action, which required a heavy touch, whereas Kate's was the light and delicate Viennese type – and frightened the life out of him, he complained, by pretty near playing itself before his fingers even touched the keys. He was further distracted by his sheer pleasure in listening to Kate's soaring voice, which he had not heard before. He had not realized she was so good.

By now, she had not only the music but the words to go with it. All she lacked, she said acidly, was the dialogue that fitted in between the songs. The work was a kind of ballad opera version of *Figaro*, called *Follies in a Maze*, with music 'after' Mozart. The dialogue, by the late Mr Holcroft, was currently being worked over by a nameless hack who was as slow as he was pedantic. 'You understand,' she explained, 'that Elliston is playing Count Almaviva, Mrs Faucit the Countess, and our Byronic-looking friend, Frederick Vining, Figaro. None of them can sing. Elliston did try, but for once heeded the opinion of his fellow players. So some of their principal songs have had to be allocated to other characters, with very odd results. As if everyone had a *doppelgänger*. And to add to it, a gardener has been inserted into the plot who will roar out a few folk songs

163

to keep the pit happy, while the *cognoscenti,* having rattled their canes and snuffboxes at every favourite air and insisted on a repetition of it, will walk out the minute the singers draw breath to oblige.'

'Whose *doppelgänger* are you?' John enquired interestedly.

'I?' she sang on an ascending note of the utmost purity, and then returned to plain speech. 'I am Susanna, and my own *doppelgänger.*'

There was a tap on the door and the footman entered. 'I'm sorry I've been so long, madam, but the gentleman seemed in no hurry to give me an answer.'

'Thank you, James.' She accepted the note, dismissed him, and turned to John with a mischievous look in her great, dark eyes. 'A wager?' she said.

'No, no! Open it.' He could scarcely contain his impatience.

Her eyes glanced over the lines. Tilting her head thoughtfully, she read it again, and then looked up. John appeared to be in imminent danger of expiring, and she took pity on him. 'He says he will call on me at three o'clock this afternoon.'

'Phew! That ought to be interesting.'

They wrangled from midday until close on three over whether John should be physically present at the interview, or remain an invisible eavesdropper in the anteroom. He was determined to stay within range, while she argued that his presence might tie Iredale's tongue. They reached a compromise that satisfied neither. John would remain, but as much in the background as possible.

Iredale was late. It was almost twenty minutes after the appointed hour before Kate's butler announced him. He came in looking so much like a respectable clergyman that John was assailed by doubts all over again.

'Mr Iredale,' Kate said, with a flirtatious smile that caused John's eyes to open before he remembered that she was, after all, an actress. It had not occurred to him that he was about to witness a performance.

The visitor's hands were clasped loosely in front of his stomach and his shoulders slightly hunched, for all the world as if he were modelling for a caricaturist's portrait of an obsequious parson. His answering smile was less a widening of the mouth than a lift of the upper lip. The mane of pale hair suggested vanity, but there was nothing else positive about him. Suddenly, he caught sight of John, and his lip descended again. 'I – uh – expected this to be a private talk,' he said.

'I imagine you did,' Kate replied, and pouted becomingly. 'But I thought I should be careful, so I asked my gentleman friend here to be present.' John cringed inside, and hoped she was not going to overdo it. 'Have you brought the money?'

Iredale's eyes were flickering behind the steel-rimmed spectacles. 'I'm afraid there has been some mistake. I think you ... '

'Pray do sit down,' she said, gesturing towards a chair that was carefully positioned so that he would be facing her, but half turned away from John. He did not like it, but without resorting to downright rudeness could do very little about it. Compromising, he perched sideways on the edge.

'Thank you,' he said automatically. 'Yes, I think you must have misunderstood something Miss Reece said to you.'

'Oh, no!' Her tone was final.

He floundered. 'But she ... That *must* have been it. I cannot believe – I cannot think of any reason why my wife's own sister should invent stories about me. I have never been anything but kindly disposed towards her.'

It was very well done. The light eyes glinted worriedly behind the spectacles, and he unclasped his hands and spread them openly – innocently – before him. When he had finished speaking, he shook his head a few times, so that the beautifully tended hair shone in the afternoon sun. He did not chew his lip.

Kate looked at him doubtfully. 'I can't have misunderstood.'

'What did she actually say?'

'We-e-ell,' Kate pondered, her brow prettily furrowed. 'She said you were holding her Mr C. up to ransom, getting money from him in exchange for keeping quiet ... ' Her voice tailed off artistically. John almost began to feel sorry for the man.

He fell plump into the trap. His eyes widened in enlightenment, and his rather slack smile appeared. 'Oh, I see!' he announced, in the tones that no doubt went down well in the pulpit. '*Now* I understand your confusion! Ah, yes.'

Get on with it, man! John thought irritably. Kate wore her melancholy look.

'Merely a private arrangement,' Iredale explained with a touch of deprecation. 'I was afflicted by a temporary embarrassment, and – uh – Mr C. kindly offered to help me out. A loan. And the confusion in your – Imogen's – mind must have arisen because I hoped to keep the transaction secret,' he looked at Kate appealingly, 'from my wife. Mrs Iredale is so highly strung, and so proud, that I could not bring myself to let her discover that I had been reduced to begging. Do you understand? *Can* you understand?'

Kate was beginning to enjoy herself, and only regretted that Robert's *violin obbligato* was not available to underline the pathos. 'Oh, yes!' she exclaimed, and John was dumbfounded to see that her magnificent eyes were sparkling with tears. 'I do, I really *do* understand. And not only begging, but theft. And murder.' The tears brimmed over.

John estimated that it was well over thirty seconds before Iredale absorbed what she had said. Then he asked stupidly, 'What did you say?'

She patted her cheeks delicately with a lacy handkerchief. 'I feel for you. I might almost have been convinced, I think, if it had not been for the Melancholy Virgin.'

'The Melancholy Virgin?' he repeated blankly.

'Of course, you didn't know her long enough even to learn her name. The illuminated manuscript, Mr Iredale, which you stole from your employer and have been selling, page by page, to – Mr C. For so much money that you were prepared to kill Imogen rather than give up your scheme.'

Iredale looked at her as if he had been magnetized. 'I don't know what you are talking about. You are mad. You must be!'

She smiled sweetly. 'Not at all. The only reason I have not told all this to Bow Street is that I believe Imogen would have preferred me not to. She had a very well-developed sense of justice, you know. I think it would have given her much more satisfaction to know that I had taken the money away from you. As I intend to. And I also think she might have wanted me to tell her sister. But,' she paused carefully, 'I have a very well-developed sense of priorities, as well as of justice. One has to, if one is an actress. It's rather like being a parson, Mr Iredale. One is inadequately paid.' The lovely eyes glowed at him. 'So I will have the money first. And afterwards I will decide whether to tell your wife. She might persuade you to return what you have stolen from Lord Ballinton's library.' She paused. 'Did you bring the money with you?'

'No! Really, Miss Kenwood ...'

She turned sharply to John. He thought, *The Taming of the Shrew*! He was catching on fast. 'What do *you* think, sir?' she asked imperatively.

He shrugged as coolly as he could. 'I think you have been wasting your time. I think you should send for the Runners. Preferably Townsend,' he said, and added cunningly, 'who, I am told, has been in charge of the investigation into Miss Reece's murder.'

'No,' said Iredale, who was by now chewing his lip in earnest. 'I'll bring you the money. I couldn't get it today at such short notice. Wednesday. I'll bring it to you on Wednesday!'

'All of it,' Miss Kenwood said coolly. 'Two thousand pounds.'

He responded on a wave of panic. 'I don't have it. Not all of it. I had to spend some.'

'Then I want what remains.' She could not resist it. 'And, of course, some evidence, on paper, of where the rest has gone.'

Clearly, he would have liked to call her a harpy or, more canonically, a Jezebel. But he stopped himself, although they could see what a struggle it was for him to say beseechingly, 'But since I am going to give you the money, you won't tell my wife, will you? I know Miss Reece would not have wanted it!'

Miss Kenwood succeeded in looking like a Jezebel temporarily wrapped in thought and said, lips pursed, 'I can't promise.'

'Not before Thursday, anyway. I'll bring you the money tomorrow or Wednesday, I don't know what time. We can talk again. Not before Thursday, please.'

'Oh, very well,' Kate said generously. 'We'll see. *After* you have given me the money.'

She rang for the butler, and they watched Iredale walk away across the square. Kate turned to John. 'Poof!' she said. 'What an experience! I am going to have some tea, but I imagine you could do with some brandy?' He nodded weakly.

She sighed. 'I suppose that ends the day's entertainment. Thank goodness I don't have to go to the theatre this evening. I feel quite worn down. When did you order your curricle?' It sounded, perhaps, a little inhospitable.

'Midnight.'

She sat up abruptly. 'Good gracious!'

John had not lived with his brother for nothing. 'You don't think that's the end of the story, do you? He could be back here with a blunt instrument in his hand within five minutes.'

'Oh,' she said blankly. 'You don't think he'll wait until tomorrow to decide what to do?'

'I don't know,' he replied grimly. 'But I don't propose to leave here without seeing all the servants to bed and every single door and window infallibly bolted and barred for the night.'

Chapter 14

John let himself into the house very quietly, intending to go straight to bed. It had been a fatiguing day. But the doors from the staircase hall into the dining room were wide open, and so were those from the dining room to the library, which was fully illuminated. As he hesitated, Adam's figure appeared in the library doorway.

Obedient to his beckoning, John strolled through. 'Did you have a pleasant time?' he asked.

'Very.' Adam and Lady Susan had been to an evening party. It was when the captain had told Fielding to collect them from it at about eleven-thirty p.m. that Fielding had said, 'Pardon me, sir, but I have to go back and pick up Mr John from Cavendish Square at midnight, and I'm not sure I can do both. It's difficult,' he had added apologetically, 'with Anderson still being away and young Jamie not quite up to London traffic yet.'

Adam, not altogether displeased at having an excuse to leave the party early, had merely said, 'Well, make it eleven o'clock, then'. But he was uneasy.

When he mentioned it to Susan, she exclaimed, 'He can't have been there all day, can he?'

'Might he have been visiting Verona?'

'Never!' She looked up into his kindly, concerned brown eyes, and said, 'Could you talk to him, do you think? It would come better from you than from me.'

Handing John a glass of brandy, Adam said, 'You will be pleased to know that, not just one, but two of the young men on your interview list were there, and I talked to both of them. You may therefore cross off Darius Thornton and young Ponsonby.'

169

John's 'How splendid!' did not carry a great deal of conviction.

'Lost interest?' Adam asked politely.

'No! Not at all. Thank you very much.'

'How was Miss Kenwood?'

The tone was innocent enough, but John coloured to the roots of his hair. 'Very well. Preparing for the new ballad opera that goes on tomorrow night.'

'Were you in the audience tonight? I deduced from Fielding's timetable that you must have escorted her home.'

'No, she was not appearing tonight.'

Adam sighed, and went to replace his glass on the tray. His back still turned, he said, 'John, I don't wish to interfere, but I would recommend you not to spend too much time dancing attendance on Miss Kenwood.'

John flared up. 'Why? Because she's on the stage? I'll wager she's every bit as respectable as anyone else you can think of – and a deal more respectable than some!'

Exasperated, Adam said, 'I'm sure she is, you young idiot! But that's scarcely the point. She is also a very attractive young woman, and your brother is head over heels in love with her!'

John was momentarily deprived of speech. Then he said, 'Charles?'

'It's hardly surprising, is it?'

'How do you know? Has he said something?'

'Far from it. He's trying desperately not to give any sign of it – until he knows her feelings, I presume. In fact, I wouldn't have mentioned it if I hadn't thought there was a danger you might fall in love with her, too.'

John shook his head gloomily. 'She can't be much more than a year older than I am, but she makes me feel as if I were still in kindergarten. I think she's marvellous, but ... ' He was wholly intrigued. 'Is Charles truly in love with her, do you think?'

'Yes.'

He thought over their conversations of the last two days. 'I don't think she feels the same way about him, you know. In fact, I'd say she considered him high handed and autocratic, and in need of taking down a peg or two. That's partly why ...

Oh, Gemini!' For the first time, he realized the scale of the trouble he was going to find himself in when Charles got back. He had known his brother would be angry at having the case taken out of his hands. And angrier because it involved letting Miss Kenwood run into danger – even if it was a danger in which neither Miss Kenwood nor John himself altogether believed. But if he were head over heels in love with Miss Kenwood!

'Gemini!' he said again.

Adam looked at his white face and said, 'John, what have you done? Sit down and tell me about it.' He pushed him gently into a chair, took the empty glass from him, and went to refill it.

John said unhappily, 'I'm going to need an ally, Adam. Miss Kenwood and I thought we might force a solution, and we've started to blackmail the blackmailer.'

'*What?*'

'She wrote to Iredale and said she wanted to talk to him, and when he came she told him that Imogen had told her everything, and that unless he handed the money over to her, she would tell Bow Street. She thought that if he submitted to blackmail it would be proof of his guilt.'

He had never seen Adam angry before. For a moment, the captain could not trust himself to speak. Then, his teeth gritted, he said, 'Have you taken leave of your senses? Of all the imbecile games to embark on! This man is almost certainly a murderer, with nothing to lose, and perhaps everything to gain by killing again. If he really believes that Miss Kenwood heard from Imogen Reece what was going on, then she is a direct witness against him, and the only threat to his security. I warn you. If anything happens to that girl ... '

'Well, I've ... '

'And, my God! If Charles chooses to tear you limb from limb when he gets home, I'll help him – not hinder him!'

'Yes, but ... '

'Is she protected in that house? Did you have enough sense to see that everything was bolted and barred before you left? When are the servants about in the morning? When does Miss Kenwood get up?'

John gulped, and said with unsteady indignation, 'Dammit, Adam, I'm not *that* much of a fool. I stayed with her all day and, yes, I did make sure everything was bolted and barred. I don't know what time the servants get up, or Miss Kenwood. Why should I?'

'Because when the servants are about, doors and windows are usually open. And since the day's work begins in the basement, a determined man might very well succeed in reaching Miss Kenwood's room unobserved while she is still asleep. You know the house. Is that possible?'

'Oh, God!' John said. 'Yes.'

'There's no help for it, then, is there? We should manage about three hours' sleep. If it were not that I doubt whether Iredale would risk slipping out of his own house in the middle of the night, I'd say we ought to go straight back to Cavendish Square now. But we certainly dare not leave it later than five o'clock. You can take the back of the house, and I'll take the front, and we'll stand watch until Miss Kenwood is up and about. Then we can go indoors and see what can be arranged for the rest of the day.'

He looked at John's horrified countenance and relented slightly. 'Cheer up, you young cloth-head. We'll do what we can.'

At about three o'clock next afternoon, the rather lanky young man who had been strolling up and down Jermyn Street, waiting, it might have been thought, for an illicit assignation with a young lady, crossed the top of Duke Street for the dozenth time in an hour and, glancing down it, observed a tall, well set up, slightly older gentleman strolling with equal lack of purpose along King Street at the foot. The crossing sweeper, trying to catch a glimpse of either gentleman's face, had several times been distracted by the demands of his profession just as he had thought himself about to succeed. It was precisely his luck, he thought balefully, employing his broom in the wake of yet another carriage and pair, to find himself pursuing his unsavoury task in a street full of stables.

Just then, the lanky young man let out a shout of 'Hello, there!' and waved furiously to the gentleman down in King Street. The gentleman stopped, and the younger one came running down towards him, crying, 'I wasn't sure it was you, Adam! How are you?' The gentleman whose name appeared

172

to be Adam glanced over his shoulder in a way that made the sweeper very suspicious indeed, and caused him to start drifting hurriedly towards King Street. He was nearly there when two ladies in very fashionable bonnets turned the corner.

One of them beckoned him imperiously. 'Here, my man! We wish to cross!' The street was perfectly clean, and the sweeper might have been tempted to reply in a democratic way, 'What's stopping you?' if he had not learned during the course of his week's masquerade that ladies of the Quality always expected you to wield your broom for them, regardless. Not that he minded, since a tip was always forthcoming. But, his attention already divided between trying to keep an eye on the two gentlemen and the task of pushing his broom across the road, he was further diverted when the lady who had summoned him turned her ankle and almost fell, clutching at his arm to save herself and then complaining that it was his fault for not having swept properly. If she had not been such a beauty, he would have been tempted to answer more sharply than a crossing sweeper had any right to. As it was, he was opening his mouth to placate her when he realized that he had almost missed something – the sound of a carriage entering Duke Street from the top. He turned abruptly, but he was too late. The driver had already backed the coach into one of the stables further up, and all that was visible were two horses, which the sweeper bitterly recognized as the handsome bays the Earl of Moriston had driven out with on Saturday afternoon. A groom emerged from the stable door and ran to the horses' heads, patting and gentling them before he embarked on the task of unharnessing them.

When the sweeper turned back, fuming inside, both the gentlemen who had attracted his interest had disappeared. He could not even tell whether they had gone in the direction of St James's Square or of St James's Street. Frustration in his eye, he looked at the ladies who had appeared at such an inconvenient moment. Sourly, he accepted a coin from the second one, whom he recognized, now that her face was turned towards him instead of being hidden by the extremely large poke of her bonnet, as his lordship's sister.

Rolled up, he thought, horse, foot and guns! There might be

173

nothing to it, but he'd mention it to Mr Townsend just the same.

The four red herrings, as Kate had christened them, entered the library a few minutes after his lordship and Mr Mervyn, to find the two men consulting a small, stout volume of the Clerical Directory. Francis, Lady Susan noticed at once, looked as if the hounds of Hell had been after him. The saturnine, high-boned face, with its dark brows and slanting eyes, its calm competence, its controlled reserve, had become indefinably haggard.

The earl's first interview with Francis at Atherton had been uneasy. His lordship, hoping to preserve the normal tenor of their relationship, had been businesslike, impersonal, faintly bracing. But Francis had spent ten days convincing himself that he had been responsible, however indirectly, for the murder of a young woman whom he had almost, but not quite, loved; recognizing that he himself might well be suspected of the murder; and fearing, above all, that his employer, a man whom he respected more than anyone else in the world, would on this one, vital occasion withhold his support.

It took a good deal of time, and even more delicacy, before the earl succeeded in penetrating the silent reserve that met him, but his crisp account of the measures he had taken to find the real murderer broke it down. For the first time since the earl had known him, Francis began to talk freely, not as a valued employee to an employer who suffered fools courteously but not gladly, but as one man to another, wiser one. Even his lordship's tactful version of his sister's encounter with Miss Lang – the part of his revelations that he had approached with the deepest foreboding – did not destroy the new openness.

'I suppose,' Francis said during the torrent of his explanations, 'that in Imogen Reece I found the kind of relaxation I had never known before – a warmth, a feeling of being needed *for myself*. It was not my parents' fault that I never had any experience of this at home. It would take the most saintly dedication to nurture eighteen children as individually as they ought to be nurtured. But although Miss Reece gave me this warmth, in a curious way she gave me too much. I suppose that, having been solitary for so long, it frightened me, however grateful for it I was – and am. What she did was make me recognize my need, without herself fulfilling it. So I persuaded myself that, in Miss Lang, I had found what I was looking for, someone who would love me and yet not focus the whole of her life upon me.' His eyes darkened. 'In the last ten days I have dissected my thoughts and emotions more honestly than ever in my life before, and realized in the process that I have been idealizing something that even in the beginning could be little more than a marriage of convenience. But I had hoped that she might have felt more for me than apparently she does.' He stopped. 'I didn't know the plans her father had for me. I would have been *owned*, wouldn't I?' He sighed abruptly, and said with an honest human irritability that reduced the temperature several degrees, 'God! What a coil!'

Very much relieved, the earl said, 'Francis, you are a fool! Did you have to pay such a terrible price for that unruffled manner of yours?'

'Yes,' he replied sardonically. 'The trembling hand within the steely glove. But never again, I promise you!'

After that, the earl had taken him through everything Imogen had ever said to him about the people she knew. There was virtually nothing he had not already discovered, except for one detail. It had always been Francis's impression that Imogen had disliked her brother-in-law. There was something she had said once, nothing precise, that had given him the impression that Iredale had tried to make love to her and been decisively repulsed. She had said something like, 'That apology for a man! That moonling! I may not be as respectable as my sister, but at least I have better taste.' It was an attitude that could have helped to lead to violence.

All the way back to London the two men discussed possibilities. But they could find nothing to go on, no way of pinning responsibility for the murder where it almost certainly belonged. As they turned out of Piccadilly, Francis had said in desperation, 'Perhaps if we talked to a few people who knew him in the past, the pupils he tutored, or his fellow students at university, we might come across some hint of violence that would lend credence to the whole business. We can look up his college in the Clerical Directory when we get back.'

But the directory, curiously enough, proved uninformative

on the matter. His lordship, his finger still in the page, turned to the four newcomers and smiled. 'Thank you,' he said. 'That was very neatly arranged. And obliging of you to come to our assistance, Miss Kenwood, when I am sure you have many other things to do.'

Lady Susan said, 'Miss Kenwood has consented to be our guest for a few days, Charles.'

'How delightful!' He surveyed the three slightly wary faces of his family, and noted the suspicious melancholy of his beloved's large, dark eyes. He said again, 'How delightful. Has anything – er – interesting happened while I have been away?'

John rushed his fences. 'We thought she might be safer here. You see, Iredale knows Miss Kenwood knows about the manuscript and the blackmail.'

His face perfectly still, the earl asked, 'How does he know?'

Kate intervened. 'I told him,' she said crisply, and then stopped.

His gentian eyes were ice cold. He slammed the book closed and threw it down on the desk with a crash that seemed to reverberate throughout the house. But when he spoke, his voice was calm and almost pleasant. 'And what else did you tell him?'

It took all her self-control to still the tremor in her voice as she replied, 'That it was Imogen who first told me. And that I wanted the money he had extracted from Considine. Or I would tell Bow Street.'

'I see,' he said conversationally. He looked at John. 'And I imagine you had some part in these proceedings?'

Manfully, John said, 'Yes.'

'The idea, however, was mine,' Kate said.

'Indeed? I had been going to use the word childish, but perhaps melodramatic would be more appropriate in the circumstances. This is real life, Miss Kenwood, not the theatre. In real life, daggers are made of steel, and bullets of lead. Blood is real, too, and corpses do not sit up and sneeze. You would be well advised to remember it.'

It hurt, and there was just enough truth in what he had said to rouse her own temper. Later, she recognized that it would have been more dignified to hold her tongue, but at the time it was either hit back or weep.

She said, 'Perhaps we should review our priorities, my lord. Your interest is in saving Mr Mervyn's skin.' Ridiculously, she inclined her head towards Mr Mervyn, who bowed back politely. 'Mine is in bringing the murderer of a very dear friend to justice. Perhaps I am prepared to go further than you are.'

It was unforgivable. The earl drew a long breath. But before he could speak, Adam, silencing John with one savage look, said, 'Charles, I would remind you that the damage is done. We should be concerned with protecting Miss Kenwood, not with useless recriminations.'

His matter-of-fact approach cooled the atmosphere slightly.

The earl, his face bleak, said, 'Yes.' His eyes detached themselves from Miss Kenwood's, and he added, with an effort, 'You are right, of course.'

Lady Susan did her best to help. 'In the meantime,' she said, 'I have arranged with Brandon for Francis to stay in his rooms without being disturbed.' She smiled at him a little nervously. 'I am so sorry, Francis. Either you were being pursued by Bow Street, or the bailiffs, or an irate husband, or were suffering from an acute irritation of the nerves, for which absolute quiet is the only remedy. The last seemed the least objectionable alternative. Brandon knows as well as we do that all problems and all visitors are automatically referred to you, so he quite understands that it will be necessary to deny your presence in the house, and he has instructed all the staff on the subject. However, I very much fear that you ought to retire to bed on an invalid diet!'

Mr Mervyn's saturnine expression looked as if it might crumble at any moment. Adam took him firmly by the arm, and hustled him out into the back corridor, and thence to the suite of rooms behind the library that were his private preserve – the office, tiny drawing room, bedroom and bathroom. As he left him there, Francis's rare smile lit his face. 'Thank Lady Susan for me,' he said with a slight break in his voice. Adam smiled back.

In the library, the earl was saying to John, 'I'll talk to you later. In the meantime, we had better try to retrieve something from the wreckage. Perhaps someone would be good enough to tell me what exactly had been going on.'

At that moment, Brandon entered with a tray, followed by the second footman, bearing another. The butler gave a most convincing start at the sight of his lordship. 'Welcome home, my lord,' he said, as if he had not been an interested witness of the goings-on in Duke Street a short while before. 'I took the liberty of bringing in some tea for my lady, in case she should fancy some refreshment.'

Noting at a glance the presence, not of four but six cups and saucers on the tray, his lordship said cordially, 'Thank you, Brandon. Your instinct never fails.'

When his lordship had been more fully apprised of the plot concocted by Miss Kenwood and John, he graciously admitted that it had been done well, even if he would have preferred that it had not been done at all. Apart from the personal danger to Miss Kenwood, which was his overriding concern – although he did not say so – he could detect only one real flaw. This was that if Iredale knew of Miss Kenwood's acquaintance with the man who was investigating Imogen's death, he might decide that his only solution was to brazen things out. In which case, the earl said, they were no further forward than before. On the contrary, they were now inhibited by the need to protect Miss Kenwood who, as the only apparently first-hand witness, would be in constant danger.

Miss Kenwood, somewhat recovered, said that on Captain Gregory's advice she had told her servants she would be spending a few nights with a friend, Lady Susan Gregory, in St James's Square, and that Iredale might not make the connection. But whether he did or not, it was high time she left for the theatre, otherwise there would be immortal chaos. This very nearly precipitated another crisis. The earl, staring at her, enquired whether she seriously thought he would permit her to go to the theatre under such circumstances, and she replied that he obviously did not understand that there were certain obligations involved in working for a living. It took the combined efforts of Lady Susan and Captain Gregory to achieve a truce satisfactory to Miss Kenwood, and acceptable (though only just) to his lordship. John remained silent throughout, becoming progressively more certain that Adam was mistaken, and that Charles had no feeling for Miss Kenwood other than dislike.

The outcome was that Miss Kenwood left for the theatre, with John and Adam accompanying her, in a town carriage borrowed from, and bearing the arms of, a surprised Lord Jersey, who resided next door and by the greatest good fortune did not require it that evening. When they arrived at the stage door there was the usual handful of early arrivals, waiting for a glimpse of the players.

Turning to the footman who had assisted them to descend, Captain Gregory said in a superior tone, 'You may come in with us, James, and Miss Kenwood will see if she can find some unobtrusive corner from which you may watch.'

'Thank you, sir,' said the footman, and at a respectful distance followed the little group into the theatre.

Safely inside, his lordship tucked the footman's silver-topped staff of office under his arm, removed his white gloves and cocked hat, and ran a fastidious palm over his powdered hair. 'Ugh!' he said, 'How disgusting! It will take me days to rinse this stuff out.'

'Have some egg nog,' his brother recommended unsympathetically. 'That should make you feel better, I've always suspected the real James of being something of a connoisseur.'

The earl looked at him, and then turned his attention to the knob of his staff. Twisting the top, he peered into the cavity. 'By God, you're right!' he exclaimed and took a tentative sip. 'It's not bad, either. Fresh egg, and,' he rolled the mixture round upon his tongue, 'my best Volnay, if I'm any judge. Well, I'll be damned!'

Chapter 15

Two hours later, Miss Kenwood was seated at the table in her dressing-room with her hands over her ears to shut out the roistering noises of the comedy that was the first item on the evening's programme. She was dressed for her part in *Follies in a Maze* in a seductive bright blue gown, low necked and short sleeved, Susanna's status of maid being indicated by a very small frilly apron and a gossamer froth of cap perched on top of a tumble of honey-blonde curls. On the table before her was an untidy sheaf of papers. The script for Acts III and IV had finally arrived, but there were insufficient copies, so that the pages were being passed in instalments from one dressing-room to another. Since Kate was one of the few singers in the cast and could therefore, at a pinch, fall back on the original libretto, she was the last to see them. It was not that she needed to study the words of the songs themselves, but it was useful to know, as she remarked acidly to John, when someone had seen fit to change the plot by inserting new snatches of dialogue in between. At last came the cry of, 'Signora Katarina is called for the stage!' and Kate raised her eyes to the ceiling in silent prayer, gathered up her skirts, and with John beside her threaded her way through the backstage clutter and into the wings.

Though she was perfectly at home in tragedy, Kate revelled in comedy, and her voice soon soared with mischievous purity and clarity through the auditorium as Susanna entered into all the schemes designed to extricate the Countess and herself from the dilemmas in which they were continuingly involved. Out in the pit lobby, the earl, still in his footman's rig and positioned to keep an eye not only on the main entrance but the stairways leading to the galleries and boxes, caught only an occasional glimpse of the stage on his patrols. But though he was unable to see much, he could hear, and he judged Kate to be superior to Catalani even in the role that grasping lady had made so peculiarly her own. It was, in fact, the only role in which a number of carping critics, including his lordship, had been able to admire her. Her habit of holding a note until her lungs were as empty as an exhausted air pump, or drowning a composer's music in a perfect cascade of extemporized vocal ornament, quite offset the pleasure they would otherwise have derived from the power, richness, and astonishing agility of her voice. Kate's voice, if more restricted in range, was quite as free and mellow, with a remarkable capacity for conveying the pure joy of the music.

The earl had to make a conscious effort to block it out. He could not afford to have his attention seduced, his vigilance relaxed, by lending an ear to the song of the sirens. The appalled awareness of danger that had expressed itself in bitter words a few hours ago had not diminished. He thought Iredale would probably not risk anything in the theatre itself, for he was not the type of unstoppable, nightmare killer who did not care what happened to him afterwards. Iredale would want to kill and go free. But Kate had threatened to go to Bow Street on Thursday, and he would not dare leave his attempt too late. Time was short.

Adam, inside the auditorium, was feeling slightly foolish, leaning negligently against the wall down by the orchestra and watching, not the stage, but the audience. What he was expected to do if someone on the far side of the pit rose from one of the hard, backless wooden benches and pointed a pistol at the stage he was not quite sure. There would certainly be no chance of stopping him, although a quarterdeck bellow might alert his neighbours. However, since a large and excitable part of the audience was on its feet half the time anyway, there would be little possibility of even a good marksman hitting a target on stage. In fact, despite his earlier reaction, the more Adam thought about it the less did he believe it likely that Iredale would risk another murder, especially when he saw that Miss Kenwood was guarded. From what Adam had heard about him, he was the kind of man who would always use his brains in preference to his hands. The kind of man who, having killed Miss Reece in a moment of uncharacteristic rage, might well have been so horrified that he would never lay hands on a weapon again. Adam suspected that Charles, because of his feeling for Miss Kenwood, was exaggerating the danger. He shifted his position slightly against the wall, which was remarkably hard. But at least it kept him awake after last night's vigil. And the music, too, of course. He supposed he might learn to enjoy opera some day, but a whole adult lifetime at sea had left something of a gap in his musical education.

John, assigned to duty in the wings, was having the time of his life, patrolling up one side, round the back, and down the other, to the considerable annoyance of several actors who crashed into him while attempting to leave the stage with appropriate bravura. After having been abused in comprehensive and extremely heated undertones by a number of persons in false moustaches – worn to show, Miss Kenwood had said, that they were Foreigners – John carefully scanned every figure lurking in, over, or near the wings, and then detailed Betsy to guard one of the doorways on to the stage while he took the other. Betsy, as devoted as Brandon to vicarious excitement and persuaded that Miss Kate was being importuned by some unknown admirer, happily obliged, and John, from his new position, was afforded an excellent and unusual view of the proceedings on stage.

He already knew that neither Elliston, who was playing the Count, nor Vining, who was Figaro, could sing a note, and was very impressed by the stratagems to which they resorted to disguise the fact. He did not even observe one of them until a stout little Italian in everyday clothes pushed past him, muttering, into the wings, and remained there singing his heart out. Startled, John looked more closely at Elliston, who was at the side of the stage with his back half turned to the audience, and discovered that he was simply gesticulating and mouthing, with the greatest enthusiasm, in time to the music. Some songs had been rewritten in such a way that the actor involved was able to declaim them as a kind of recitative. Vining was particularly good at that. And when neither ruse would serve, the songs were merely delegated, not always appropriately, to another character.

The high spot of the evening came when the singer who was

playing Bartolo opened his mouth in preparation for a *sforzando* passage, inhaled deeply and dramatically, and swallowed his moustache.

The audience howled. And howled again, even louder, as all the other male members of the cast automatically clapped a hand to their upper lips to reassure themselves that the glue was holding.

After that, very little could be heard of the remainder of the play. Coming off stage, breathless with suppressed laughter, for the third interval, Kate gasped, 'The rest of us might as well go home! I have never seen *a whole cast* so ruthlessly upstaged!' Bartolo himself passed, scarlet in the face, and accompanied by Elliston who, with no doubt kindly intent, was advising him on the relative merits of a number of cathartic remedies.

It was dark when they left the theatre, with Kate, still effervescing slightly, closely surrounded by her three tall bodyguards. Lord Jersey's closed carriage was standing, as instructed, directly outside the entrance in Wych Street, and as soon as Adam and John had joined Miss Kenwood inside, the earl swung himself up next to Fielding on the box and they set off for home. His lordship scanned the streets carefully, but they were still too full of carriages and carts and barrows and horsemen for him to judge whether or not anyone might be following them. He had seen no sign of anyone resembling Iredale at the theatre, but that did not mean very much.

When the carriage stopped in St James's Square, Brandon already had the house door open. The earl jumped down from the box and strode round to open the carriage door, so that first Adam, and then Miss Kenwood, and then John might descend. As the little group on the pavement turned towards the front steps, Fielding drove off.

It was then that the first shot was fired. It was the earl, the only one among them who had been taking the danger quite seriously, whose ear separated the sharp crack of the pistol from the dominant clatter of horses' hooves, and he reacted on the instant. The front door might as well have been a hundred miles away for all the refuge it offered. With brutal hands he threw Miss Kenwood flat on the ground and flung his body on top of hers. As he did so, he heard the sound of another shot, followed almost at once by a cry from John. Twisting his head up, he saw Brandon standing frozen in the doorway and Adam pushing a reeling John up the steps towards the house. John's right hand was clasped round the upper part of his left arm, and the earl had a moment of overwhelming relief as he realized that it was nothing worse.

Two shots. Two pistols. The odds were against a third. The earl looked down again at a silent Miss Kenwood, and said on an indrawn breath, 'Stay flat. On no account move.' As he was rising to his feet, Brandon exclaimed, 'Over there by the south entrance to the gardens, my lord. That's where the shots came from!' With Adam hard on his heels, his lordship set off at a silent run. The distance was perhaps no more than fifty yards, but when they reached the corner there was no one in sight. The two men stopped, breathing lightly and quietly, and as they hesitated they heard the faintest rustling sound coming from inside the gardens, which were cut off from the street by a high railing. The earl felt for his keys, separated out the one for the gardens, and with extreme stealth began to unlock the gate. Like wraiths, the two men slipped through and then stood in the pitch blackness under the trees, listening. Their quarry did not even know they were there until he felt his arms grasped brusquely and firmly on both sides.

The earl knew it was not Iredale as soon as he laid hands on him, but he and Adam dragged him out and into the light of the street just the same. Looking at him disgustedly, his lordship said, 'I might have known it. Townsend's man.'

Flustered, the man said, 'Yes, my lord. I mean, no, my lord. I'm the gardener. I sleep in the shed over there.'

'You heard the shots? Was the man inside the gardens?'

'No, my lord, outside. I was tiptoing down thinking I might catch a glimpse of him when you nabbed me. If you didn't see him, he must have got away into Pall Mall.'

The earl looked at Captain Gregory. 'That's probably true. If so, there's no point in pursuing him. He could be strolling along quite openly, and we couldn't prove a thing even if he had the pistols in his pocket.'

The captain, his theories about Iredale in ruins, said, 'No. No point. But I owe you an apology. I didn't think he'd try it.'

His lordship turned back to Townsend's man. 'What did you see?'

'Nothing much, my lord. I'd heard the sound of the carriage, so I was up at the top of the square.'

'Interested to see who descended from it?' his lordship enquired drily.

'Well, yes, my lord. Then I just heard the shots, same as you did, and started to move down as quiet as I could, not to frighten him off, see? But you was too quick for me. I disremember when I've seen a gentleman move so fast as you when you threw the lady down, my lord. I hope she's all right. Enough to give any lady the vapours, that sort of thing.'

Miss Kenwood, however, as she had pointed out to his lordship on a previous occasion, was not just 'any lady', and she was not having the vapours. As soon as she had recovered her breath, she had risen to her feet in a very stately fashion, studiously ignoring a faint but unmistakable tendency to tremble at the knees, and had proceeded indoors with Mrs Jameson, the housekeeper, and Sanderson, the earl's valet, clucking worriedly at either side and making darting attempts to brush her down.

At the sight of John, sheet white and bloodstained in one of the dining room chairs, being ministered to by Lady Susan and Brandon, she stopped short. That her partner in the extremely risky game she had instigated should have been the one to suffer caused her the most severe pang of conscience. She ran forward and knelt beside him. 'Oh, John!' she exclaimed distressfully. 'I am so very sorry! Is it bad?'

His senses swimming, he contrived a smile. 'Only a flesh wound,' he said. 'And thank God it was me. We would all have looked remarkably silly if it had been you.'

His lordship, appearing in the doorway at this moment, said rather sharply, 'Well, that's one way of looking at it, I suppose. Are you all right, Miss Kenwood?'

'Yes, thank you,' she replied untruthfully, aware of a stinging graze all the way down her left side, but perversely determined not to mention it.

He turned back to John. 'Does it pain you very much?'

'Oh, no,' said John bravely, and passed out for the second time.

185

Adam said, 'Best to move him upstairs while he's unconscious, Charles.' They lifted him between them, and with Brandon and Sanderson hovering on either side, and Lady Susan following, vanished in the direction of the marble staircase.

Miss Kenwood was left with Mrs Jameson, who said briskly, 'I know what you need, miss! Just you go into the library and I'll bring it up directly.' She held the library door open for Kate, and then whisked off, closing it behind her.

Kate, feeling very useless, continued to gaze at the door for a moment, and then began to remove her bonnet, turning into the room as she did so. She found herself looking straight into the dark, concerned face of Francis Mervyn.

'Is it all right?' he said. 'I came out to help, but Lady Susan sent me straight back in here again. She said she thought nothing was solved yet, and his lordship would not be pleased if I showed myself before he thought the time was right. *Please*, Miss Kenwood, tell me what happened?'

She sat down with a sigh, and said, 'What a pair we make! I precipitate a situation in which John is shot. You precipitate one in which Imogen is murdered. It's other people who suffer for our foolishness.'

He flinched. 'That's hardly fair, Miss Kenwood.'

She looked at him for a moment with no change of expression, and suddenly realized just how unfair it was. She said contritely, 'I am sorry, Mr Mervyn! An acute attack of self-disgust, I fear. In your case, it was not only unfair but untrue. Nothing you did, or did not do, was in any way related to Imogen's murder. In some ways, I think you are as much a victim as she was. Forgive me?'

She smiled enchantingly, a little sadly, and Mr Mervyn began to revise his opinion of her. The earl, describing to him what had happened during his absence from London, had told him what she had said, and what she had done, but not what she was. He had been inclined to blame her for most of his own predicament, but he thought now that he, too, perhaps, had been unfair.

'Shall we call a truce?' he suggested, and she smiled again. 'Now, do please tell me what happened!'

She had just finished when the earl and Captain Gregory

reappeared, with Mrs Jameson just behind them, bearing a tray of steaming cups. Miss Kenwood looked at hers with extreme suspicion.

'It'll not harm you,' Mrs Jameson said with a twinkle. 'Just you drink it down and you'll feel much better.'

Kate dutifully took a sip, being careful not to inhale the fumes that assailed her nostrils, and was rewarded with an uncontrollable shudder that started somewhere about her shoulders and ran powerfully down her spine. 'What is it?' she gasped, when she could speak.

'And another one!' Mrs Jameson instructed.

With the amused eyes of her host upon her, Kate braced herself to swallow again. This time it was better, a small river of warm and comfortable fire inside her. She looked up doubtfully.

The earl said, 'Thank you, Mrs Jameson. An excellent idea under the circumstances. I think you might take some up to Lady Susan, too.'

'A version of a traditional Highland reviver,' the earl explained after she had left. 'Illicit whisky mixed with hot milk and a dash of salt. Strictly speaking, it should be whisky, sugar, and hot water, but Susan can't drink it like that, and since it is such an infallible medicine for all ills, we allow her to have her way.'

'Does the whisky *have* to be illicit?' Kate asked, sipping again.

'It is a sad fact that the stuff secretly distilled in Highland glens, to evade the excise duty, is almost without exception vastly superior to the product of the legal distilleries in the Lowlands. And it's easy enough to come by. There are said,' his lordship added meditatively, 'to be about fourteen thousand illicit stills in the Highlands, which must work out at about one to every family in the area!'

She was feeling considerably better. 'How is John?'

'Settled down for the night. I think we should all go to bed, for though there is a good deal to be talked about, I, for one, see no possibility of being able to think rationally until I have changed into civilized attire and rid my hair of this powder. I had not realized what an inhuman imposition it was. What do you think, Miss Kenwood? Should the Dornay family set a new fashion by forbidding its footmen to powder their hair?'

She looked at him a little sleepily. On Saturday, she had quite liked him. His manners had been pleasant, easy, and open, in comparison with the curtness he had shown on their first meeting and the detachment on their second. Even though the curtness and detachment had been leavened with quite human gleams, she had still thought them his natural style. But Saturday had made her wonder. Despite the trials of the visit to Richmond, he had seemed relaxed and friendly. He had seemed genuinely to like her. Yet here he was today, as authoritarian as ever, raking her down over the Iredale enterprise, incapable of understanding that she *had* to go the theatre, throwing her roughly to the ground when the shot was fired, as if she were no more than a sack of barleymeal.

She said in a small voice, 'I have to thank you for saving my life, but was it necessary to be quite so decisive about it?'

His lordship was taken aback by the inconsequence of it, and distracted by the most urgent desire to take her in his arms. In a carefully reasonable voice that had the unfortunate effect of making her feel foolish for not having thought of it herself, he said, 'I would, I assure you, have been less drastic if I had known which direction the shots were coming from. But to cover your right side when they were coming from the left would, you must admit, have been worse than useless. I fear that horizontality was the only pose.' He smiled. 'I have been remiss in failing to congratulate you on the coolness with which you reacted to the whole episode. As Townsend's man said just now, most ladies would have succumbed, quite justifiably, to a fit of the vapours.'

His remark, earlier in the afternoon, that this was real life, not the stage, still rankled. She said, with slightly muzzy dignity, 'You forget how often the heroines of tragedy are required to submit to the most brutal treatment. The theatre is not, as you believe, an entirely bloodless substitute for life.'

He had the grace to say, '*Touché*' and even to add that the attack had virtually proved what hitherto they had only assumed, that Iredale was not only a blackmailer but a murderer. So when he took her by the hand and coaxed her to her feet, saying, 'Come along, Miss Kenwood. Mrs Jameson has prepared your room,' she was able to admit to being tired, and to go upstairs feeling rather more in charity with him than she would have expected.

Chapter 16

Adam said, 'But even if the man didn't realize we were acting as a bodyguard to Miss Kenwood ... '

'Or trying to!' John interrupted.

' ... he must realize that he may have frightened her into going straight to Bow Street.'

'So what do you think he did last night? Would he risk going home?' John was sitting up in bed, his left arm reposing in a sling, his right hand toying unenthusiastically with a cup of beef tea, a potion in which Lady Susan, like her mother before her, reposed the greatest faith. In John's opinion, a cup of claret would have been a good deal more restorative, but he had been overruled, as he had been when he demanded to be allowed up. 'I've only lost a pint or two of blood,' he had complained, but his sister replied with an exceedingly firm 'No!', and the earl, appealed to, had recommended him to do as he was bid, saying 'You should know better than to argue with Susan.'

'We think,' Adam replied, 'that he probably did go home. Nothing would have been a surer indication of guilt than to stay away, and he might think that by the time the fuss had died down here, we would leave Bow Street until the morning. No. Charles's guess is – and I think he's right – that Iredale would go home last night, but probably leave promptly this morning, on some mythical business that could be relied on to keep him out for most of the day. If he returns home and finds everything quiet, he may think he has got away with it.'

'And in the meantime, of course, he's still on the loose.' John's eyes widened. 'You think he might try again?'

Adam nodded. 'And again. And again. Thanks to you and Miss Kenwood, unless we lay him by the heels Miss Kenwood will never be free from danger.'

John gulped. 'We really ought to take the whole thing to Bow Street, oughtn't we? There's enough now to convince Townsend that Francis is innocent, I should have thought.'

At that moment, his lordship walked in the door. 'Miss Kenwood won't have it,' he said. 'Because to clear Francis means to present Townsend with Iredale, and Iredale is bound to bring Considine into it. And Miss Kenwood is strongly of the opinion that he – and, more important, Lady Considine – should be protected if it is humanly possible. Having promised Considine that I would do my best to keep his name out of it, I feel the same. And furthermore, we dare not give Iredale to Bow Street save in the absolute certainty that he will be tried and convicted. For as long as he is free, Miss Kenwood is at risk.'

Adam said, 'But if he is arrested on Miss Kenwood's evidence, and then freed, surely he would have nothing to gain in killing her afterwards?'

'Perhaps not. But would you care to take a chance on his having a forgiving disposition? A desire for vengeance can be very corrosive.' He paused. 'However, I have the glimmer of an idea that might settle matters. Come in!'

The discreet visage of the first footman appeared.

'Yes, Dennis?' John said.

'Yes, James?' said his lordship.

In polite society, the first footman was always known as James. But the stalwart young man who held this post in the earl's household was no longer thrown off balance by the Dornays' blithe disregard for convention. Well accustomed to being addressed in traditional style by his master, and by his real name by Mr John, who did not hold with such old-fashioned flummery, he said calmly, 'There is a Mr Townsend to see you, my lord.'

'Is there, indeed? Very well. In the library in ten minutes. Oh, and James! Do, please, have a word with Sanderson, and tell him how the devil I am to get the last of the powder out of my hair. I'm damned if I'll stay grey any longer!'

'I don't know,' John said critically. 'I like those patches over the ears. They look rather distinguished.'

With a searing glance, the earl followed Dennis/James out of the room, descending to the ground floor by way of the family backstairs, which ended just outside Francis Mervyn's personal suite. He tapped on the door of the office and entered. 'Francis,' he said, 'I am sorry to disturb you, but Townsend is here. If you were to lose yourself somewhere in the upper reaches of the house, I could tell him truthfully that I didn't know where you were.'

Mr Mervyn had recovered sufficiently to respond to this with an amused grin. 'You could,' he said, and, gathering up some of his lordship's neglected correspondence, departed briskly in the direction of the stairs.

When Brandon ushered Townsend into the library a few minutes later, his lordship – with the appearance of one who had been sitting there peacefully ever since the Runner's visit of a week before – looked up and greeted him with polite surprise.

Townsend was legitimately annoyed. His little dark eyes were snapping, and his flat cheeks sucked in. 'Eventful doings around here, my lord,' he said without preamble. 'I'm disappointed you didn't see fit to inform Bow Street about last night's shooting!'

The earl raised his brows. 'And *I* was disappointed to see no sign of the Foot Patrol. I understood it was their task to prevent this kind of occurrence or, at the very least, to turn up in time to chase the culprits.'

Townsend's lips thinned. 'You know as well as I do, my lord, that five parties of four or five men can't be expected to be everywhere at once. Anyway, as you've guessed, my man in the gardens reported to me this morning. And from his description, the lady who was being shot at was Miss Kenwood. And you must have expected it, because you and two other gentlemen were gathered round guarding her. I've a right to ask why, my lord. And to ask why you were disguised. And why you were using someone else's carriage.'

'Congratulations!' the earl said amiably. 'Your man obviously keeps his eyes open. What a pity he was looking in the wrong direction, and not at the man who fired the shots.'

The Runner's temper snapped. 'He might have been, if you hadn't been playing hares and hounds in Duke Street earlier on! When I heard about that, I took it to be a bluff. You wouldn't risk bringing Francis Mervyn here in broad daylight,

I thought. Seemed to me it was a diversion and that you might smuggle him in after dark – which is why my man was so interested last night. I ask you straight, my lord. Do you know where Francis Mervyn is?'

'No, I don't,' said his lordship.

The Runner did not believe him. On the other hand, he had taken the precaution of asking Brandon, when he arrived, if Mr Mervyn was at home, and Brandon had also denied it – salving his churchgoer's conscience, if Townsend had but known, with the reflection that Mr Mervyn's home, strictly speaking, was not in London but at Worthing.

'Ay. Well, we'll leave that for the moment. For I've another question to ask. If you expected Miss Kenwood to be shot at, you must have known who was likely to do the shooting. And I must require you to tell me, in my capacity as an officer of the law.'

The earl said suavely, 'Tut! tut! Threats? I can assure you it wasn't Francis Mervyn, if that's what you think.'

'How do you know?'

The earl ignored the question. 'Cool down, Townsend. And for God's sake, sit down. You are giving me a crick in my neck. You should know you won't get anything out of me by taking this tone.'

Townsend did know it. After a moment, he propped his stick against the desk and sat down on the straight chinoiserie chair he had occupied on his last visit. 'I won't go without an answer of *some* sort, my lord. That I do say.'

'If I told you that the other gentlemen and I were merely escorting Miss Kenwood back from the theatre, and that I was dressed as a footman in order to win a wager, and that I borrowed a carriage because my own was in need of attention from a wheelwright, and that I believe the shots to have been fired to distract our attention from a burglary that was in progress further round the square, what would you say?'

'Nothing that could be repeated in front of a lady, my lord.'

'That's what I thought. You are clearly of the opinion that last night's incident was related to the murder of Miss Reece. Do you still think Francis Mervyn did it?'

'I've come across nothing to disprove it.'

193

'Do you seriously believe that my secretary, whom I am trying to free from suspicion, would shoot at a group of people that included not only Miss Kenwood, but myself, my younger brother, and my sister's husband?'

'I don't know how he feels about you all,' the Runner said caustically. 'And if you don't think Mervyn fired the shots, you must know who did. Who was it?'

'I don't *know*. Just as I have no firm evidence that would help to convict the murderer of Imogen Reece. What I have is a very strong suspicion – enough to convince me, and possibly you, but not a magistrate trained in the requirements of the law. What I am now doing is trying to find the evidence. Why do you complain? You yourself encouraged me to embark on this investigation.'

'Ay. But I never said I'd be agreeable to your investigation hampering mine.'

'Is it? How?'

'You're withholding information, my lord. That's how!'

'But none, I solemnly swear, that would help to prove Francis Mervyn guilty.'

The Runner, frustrated, pushed out his lower lip and exhaled vigorously, so that his fringe flipped in the little gust of air. He recognized that the conversation had gone astray somewhere, and that the earl was holding back. But there was nothing he could do about it. It was, after all, no crime to be shot at, and as far as Townsend knew that was all that had occurred to interest him in the last week. His instinct, however, told him that a great deal more had been going on.

Stubbornly, he said, 'Do I understand Miss Kenwood is staying here? May I ask why?'

The earl smiled sympathetically. 'Merely a private visit.'

'I would like to talk to her.' He was surprised, and then suspicious, when the earl tugged the bell pull and said, 'If you insist.' If it was going to be as easy as that, he might as well save himself a bit of time and leave right now. But a small voice in his head suggested that Miss Katharine might be more likely to let something slip than his lordship, and besides, he was beginning to wonder what kind of May-game she was playing.

Brandon appeared, and his lordship said, 'I believe Miss

194

Kenwood may be in the drawing room. Would you ask her whether she will see Mr Townsend, and then take him up to her?'

Brandon inclined his head a fraction. That was more like it, he thought. No refreshments this time, and the Runner to be kept waiting in the hall. What a splendid week it had been, to be sure! He had not enjoyed himself so much in years. He still had not quite discovered the details of the misunderstanding that had led Mr Mervyn to incur Bow Street's disapproval, but had not the slightest doubt that it would be resolved. Far more interesting was having his lordship's future lady staying in the house, even if neither of them knew it yet.

Kate was seated in the drawing room wearing a long-sleeved muslin gown that concealed the grazes on her arm. Betsy, arriving after the uproar had subsided last night, had tried to persuade her to have the arm bandaged, but Kate was determined to appear untouched. An application of salve was all that was required, she had said, and was now paying for her vanity by suffering a twinge every time she moved her arm.

'Well, now, young lady,' said Townsend, in the avuncular manner he sometimes affected. 'That was a nasty fright you had last night!'

'Yes, indeed. But so exciting. Almost as good as a play.'

He sighed. 'It's like that, is it? At any rate, I'm glad you didn't come to harm. What was it all about, though? You'd better tell me.'

'I? I doubt if I can tell you any more than Lord Moriston. You have already seen him, I take it?'

Exasperated, he said, 'Miss Katharine! We've known each other this past three years, so don't play off any of your tricks on me. *You* called me in to begin with, *you* told me Francis Mervyn was the murderer. Drat it! You're even paying me. But now I find you "just visiting",' he mimicked, 'the home of Francis Mervyn's employer. And telling me – or as good as – that anything he says you'll back up. What I want to know is, whose side are you on?'

'I'm sorry,' she said remorsefully. 'But if it's any consolation, I'm being unfair to everyone I meet these days. In rotation.

195

There's really nothing I can tell you, except that I now believe Francis Mervyn was not guilty of murdering Imogen.'

'Oh, that's fine, that is!' he exclaimed wrathfully. 'Women! You think you've found one whose judgement you can trust, and then she starts behaving like a weathercock, just like all the rest!'

She giggled.

'And I don't suppose,' he went on sarcastically, '*you* know who popped off at you, either?'

Hopefully, she added a small twig to the blaze. 'I don't even know whether it was I who was shot at. After all, I imagine that someone like Lord Moriston must have his fair share of enemies. Perhaps the shots were directed at him?'

He glowered at her. 'Thank you very much,' he said. 'I don't know why I waste my time, really I don't. How does Mr John Dornay feel about it all? I'm told he's the one who got hit.'

'Fortunately, the shot only carved a furrow along his arm. It was very messy and alarming at the time, but no more. A day or two in bed should see him cured.'

'Ay. I'm glad to know that, even if it's not quite what I asked.' He turned towards the door, but paused there. 'If so be as you should think better of it, you can always send for me, you know. The sooner it's settled, the happier I'll be.'

'The happier we'll all be,' she said.

He clapped his hat on his head, and went out without a goodbye.

When the earl strolled into the drawing room a few minutes later, he found Miss Kenwood looking pale and a little subdued. 'Poor Townsend,' she said. 'We are treating him very badly.'

He smiled understandingly. 'I'm afraid it's either him, or Francis *and* Considine *and* Lady Considine.'

'Yes, I know. But my conscience troubles me.' Making a visible effort, she went on interestedly, 'And what do we do now, other than remain here with the doors and windows bolted and barred?'

'We must force a conclusion. Would you mind very much coming to John's room, so that we can discuss things without his feeling left out?'

Lady Susan, Captain Gregory, and Francis Mervyn were already in residence, and the arrival of two more visitors led John to remark, in a satisfied fashion, 'My God! It's like a royal levée in here.'

'You are not getting up,' said his sister automatically, for what was obviously not the first time that morning. Kate laughed, and asked how he felt. 'Full of b-b-b-beef tea!' he said.

When, after what resembled a game of unmusical chairs – in which Francis Mervyn was the loser, and had to perch on the end of the bed – everyone was seated, the earl began. 'We have to settle this matter as soon as may be. As far as I can see, Francis can be cleared whatever happens. And if necessary we can lock Miss Kenwood up in the wine cellar to keep her out of harm's way.' Miss Kenwood looked at him doubtfully. 'Which leaves the identity of Considine as our main problem. Now, the only people who know it, other than ourselves, are Mr and Mrs Iredale. So they are the only people who could reveal it.'

'We all know that,' John said impatiently.

'I just want to be sure you remember it. Because there is only one person who knows of it *and* who fears the disclosure of Considine's relationship with Imogen more than Considine himself.'

'Of course!' Susan exclaimed. 'Mrs Iredale!'

Adam remarked, 'I don't see how that helps.'

'You might, if you had had the doubtful privilege of meeting her. How much do you think she knows about her husband's activities?'

Kate said, 'She can't know anything. When he came to see me, he was in more of a panic about my telling her than telling Bow Street. And I think it was genuine, wasn't it?' She looked at John.

'It seemed so to me,' he agreed.

His lordship said, 'But he may be deluding himself. She might, at the very least, have her suspicions. Looking back, I wonder whether her hysterics when I went to see her may not have had their source in a division of loyalty. Between her sister and her husband. Is *any* woman so much a slave to

197

respectability that she would, for that reason alone, prefer her sister's murderer to go unpunished?'

They were silent.

'What I wonder is – what would she do if she discovered that he was likely to be arrested and charged?'

'Lie herself purple in the face, I should have thought,' John said.

'But if she also discovered that no amount of lying on her part would save him? What does she feel about him? You have had no opportunity to judge, but it's my guess that, deep down, she feels nothing but contempt. I believe she'd try to save *some*thing from the wreckage – and that "something" might well be her sister's reputation.'

'A rational woman,' Adam said, 'would simply persuade him to leave town. Or leave the country. They could, now that the wars are over. And they have £2,000 to do it on.'

'It's a possibility,' the earl agreed. 'And one that would suit us quite well.'

Kate said tentatively, 'She doesn't sound like the kind of woman who would be happy outside her own country, especially with a man she didn't care for.'

The earl smiled without humour. 'I think you may be right. But the one thing she cannot do is expose Considine, for by doing that she publicly ruins her sister's reputation *and* invites testimony from the only firsthand witness to her husband's iniquities. To be frank, I don't know what she'll do, but if we are to put an end to this case quickly, I believe we must tell her everything, and then wait and see.'

There was another silence. His lordship look round the thoughtful faces in the room and said, 'And when I say "we", I'm afraid I mean Miss Kenwood.'

She looked at him, startled. 'But ... '

'She wouldn't believe anyone else. You were Imogen's oldest and closest friend, and she must know that Imogen confided in you. All you have to do is tell her what you told her husband. But a little more explicitly, and with the addition of what has happened since then.'

'Does she deserve it?' Kate queried.

It was an odd question.

She went on, 'I didn't mind lying to Iredale. After all ... '

198

'You knew that he had blackmailed Considine. You knew he had stolen the manuscript. You suspected he had murdered Imogen. And now you are almost sure he has tried to murder you – which he would scarcely have done if he had not also killed Imogen. Do you doubt his guilt?'

'No.'

'Then you know that he has to be caught, and stopped. And that, when he is, Mrs Iredale is bound to discover everything.'

'Yes.'

'Then why are you hesitating? How does your intervention alter the course of events, except by hastening them? Perhaps mercifully.'

'But . . . ' she said again.

'But you prefer not to lie. Yet you know all these things, don't you?'

'Yes.'

'And the only real lie is that it was Imogen who told you?'

'Yes.'

'Very well, then!'

Put like that, it seemed perfectly reasonable.

'Very well,' she said.

Half an hour later, as they left John's room, Adam murmured, 'You're right, of course, Charles. But I don't like it.'

'Neither do I,' said his lordship.

Chapter 17

Mrs Iredale was a disappointment to Brandon. He was not accustomed to strange women paying off hackneys in front of the house, and failing, if the jarvey's parting remarks were anything to go by, to tip properly. His stateliness did not falter, but he put the lady in her place by leaving her to wait in the hall while he dispatched a footman to tell his lordship that she had arrived. The earl had not bargained for his butler's private war against a class of society that he stigmatized, all-embracingly and not always accurately, as Cits, and was irritated to find that Mrs Iredale, when she was ushered into his presence, had the high colour in her cheeks that, in his limited experience of her, betokened an explosive mood.

'I received your note, my lord,' she said stiffly, but with a glitter in her eye. 'I cannot imagine why you wished to see me, but since I happened to be in the vicinity I thought I might as well call.'

He said soothingly, 'I am most grateful. It seemed to me that we might talk more privately here than at your house.' And that, he thought, was a remark that might have been open to misinterpretation if Miss Kenwood had not been present. 'I believe you are acquainted with Miss Kenwood, who was a friend of your sister?'

Mrs Iredale glanced briefly at Kate, and said, 'We have been introduced.' It had not, his lordship deduced, been a meeting of souls.

Kate studied her curiously while she settled herself in a chair. She had forgotten what a drab imitation of Imogen she was, despite the resemblances. Imogen's sunny hair, in Olivia, had been dulled to a light brown. Imogen's huge, pansy-blue eyes had diminished and narrowed. Imogen's seductively pouting lips had taken on, in her sister's countenance, a sulky and wilful cast.

Mrs Iredale said, 'Your message claimed that you had discovered who killed my sister, and said you wanted to consult me about how to proceed. I don't understand. Presumably, there is some sort of routine in these matters, which I am happy to say I know nothing about.'

'There is,' the earl replied. He had been intending to break it gently, but changed his mind. It might be a mistake to give her time to think. 'And if it had been followed, your husband would now be under arrest for trying to murder Miss Kenwood.'

'For trying to ... For *what*?'

'Last night, your husband tried to shoot Miss Kenwood, as she returned here from the theatre. Fortunately, he missed.'

'I don't believe it. Why should he try to shoot her?' She looked at Kate suspiciously. 'What had you done?'

The earl said, 'She wrote to him a few days ago. Perhaps I should read the letter to you.'

Mrs Iredale's eyes were still on Kate. 'You wrote to him?' She held out her hand. 'Let me see!'

The earl placed the letter in her hand. 'This, of course, is only a copy.'

She scanned it rapidly, and then went back to the beginning. Her face did not change at all. At last she looked up at Kate. 'What is this all about? I don't understand it. Money? And who is this person "Spencer" you refer to?'

Kate said, almost apologetically, 'It was the name your husband used when he was extracting money from Imogen's Mr C. I'm afraid Mr Iredale took advantage of his position as Lord Ballinton's librarian to remove an extremely valuable illuminated manuscript from the as yet uncatalogued part of his collection. He replaced it with a much inferior one which he had bought for a song' – she nearly made the mistake of adding, 'we believe' – 'from a Belgian refugee. Then he sold the first manuscript, page by page, to Mr C. at an astronomical price. It was theft first, and then blackmail, I'm afraid.'

Mrs Iredale had lost her high colour. 'It's all lies.'

'No. Please let me explain. Imogen never told me the name of the man who was ... ' Hastily, she changed what she had

201

been going to say. ' . . . the gentleman who so kindly helped her meet her expenses. He preferred to remain anonymous. But she did tell you.'

'You're lying. She didn't.'

In for a penny, in for a pound, Kate thought. 'She told *me* she did. After all, you were her sister. If she could confide in anyone, she could confide in you. The result was that when Mr C. began to receive blackmail demands, she knew that the only person who could be responsible was your husband, because he was the only person, other than yourself, who could possibly know what the blackmailer apparently knew. She realized that you must have told him. Naturally enough,' she added understandingly.

'I didn't. It's all lies. Neither of us knew.' They could almost see her mind racing.

The earl said, 'I am afraid it's too late to deny it, Mrs Iredale. Your husband received that letter from Miss Kenwood on Monday morning, and went to see her the same afternoon. He admitted accepting money from Mr C. He even agreed to hand it over to Miss Kenwood, but said he needed time to produce it. She gave him until today.' He held up his hand. 'And before you say again that it is all lies, I must tell you that there was a witness to the conversation.'

The silence was punctuated by muffled street noises and the sound of Mrs Iredale's breathing. A young mistle thrush, fat and speckled, chattered for parental attention from the balcony rail outside. Miss Kenwood moved slightly in her chair.

His lordship said, 'What time did your husband arrive home last night?'

She was staring right through him, her mouth drooping and a little open. She said nothing.

'It must have been late, because at eleven o'clock he was here in St James's Square shooting at Miss Kenwood – and, I may add, injuring my younger brother. We don't know whether he has tried to get in touch with Miss Kenwood by less lethal means, as she has been staying here in the interests of safety, but her servants at home report that he has not come calling at the front door.' Still she said nothing. Incisively, the earl summed up. 'The essential points are that you did tell your

202

husband Mr C.'s name; that he did blackmail Mr C; and that your sister knew it.'

Her hands were clenched together so tightly in her lap that they were patterned in white and pink. Her gown was a dull blue printed cotton, with white muslin filling in the neckline, and from under the matching blue and white bonnet her eyes continued to look at him blankly.

Kate's voice, however, woke her to attention. 'Bow Street don't know about the blackmail, Mrs Iredale,' she said. 'I didn't tell them about it at first, because I didn't connect it with Imogen's death. But – I'm sorry – I must tell them now, so that they will be forced to arrest your husband. You have to understand that I can't allow him to remain free if he is determined to kill *me*. As well as Imogen.'

At last she opened her mouth, and it was clear that she had now accepted everything as comprehensively as she had denied it a few minutes earlier. She said huskily, 'I could persuade him not to, if you promised not to go to Bow Street.'

Kate was feeling sorry for her, but she said, 'That would be a very poor bargain, Mrs Iredale. He would go unpunished, while I would spend the next few years wondering how long he would keep his promise! The answer, I fear, is no.'

Mrs Iredale was still half immersed in her own thoughts. 'Yes,' she said to herself. 'I see.' Whatever it was she saw, she did not disclose it. Tiny, unexplained incidents, the earl thought, were probably beginning to appear to her in a new light.

Her eyes suddenly came right back into focus. She looked at Kate and then at his lordship. 'It's all settled, then, is it?' Her lips curled sarcastically. 'You just very kindly wished to warn me what I had to look forward to?'

The earl said gently, '*Almost* all settled, Mrs Iredale.' Now came the delicate part. 'I remembered what you said to me last week, about your sister's reputation being the most important thing in the world to you. Whatever happens, your husband will have to pay the penalty for his crimes. Make no mistake about that. But it occurred to me that you might be able to save your sister's reputation. If the story of the blackmail comes out, then the reason for it must come out, too. That your sister was,' his eyes flicked briskly over the desk and table surfaces to make quite sure that he *had* moved all potential missiles out of reach, 'a kept woman.'

She flushed darkly but, rather to his surprise, made no move.

He went on, with a stirring of relief, 'But if you were to persuade your husband to go to Bow Street and confess that he murdered your sister for some quite different reason – perhaps in a fit of rage because she had criticized him – then perhaps nothing need come out at all. Whether that's possible, only you know. But I thought I should give you the opportunity.'

'I see.' She rose to her feet as if there was nothing more to be said, and picked up her shawl and reticule.

'But very soon,' his lordship added. 'You must decide by tomorrow.'

She said, 'Thank you.'

The earl started across the room to open the door. Olivia Iredale, who like her husband was not a fool, turned to Kate and said, 'Why did you write that letter in the first place?' Before Kate could reply, she went on, 'You said you wanted the money, but it was to trap him, wasn't it? It was to trap him!'

The earl swung round as he caught the note of rising hysteria in her voice.

Kate said, 'I ... ' and stopped.

Mrs Iredale had a little dagger in her hand, pointed at Kate's breastbone. There was no more than a yard between the two women. Mrs Iredale's shawl and reticule had dropped to the floor, with the scabbard on top.

She was breathing in deep, noisy gusts, her diaphragm jerking in and out and pulling on the ribbon band under the high bosom of her dress. She said, 'It's your fault, isn't it! All your fault. It was the theatre and people like you who led Imogen astray in the first place.' Kate opened her mouth. 'And it's you who are responsible for all this trouble now. Well, you won't be responsible for any more!'

Kate's eyes were fixed on the knife. Violence quivered on the air, and the Iredale woman's control was as fragile as blown glass. The earl dared not move. He was too far away, and his own foresight had ensured that there was nothing within range for him to throw. Kate had been frozen in the act of rising from her chair, and was still penned in by it on three sides with no hope of slipping out of range.

Mrs Iredale went on, 'You didn't expect this, did you! But London is a dangerous city, and I always carry it to protect myself.' She laughed spitefully. 'Say goodbye, Miss Kenwood!'

Everything exploded. She raised her arm to lunge, and as she did so the earl hurled himself across the intervening space, while Kate did the only possible thing and threw herself hard back and sideways into the chair, so that it shuddered, teetered, and finally keeled over with its occupant on to the floor. She felt a searing pain in her arm, and then her head connected with something hard and she lost all interest in the proceedings.

When she recovered consciousness, she was lying on the chaise-longue. The library was empty except for his lordship, whose unreadable face was bent closely over hers while he possessed both her hands in a grip that threatened to crush them. When her long, silky lashes were fully open, he withdrew his head a fraction.

It took her a moment to bring the blue gaze into focus, but her mind felt surprisingly clear. It was irresistible. 'Where am I?' she murmured. 'What happened?'

The corners of his mouth twitched, and the betraying creases appeared below his eyes. His grip on her hands tightened, and he said in a voice she scarcely recognized, 'Oh, Kate! You little witch. I ... '

The door opened and Lady Susan came in, vinaigrette in hand, followed by Mrs Jameson with towels and a bowl of ice from the store in the cellar.

'Thank goodness,' exclaimed her ladyship. 'Take this, my dear, in case you feel faint again.'

Kate accepted the vinaigrette politely, a charming little porcelain bottle in the shape of a teardrop, decorated with painted flowers and with a gilded dove perched on the stopper. With impressive serenity, she said, 'How pretty!' and raised her head to examine it more closely. A small cannonball began to ricochet around inside her skull. Gently, she closed her eyes, and even more gently returned her head to its resting place among the cushions.

Mrs Jameson said with a touch of impatience. 'If you'd just move over, my lord! The sooner I put a cold compress on the bump, the sooner Miss Kenwood will feel better.'

'*What* a household!' exclaimed Lady Susan with soft-voiced vehemence. 'If anyone deserves a bump on the head it should be you, Charles.'

He was not attending. Obedient to Mrs Jameson's instructions, he had inserted an arm under Miss Kenwood's shoulders to raise her head from the cushion while Mrs Jameson wrung out a towel in cold water, wrapped it round some slivers of ice, and applied it with gentle hands. Kate sighed with relief and subsided again, only to let out a startled exclamation as her left arm began to sting furiously. The sleeve of her dress, she now saw, had been ripped from shoulder to wrist, and Mrs Jameson was washing the grazes.

His lordship, the large, questioning eyes upon him, said, 'I did not know you had been hurt last night. There was blood on your sleeve, and I thought the knife had caught you. I am sorry about your gown.'

'Oh, yes,' she said interestedly. 'The knife.'

He went over to his desk. 'I have it here.' Turning, he brought it back to her in its scabbard, resting ceremonially across his open palms. 'I don't know whether you collect mementoes of your triumphs, but I should think this deserves a place of honour somewhere.' There was an embarrassed look in his eye.

'What a splendid idea,' she agreed cordially. 'I can think of a multitude of uses for it. What has happened to its owner?'

'She has gone home, I hope.'

Kate stared at him. 'I see,' she said at last. 'Home. Not under guard to Bow Street?'

'I – er – thought it better to allow the original plan to proceed, since no serious harm had been done.'

'I see,' she said again, much struck. 'How very clear-headed of you.'

'Charles,' remarked his sister acidly, 'is invariably clear-headed. It is the rest of us who become distracted.'

206

He said, 'I have the strangest feeling that I am *de trop*. Miss Kenwood, Adam has gone to find Doctor Essex for you.'

'There was no need for that!'

'Perhaps not, but he may like to give you a soothing draught and recommend that you lie down for a while.'

'May he? I suppose when he is summoned to this house he instinctively brings his stock of soothing draughts with him.'

He laughed. 'Not infallibly. We are a remarkably healthy family, in general, and quite tranquil by nature. Now, if you will forgive me? I hope to see you recovered soon.'

Chapter 18

Miss Kenwood recovered swiftly, thanks to the natural vitality that enabled her not only to survive but enjoy life in the theatre. When she descended to dinner that evening, she was suffering from no more than the faint echo of a headache. As she pinned her long, thick hair up into its accustomed coil, she thought it had probably helped to cushion the blow.

John had also been permitted to rise from his bed, and Francis Mervyn, the myth of his illness already somewhat tattered round the edges, emerged from his sanctum to join the others at table. There was a faint air of suspense about everyone, but with the servants present it was impossible to discuss the matter that preoccupied all their minds, so that the beginning of the meal was a little subdued. Alexandre's superlative green pea soup went past, and then the trout stuffed with prawn mousse, and the whitebait, and then the *médaillons de boeuf*, and the chaudfroid of quails. The first course was cleared away, and the second began. Roast grouse were set on the table, and various dishes of entremets, ranging from butter-gleaming new potatoes through artichoke hearts to fresh peaches and raspberries.

All the way through, the slightly strained and desultory conversation persisted until Miss Kenwood's sense of humour overcame her when she was asking for the salad to be passed to her. 'Give *me* the bowl!' she said in precisely the deep, throbbing tone in which Lady Macbeth might have said, 'Give *me* the dagger!' Everyone looked at her in astonishment.

After a moment, John exclaimed triumphantly, 'Mrs Siddons!' and Kate smiled. 'Correct,' she said. 'I was once a guest at the same dinner table, and she asked for the salad *just* like

208

that. She was perfectly serious, but I'm afraid everyone else began to laugh.'

'I understand that she has a naturally grave disposition?' the earl said.

'Indeed, and it has the most salutary effect on her fellow players. They always behave with perfect propriety when she is on stage. I wish I could say the same,' she added in hollow tones.

John's eyes lit up. 'What do you mean?'

She chuckled. 'My little contretemps this afternoon reminded me of the kind of thing that happens to me, but could never happen to Sarah Siddons.' She looked round the circle of expectant faces and was encouraged to go on. 'You know how, in *Romeo and Juliet,* Romeo drinks poison and falls dead by the apparently lifeless body of Juliet – who then promptly revives? Whereupon she first tries to drink from the poison phial, and then stabs herself with Romeo's dagger?'

They nodded.

'Well, I was involved in one production in the provinces that I shall never forget. The first disaster was Romeo's costume. He was clad in breeches that looked as if they had been borrowed from some ancient Dutchman, and he was wearing a pair of red slippers, if you please! The next thing was that the curtain rose a little too soon on one of the scenes in Juliet's chamber, and revealed half a dozen disreputable carpenters busy smoothing down pillows and adjusting draperies. But the high point of the evening was my final scene over Romeo's corpse. He had fallen in a most inconvenient position, so that I had the greatest difficulty casting myself on his bosom.' She paused, and thought for a moment. 'Let me try and reconstruct the dialogue for you. It went something like this:

'Juliet to Friar Lawrence: "Go, get thee hence, for I will not away."

'Juliet to Romeo's corpse, *sotto voce:* "Am I smothering you?"

'Corpse: "Not at all. But could you be so kind, do you think, as to put my wig on again for me? It seems to have fallen off."'

209

John gave a shout of laughter, and even Francis Mervyn smiled. Lady Susan, looking at him, thought that perhaps the crisis of the last two weeks might have wrought a change for the better in him.

Miss Kenwood said, 'Hush! I haven't finished. My next line should have been, "What's here? A cup, closed in my true love's hand? Poison, I see." Unfortunately, there was no cup clasped in his hand, nor any sign of one. Typically, he had fallen on it and broken it, so I had to carry on the appropriate bit of business with my back to the audience. And the last straw came when I was supposed to snatch the dagger. The dialogue, then, went like this:

'Juliet, aloud: "Someone approaches!"'

'Juliet, *sotto voce:* "Where's your dagger?"'

'Corpse, equally *sotto voce:* "Pon my soul, I don't know!"'

'Juliet, aloud: "Then I'll be brief." *Sotto voce:* "Well, find it!"'

'Juliet, aloud and very slowly indeed, while the corpse rummages under his cloak: "Oh, happy dagger. This is ... thy ... sheath ... "'

'Romeo finds the dagger, Juliet snatches it from him, and stabs herself with a heartfelt sigh of relief. "There rest, and let me die."'

'I don't know when I have been so happy to reach the end of a performance,' Kate concluded.

The atmosphere at table was very much lighter. Looking round at that moment, his lordship also surprised Brandon with a beatific smile on his face, which changed to one of extreme sheepishness as he caught his master's amused eye. Hidden depths! thought his lordship, summoning him to refill the glasses.

They had not quite finished dinner when a footman appeared at the door and murmured in Brandon's ear. The butler merely nodded. But as the ladies were preparing to rise from table, he stepped forward and spoke to the earl in low tones.

'Indeed?' said his lordship. 'Thank you.' He turned to the others. 'I wonder if you would mind retiring to the parlour for your coffee and brandy? You don't object, Susan? I shall need the library – and Miss Kenwood, I fear. Townsend wishes to see the two of us privately.'

In the few moments before Brandon brought the Bow Street Runner to the library, Miss Kenwood said, 'Has something gone wrong, do you think?'

The earl's face was preoccupied. 'I don't know. I certainly didn't expect anything to happen before tomorrow, at the earliest.'

Townsend was, if anything, less sweet-tempered than he had been earlier in the day. In deference to Kate, he removed his hat. He even sat down, and accepted a glass of brandy. But his voice was peremptory.

'You knew it was the Reverend Mr Iredale who fired those shots last night, my lord, and I'd like to know how you knew. Because I've a shrewd suspicion you knew he killed Imogen Reece as well.'

Everything's gone wrong, Kate thought. He must have arrested Iredale before Olivia had the chance to talk to him. Now Considine's part is bound to come out. Poor Lady Considine!

The earl said, his dark brows raised over careful blue eyes, 'Why are you angry, Townsend? You said last week that you proposed hunting my secretary, but that you wouldn't "take it amiss", I think were the words you used, if it could be proved to be someone else.'

'Ay, but I don't like the way it's worked out. I'm not one of those who's satisfied with a bald answer, and I've the very nasty feeling I've been manipulated.' He was too angry to add the insurance of 'No disrespect intended.'

'Take a moment to calm down,' his lordship recommended.

'I don't want to calm down, my lord! I want the answers to my questions.'

'I told you this afternoon that I had no evidence that would lead to the conviction of the man who murdered Imogen Reece, but that I was trying to find it. That remains true. I still have no evidence. Have you?'

'Ay. I'm ahead of you there.'

'Have you arrested Iredale?'

'No.'

211

They must have run away, Kate thought. But if they have, what can Townsend have discovered in the way of evidence?

The earl opened his mouth to speak, but Townsend had no intention of being stopped. 'I've been in this business for nigh on thirty-five years, my lord, and you get a nose for things. My nose tells me Iredale's guilty, and it also tells me you know more about the whys and wherefores than I do. And I repeat, I don't like it.'

His lordship ignored this speech. 'Why haven't you arrested Iredale? If you know he murdered Imogen Reece ... '

'Where's the point in arresting a dead body?'

Kate gasped, and he said, 'Drat it! Sorry, Miss Katharine, I'd forgotten you were here!'

The earl looked at him, quite without expression.

'Ay, he's dead all right,' the Runner admitted resignedly. 'Shot himself a couple of hours ago. And obligingly left a note.'

His lordship's face was oddly tired. He said flatly, 'What happened?'

'I only know what Mrs Iredale told me. She said he'd been behaving very funny-peculiar this last week or two.' The Runner's face and eyes were screwed up in frustration. 'Especially last night. So she decided to have a talk with him. When he arrived home this afternoon, she insisted on him telling her what had been going on. They talked. They argued, seemingly. He said, "All right, I'll write it all down", and took some paper and wrote a couple of pages. She said, "We'll talk about it some more, but I have to go out and get some milk from the cowkeeper first, otherwise there won't be any curds and whey for your breakfast on Saturday." When she got back, about half an hour later, he was dead. The pistol was on the floor beside him. *And* the confession – in his handwriting, unless there's a better forger around than I've had the misfortune to meet.'

He produced two sheets of lined paper from his pocket. 'The kind he used for his cataloguing work,' he said. 'I'll read it out to you.

"To whom it may concern. I hereby confess that it was I who was responsible for the death of my wife's sister, Miss Imogen

212

Reece. It was an accident. I lost my temper, under provocation, and hit her with the first thing that came to my hand. As a parson without a living, I have a small income, but because my wife was so attached to her sister I contributed something towards her household expenses. She seemed to me to manage very well on what she had, far better than we did, and I had suggested to her more than once that she could contrive without my assistance. She always refused. On Friday of the week before last, I remonstrated with her again, but she laughed at me. I had just been working out the state of my finances and found them at a very low ebb. I lost control, and hit her. I am afraid that in my rage I hit her several times. I do not expect to be forgiven, least of all by my wife, but she has insisted that I should write this down. She still refuses to believe that her sister goaded me. But I was driven beyond what any reasonable man could endure."*

'And that's all,' Townsend concluded. 'Interesting, isn't it? There's a lot missing. Nothing about Miss Reece's protector.' His head swivelled. 'And nothing about why he should have taken a shot at you, Miss Katharine. As I must presume he did.' He folded the papers up again slowly, and replaced them in his pocket. Then he leaned forward, placed his chin in his fists, and rubbed his middle fingers up and down the sides of his nose. 'It's just,' he said, 'that I wonder why. If I didn't have Mrs Iredale's Bible oath that there was no one else there, I'd think maybe it wasn't *his* confession at all. It's as if it had been dictated to him – by someone who had something to hide.'

Neither Miss Kenwood nor the earl said a word.

'Ay, well. We can't have everything, I suppose. He didn't even say he was going to shoot himself, but maybe he was just conserving energy.'

He looked at the earl, who was looking at his interlaced fingers.

His lordship said, 'You must have deduced, earlier today, that I believed there was a connection between the murder of Miss Reece and the attack on Miss Kenwood. There are things I cannot tell you because they were revealed to me in confidence, and, since the murderer has been exposed and the penalty paid, you have no real need to know.' He sighed.

'However, in fairness, I will say that I learned who it was who had Miss Reece in keeping. And that his identity led me to deduce that Iredale was the guilty man. I also – learned – that he suspected Miss Kenwood of having received confidences from Miss Reece that, if disclosed, would lead to his arrest. That was why I arranged for Miss Kenwood to be guarded. That was why she was shot at.' He looked up. 'But, I repeat, I had proof of none of this.'

Townsend surveyed him, wrinkling his nose. 'Ay. Don't think I don't believe you, my lord. I do. It's just that it's all sorted itself out a bit too pat for my liking. But it *has* sorted itself out. You can tell your Mr Mervyn, wherever he may be,' the irony was palpable, 'that he can start showing his face again without fear of being nobbled.'

He turned to Kate. 'And I have to inform you officially, madam, that the case in which you, personally, retained my services, has now been solved. Perhaps you will confirm that it has been done to your satisfaction?'

Kate said, 'Er ... Oh, yes. Thank you.'

'Very well. Perhaps you would be good enough to call in at the office tomorrow and sign it off. I'll take my leave now.'

The earl escorted him personally all the way to the front door, and saw him politely off the premises before returning to the library, where Miss Kenwood was waiting for him.

Chapter 19

'You knew this would happen,' she said. 'Didn't you!'

He was pulled up short by her tone. Choosing his words, he replied, 'I knew something of the kind was possible.'

'Did *she* shoot him?'

He faced her. 'My dear,' he said. 'I don't know. Does it matter?'

She scarcely heard him. 'Just like a Greek tragedy. A chain of dependences, with each link welded by the Fates. Iredale dependent on Olivia. Olivia dependent on Imogen. Imogen dependent on Francis Mervyn. And Francis Mervyn dependent on you.' She stared at him – and then fell victim to her own irrepressible sense of humour. Her eyes danced. 'I will *not* have you say that real life is wholly divorced from the theatre!'

'It was ill advised,' he admitted.

'Is it really over now?'

'Except for the bruises.'

'How flat!' she exclaimed. 'Oh, well. I suppose we should go and put everyone out of their misery.' Her heart was beating lightly and rapidly and out of place, somewhere around the base of her throat.

He put his hands very gently on her shoulders. 'In a minute. But I have something to say first. It will be a long time before I forgive myself for the dangers and discomforts you have had to suffer in the last few days.' He smiled. 'I abase myself.'

With a creditable attempt at objectivity, she said, 'I don't see why you should. It appears to me that it was mostly my own fault. And no doubt,' she went on in a rallying tone, 'if I had paid more attention to your opinions, all would have been resolved without any danger or discomfort at all.'

'I think it might,' he replied, to her considerable indignation. 'But not nearly as quickly. Oh, Kate!' he said quietly, looking down into her eyes. 'I do love you so much.'

She had known something was coming, and was braced for it. Under the influence of the doctor's soothing draught, she had lain on her bed for three hours and rehearsed the ways in which she might tell his lordship that she would not become his mistress. But the controlled vibrancy in his voice, the almost imperceptible quiver of his hands on her shoulders, the curious look in his dark blue eyes – at once tense and humorous, transparent and opaque – stripped her mind of its defences. Wordlessly, she looked back at him.

He said again, 'Kate!' and shook her slightly. 'I love you beyond belief. I love you, I love you, I love you most damnably, and I can't live without you. Will you – oh, God! – will you marry me?'

Still, she looked at him, and half in despair, he pulled her into his arms and kissed her.

It was gentle at first, and infinitely restrained. She could feel the faint tremor running all the way through his limbs. Gradually, as she stood within the tight circle of his arms, her mouth soft and enquiring under his, she felt all the strength being drained from her so that her very bones seemed to melt and her whole being was concentrated in the strange, passionate, increasingly demanding contact between their lips. Nothing else mattered. Nothing existed.

At length he drew his head back and gazed into the grave, surprised eyes below his. 'Kate!' he said again, with a break in his voice. 'Oh, Kate!' and buried his lips in the soft hollow at the base of her throat.

She scarcely noticed the hurt in her arm as he gripped her, leading her towards a chair and forcing her to sit, so that he might kneel before her. He took her hands in his, and held them close to his lips. 'Kate, Katharine, Signora Katarina, Miss Kenwood!' There was the ghost of a laugh in his voice. 'Will you marry me?'

At last she found her voice. 'But we have scarcely known each other a week!'

He laughed in earnest then. 'My foolish Kate! What does that matter? We have known each other a lifetime. And I knew

216

the first time I saw you, before we even met, that you were the one woman in the world for me, the only woman I ever wanted to share my life with.'

Her sardonic spirit revived slightly. 'The *only* one, my lord?' she asked a little breathlessly.

He sank his forehead on their clasped hands. 'I swear,' he said. 'Kate, I am thirty years old, and male, and not a monk. But I have never before felt what I feel for you. How can the past matter to us? *This* is where life begins.'

'Yes,' she said.

He raised his eyes, whose blue would have made the plainest woman beautiful. 'What troubles you?' he asked.

She scarcely knew. There were the contrasts in him. The curtness and reserve at their first meetings. The biting contempt and the arrogance only yesterday. The calculating intellect that could use a wife to destroy her husband. And on the other side of the account, the charm, the humour, and the companionship. More than once, when he smiled at her with his unrestrained blinding brilliance, she had felt her heart perform the strangest gyrations in her breast. She was nervous and attracted, repelled and enchanted, all at the same time. She had no idea whether she was in love with him, and even the newly found awareness that she wanted nothing more than to spend the rest of her life in his arms was enough to make her hesitate. There was more to love, she knew, than the simple chemistry of being *in* love. With increasing power, the admonitory voice deep inside her reminded her of the private purpose she had committed herself to four years earlier. Reminded her, too, of the dangers of emotional dependence, so vividly illustrated in these last few days. And whispered, persuasively, that no matter how she felt about him she would destroy herself if she entered into marriage with such a man as the Earl of Moriston without first proving to herself, and to him, that she was her own woman.

For all his perception, the earl did not realize that he had not yet succeeded in overcoming the prejudice she had formed before she ever met him, based on the certainty that he, like everyone else of his kind, had nothing but scorn and contempt for the stage and the people who performed on it. Nor could he have known that his ill-judged comments on the previous day, torn out of him by his fears for her life, had reinforced that prejudice. He knew that he had offended her. He suspected that the harsh realities of bringing a criminal to justice had been distasteful to her. But he had hoped that the rapport between them, so clear to his own awareness, might have acted as a counterbalance. The truth was that he loved her so consumingly that he could not believe she would not respond.

She said at last, 'I don't know. I don't know *you*. And I don't know how I feel.' She was very pale, and the severe contours of his face softened. 'Bear with me, please,' she said. 'I cannot say I will marry you. Sit here, beside me, and I will tell you part of the reason.'

He rose, without releasing her hands, and drew her towards the chaise-longue where they could sit together. The desire to take her back in his arms tingled through his veins like fire.

She said, 'Four years ago, my father died in an accident. My brother had been killed in the Peninsula, and my mother had simply faded out of life soon after. I was the only one left. My father was not a businesslike man. Just before he died, he had embarked on a scheme to reclaim farming land from the bracken and scrub, and because he had not sufficient income or capital to carry out the improvements himself he gathered all his tenant farmers and smallholders together and put the idea to them. It would benefit everyone, he pointed out, and the sooner it was started on, the sooner the results would begin to show. He was a very persuasive man. Almost everyone agreed. Some handed over their savings to him. Others sold stock or possessions to raise their share. They trusted him completely. And then came the accident. His horse stumbled in a rabbit burrow, and my father went headfirst into a drystone wall.'

The earl said nothing. Fragments of the story were beginning to return to him. There had been some talk about it at the time.

After a moment, she went on. 'Unfortunately, he had generated such a sense of urgency about the plan that a good deal of money had been handed over before the legal documents were completed. The estate was entailed, of course, and it went to a cousin of mine. An unpleasant man. He disclaimed all responsibility. Legally, there was nothing to prove that the money did not belong to the estate, and he claimed that every penny was needed to pull the existing land back from the verge of ruin without committing any of it to wildcat reclamation schemes. And that, as far as he was concerned, was that.

'Perhaps you may think I was foolish. After all, no one held *me* to blame. Indeed, everyone was unbearably kind. But I swore to myself that I would repay every penny that had disappeared into Cousin Reston's coffers.'

It was a confession she had never made before, to anyone, and she looked at him nervously to see how he was taking it. He was looking at her in the oddest way. She took a breath, and said gaily, 'I had a small legacy from my mother, which provided me with a little income, but not enough. And that, kind sir, is why I joined the theatre! And why I do not expect to leave it for some years yet. So far, I have repaid about half the debt, and, all things considered, I think I have done remarkably well. And when Drury Lane recognizes that they have on their hands a Catalani and a Siddons rolled into one, I expect to do even better!'

Her lovely smiled faded. 'Until that time, however, you must see that I cannot marry, although I am deeply – touched – that you should ask me.' The note on which she ended was not quite steady.

'But, my darling,' his lordship said, gripping her hands compellingly, 'if you will ... ' He stopped just in time, aware of the pit yawning at his feet. The last thing in the world he dared say to her was that, if she married him, he would gladly and gratefully repay her father's debt, whatever it cost him. Gallingly, he knew that if she had repaid half of it out of what she had earned in four years on the stage, he could settle the rest without even noticing it. Now, he began to understand the hints he had observed of pride in her achievement, which he had taken merely as expressions of an endearing trace of vanity. He had laughed, and loved her for it. But this was something he could not laugh away. When he had first seen her on the stage just over a week – a lifetime – ago, one of the words that had sprung to his mind had been 'gallant'. But this was gallantry on a different scale. For a well-bred young woman in these years of grace of the early nineteenth century even to contemplate setting out to earn thousands of pounds, in a quixotic gesture no one could possibly have expected of her, was remarkable enough. A flight in the face of all custom, all convention. But that she should be well on the way to success, her essential self not only undamaged but even strengthened by the experience, was ... He could think of no words adequate to the occasion.

He raised her hands to his lips, and it was suddenly as much as she could do not to retract. She wanted to say, 'I didn't mean it. I don't care about my father's debts. I don't care about the theatre. I will marry you tomorrow, if you still want me!' She did not think she could bear it if he accepted her refusal, and went away. But as he looked up again, she braced herself to hold to her purpose, whatever it might cost. Nothing, she told herself, could equal the cost of abandoning her self-respect.

He said with perfect simplicity, 'I understand. But don't send me away, I beg of you. When I said you were the one woman in the world for me, I meant it with every atom of my heart, body, and mind. I have no choices open. I can only wait, and hope that one day you will come to me.'

He rose, and pulled her gently to her feet. 'Will you try to learn to love me, Kate?'

The beautiful eyes looked up at him, wide and dark. His arms went round her, and he kissed her again, once, not softly.

She felt ridiculously happy. 'We-e-ell ... ' she said consideringly.

He laughed, and drew her arm through his. 'Come along, you – you Melancholy Virgin! How do you *do* that with your eyes? We must go back, or they will be sending out a search party for us.'

The door opened and John stood on the threshold. 'Oh, there you are!' he exclaimed in injured tones. 'We are about to expire from curiosity.' He took in the linked arms and the expression on his brother's face, and with a greater effort at self-control than he had ever shown in his life before, said, 'Are you coming to tell us the end of the story? Or not?'